Praise for the Hamptons Home & Garden Mysteries

"A delightful sneak peek into life in the Hamptons, with intricate plotting and a likeable, down-to-earth protagonist. A promising start to a promising series."
— *Suspense Magazine* on *Better Homes and Corpses*

"*Ghostal Living* is a marvelously entertaining tale of revenge, murder, quirky characters — and disappearing books! With a clever protagonist, wonderful details of life in the Hamptons, and plot twists on top of plot twists, Kathleen Bridge will have mystery readers clamoring for more."
— Kate Carlisle, *New York Times* bestselling author

"An excellent read."
— *RT Book Reviews* on *Hearse and Gardens*

"The descriptions of furniture and other antiques, as well as juicy tidbits on the Hamptons, make for entertaining reading for those who enjoy both antiques and lifestyles of the rich and famous."
— *Booklist* on *Better Homes and Corpses*

Books by Kathleen Bridge

Hamptons Home & Garden Mysteries

Better Homes and Corpses
Hearse and Gardens
Ghostal Living
Manor of Dying
A Design to Die For

By the Sea Mysteries

Death by the Sea
A Killing by the Sea
Murder by the Sea
Evil by the Sea

A Design to Die For

Kathleen Bridge

BEYOND THE PAGE
PUBLISHING

A Design to Die For
Kathleen Bridge
Beyond the Page Books
are published by
Beyond the Page Publishing
www.beyondthepagepub.com

ISBN: 978-1-950461-57-8

I dedicate this book to my cherished friend and fellow vintage fixer-upper enthusiast, Nancy Schoen. Your generous, loving spirit inspires me not only when it comes to home décor but also in every aspect of my life. This one's for you . . .

Acknowledgments

Thanks, as always, to my wonderful agent, Down Dowdle at Blue Ridge Literary Agency, along with my editor, Bill Harris, and everyone at Beyond the Page Publishing. Once again, thank you to gourmet home chef Lon Otremba, who provided the recipes in the back of this book and all my other cozy mysteries. I hope our collaboration continues for years to come. I'd rather eat at your table than any Michelin Star restaurant. To my family, who has supported my writing career from day one, I love you guys. And to my faithful COZY readers, I wouldn't be able to live my blissful writer's life if not for you — you guys are the best! Amy Hueston, author and friend, I so appreciate all your support. A big shout-out to Shelly Colloredo and everyone at Sweet Home Vintage Market in Sebastian, Florida. Thanks for adding Vintage Cottage by the Sea to your happy family of dealers. P.S. Stop by and see us if you are in the area!

Chapter 1

"There's nothing like Montauk in the spring," I said. "Only three weeks until Memorial Day, then the Hamptons hordes descend."

"Meg Barrett! That's a snarky way of looking at it," Elle said.

"Not being snarky, just love living here off-season. I'm very possessive of my serenity, especially after . . ."

"Cole," my best friend finished for me.

Before she could grill me about my recent breakup, I asked, "When's your fiancé coming back to town?"

Just like me, she avoided the question.

"Can you please pass the menu?"

I passed it to her, adding, "Good luck reading it in this pea-soup mist."

"Ha-ha, funny," she said. "How'd you know I was leaning toward the pea soup? Either that or Gwen's lobster chowder." Elle pulled the menu closer to her upturned freckled nose. "I can't read a thing under all this condensation." Taking her napkin, she swiped it across the menu. "Better."

Our outdoor table at the Surfside Lodge faced a fog-shrouded ocean. I'd insisted we eat outdoors. The past week had been nothing but fog and rain. Not that today was any different, but I was tired of being caged inside the teensy four-room cottage my one-woman interior design firm, Cottages by the Sea, had been hired to decorate. Instead of May flowers, as the old ditty went, it looked like we'd inherited April's showers.

I glanced down at the menu, deciding on the mussels in garlic and white wine.

When I looked up, I saw a small-framed female body appear through the miasma at the top of the deck's steps. Waving, I called out, "Jenna, over here." Not that it would be hard to find us. We were the only ones dumb enough to sit outdoors.

As she came toward us, Elle said, "Since when does Jenna need a cane?"

Newly married Jenna Eastman had once worked with Elle and me at *American Home and Garden* magazine. When I was at the helm of the magazine, Jenna was my locations editor. After I fled

Manhattan and a cheating fiancé to find serenity in Montauk, Jenna took over my spot as editor in chief. Following her marriage to Roland Cahill, Jenna moved to the easternmost tip of Long Island with her husband in order to renovate Jenna's family home, Enderly Hall. The mansion-sized fishing cottage was said to have been built by the legendary architect Stanford White on five acres of oceanfront land atop the Montauk moors. Just a hop, skip, and a jump from the Montauk Point Lighthouse. Jenna and I were neighbors. However, there was no comparing our two *cottages*, seeing mine had six rooms and hers twenty-plus.

Elle, Jenna and I were around the same age, in our early thirties, and we shared a passion for interior design and junk pickin'. Elle and Jenna were independently wealthy, so they did their treasure hunting for sport. I, on the other hand, not so much for sport, more for survival and a means to continue my blissful stress-free existence in my cozy Montauk cottage.

Jenna came toward us like she'd just stepped, more like limped, out of the *Creature from the Black Lagoon*'s lagoon. Her long auburn hair was plastered against her pale heart-shaped face. One of her hair extensions had come loose and was draped across her shoulder like a scarf. She wasn't wearing a jacket in the cool fifty-degree weather, just a long, open-weave sweater that made her look like she'd been snared in a fisherman's net.

If Jenna was anything, she was always buffed and coifed.

Not today.

I got up and pulled out a chair that Jenna slunk into. "I think my husband, soon-to-be ex-husband, is trying to kill me," she moaned, her saucer-like moss green eyes showing fear.

At a loss for words, I let Elle pose the billion-dollar question—because that was almost what Jenna Eastman was worth after the passing of her father.

"Jenna! Why would you think Roland is trying to kill you?" Elle asked, picking up the cane that had slipped from Jenna's grip. "And what happened to your ankle?"

"Yesterday," Jenna said, "I was doing my usual jog down Old Montauk Highway when a car came barreling down on me at high speed. I leapt to the shoulder and went flying into a ditch. If a bush hadn't stopped me, I would have fallen onto the rocky beach below." She must have noticed my skeptical gaze, and continued, "The car was a silver Mercedes sedan, just like Roland's. Luckily, another car came by, saw my reflective vest and took me to urgent care. My ankle is only sprained, but it could have been worse. Much worse." She took her pointer finger with its long French-manicured nail and swiped it across her throat like it was a knife's blade.

"Maybe we should go inside and chat by the fire," I interjected, glancing at Jenna's shivering form. I was also having a hard time hearing her low speaking voice over the crash of the waves. My hearing aids were in, but I hadn't set them to keep the background noise out and reading lips was near impossible in the fog. I leaned in until I was inches from Jenna's face.

"Noooo," she answered. "I don't want anyone to overhear." I shoved my cup of chai tea toward her. As she drank, I took a moment to soak it all in before I formed my next question. Jenna had a flair for the dramatic; a light sprinkle was a downpour, her glass was never half empty, it was bone-dry. "Jenna, what reason would your husband have to kill you?"

"Two days ago, I asked him for a divorce, then this hit-and-run happened." She extended her left ankle, then pulled up her pant leg, exposing bandages that went well above her knee. I could tell that the clinic probably provided the section of bandage at her ankle. The one continuing over her knee was in a completely different shade. Knowing Jenna, she'd probably bought a second bandage from Green's Department Store, wanting to make her injury look worse than it was. Jenna might be the most pessimistic person I knew, and the biggest hypochondriac, but she was also the most generous and kindhearted. In all the years I'd known her, I didn't think I'd ever seen her as angry as she was now.

"I wish I'd never thought of the idea of having Enderly Hall as a designer showhouse," she whimpered. "Roland's completely taken over. He's not the man I thought he was."

Now that the exterior and interior construction were completed, Enderly Hall was scheduled to become the first annual Montauk Designer Showhouse, with most of the proceeds going to the Montauk Volunteer Fire Department, commencing with Saturday night's invitation-only cocktail party. Sunday would be the first day Enderly Hall would be open for public viewing. Jenna had strategically coordinated the showhouse's opening with the festivities for Montauk Point Lighthouse Week.

Glancing at Jenna's hunched form, it was hard to believe this was the same lovestruck woman who'd told us six months ago how happy she was after returning from her South of France honeymoon. I wasn't a big fan of Jenna's husband, Roland, but it was still hard to picture him wanting to murder her. For one thing, I remembered the stink Roland had given Jenna about the prenup agreement before their wedding. What would be his motive?

Roland was new to the Hamptons scene. Per Jenna, he was the former owner of a Queens, New York–based construction business. He'd recently partnered with a top East Hampton architectural firm in nearby Amagansett, Klein and Associates. Since then, he'd been off to the races, trying to make his mark on the Hamptons social hierarchy with millionairess Jenna at his side. There was a big age gap between the pair. Roland was in his early fifties and was an expert at giving out backhanded compliments, walking around the estate like he was a rooster and the other decorators, including his wife, his bevy of chicks. Based on the few times I'd been around him when working at Enderly Hall and judging by the way he demeaned Jenna and the other three female decorators, including myself, I believed Roland was a first-class chauvinistic jerk.

Up until today, I'd given him a hall pass, thinking he and Jenna were passionately in love. If that had once been the case, it sure didn't seem to be so now.

"Why'd you ask Roland for a divorce?" Elle asked softly, taking Jenna's hand in hers.

"I overheard a conversation between him and Vicki . . ." Jenna hesitated for a moment, then looked around to make sure no one could overhear. The only living thing in view was a seagull, who stood patiently on the deck's railing, waiting for scraps of food. Vicki was Roland's former stepdaughter and the owner of a struggling Manhattan interior design firm called Veronica's Interiors. She was also one of the three decorators chosen to do the interior rooms for the showhouse. Continuing, Jenna said, "I heard Roland telling Vicki that after the designer showhouse closed, he planned to put Enderly Hall on the market! My estate! My family home! It hasn't been inhabited in years. Living there has been a dream of mine since I was a child. My grandfather was a recluse and hoarder. He died without a will. For the past twenty years my father and uncle fought over ownership. Two stubborn idiots. It wasn't until my father's recent passing that I was made his heir and the owner of Enderly Hall."

"So, what did you do after you overheard all this between your husband and Vicki?" Elle asked impatiently. Jenna was also good at maximizing drama.

"I confronted Roland. Then I told my treacherous husband that he'd have to kill me before the estate went on the market. I guess that's what he decided to do." She glanced down at her ankle. "I also overheard Roland tell Vicki that if he had to, he'd fake the papers proving that Enderly Hall was designed by Stanford White. My father and uncle spent years looking for the renderings that would indisputably prove White was the architect for Enderly Hall. They never found them. If Enderly Hall was ever put up for sale, having proof it is a Stanford White cottage would probably triple its worth."

She turned to Elle, then me, her eyes pleading. "Don't you see? I told Roland, then and there, Enderly Hall would never be sold, and I wanted a divorce a.s.a.p. He tried to play it off that I'd misconstrued his words, saying what he meant was that *after* we had children and they were grown, *then* we would sell, so we could retire and live abroad. Like I believe that malarkey. I don't want a scandal to ruin Enderly Hall's showhouse unveiling. Now it looks like I'm stuck with Roland for at least the next month and a half. For better or worse."

I had a feeling it would be for worse.

"Do you believe Stanford White was Enderly Hall's architect?" Elle asked.

"I do. But I would never forge papers saying so."

A waitress had stepped onto the deck carrying a water pitcher. I motioned for her to go back inside. She took one look at Jenna's bedraggled form and the tears running down her face, then hurried back through the open French doors leading into the restaurant.

I handed Jenna my napkin. She used it to wipe her face and blow her nose, then said, "My father and uncle were sure that at one time, when they were teenagers, they saw handwritten architectural plans by Stanford White in grandfather's study. Proof that the same man who erected the second Madison Square Garden, Washington Square Arch in Greenwich Village, and the Gilded Age *cottage* Rosecliff in Newport, Rhode Island, had been the same architect who built Enderly Hall."

Most locals knew about Stanford White and his ties to the Hamptons. Dick Cavett had bought Stanford White's Tick Hall, only a short distance from Enderly Hall. Tick Hall was one of three sister fishing cottages that White had built in Montauk. "If I remember correctly," I said, "Tick Hall doesn't have documented architectural renderings by Stanford White. But it's common knowledge that he'd built it."

Jenna moaned, exasperation in her voice when she said, "They have other proof: photographs, receipts that the interior furnishings came from Stanford White's huge warehouse, along with files found at the firm of McKim, Mead, and White and also at Tick Hall."

"So, your father couldn't find one shred of evidence that Stanford White was Enderly's architect?" I asked gently, noticing the pink on her cheeks.

"None," Jenna said. "Grandfather probably burned everything. Now Roland wants to produce false papers and sell Enderly Hall from under me. It's ludicrous, just like my grandfather's last years, when he refused to see either of his sons, or anyone else in the family. Thomas Stanton Eastman died with no will. The only way probate could go through was if my father and uncle sold Enderly Hall and split the profit. They refused, each wanting it for themselves because of the Stanford White lineage. It wasn't until my uncle died that my father took possession. Six months later, Father died from lung cancer. He was a big smoker. Mother predeceased him by a year. She had breast cancer."

"Oh, Jenna," I said sympathetically, "how tragic." My own mother had died from the same disease.

Elle patted her hand. "At least now your parents are reunited."

Jenna kept going, her malaise mushrooming to its crescendo. "To top things off," she said, her eyes narrowing in anger, "there's a crew of paranormal investigators camped outside our gates. Once the showhouse was announced they must have discovered the link to Shepherds Cottage, the lighthouse ghost and Captain Kidd's curse. Or maybe it's my grandfather's ghost they've come looking for."

I had to ask, "Why would paranormal investigators be looking for your grandfather's ghost?" I'd seen the paranormal crew she was talking about and had assumed they were from a local television station wanting to promote the showhouse.

Elle retrieved a tissue from her handbag and handed it to Jenna.

"For the years that Enderly Hall had been left empty, there've been rumors of unusual happenings. They ascribed them to Shepherds Cottage's history. Only I've had my suspicions something else might be going on. You see, Grandfather died in an unusual way . . ."

Elle looked at me and rolled her big brown eyes. Jenna continued, "It's a long story. My grandfather was on the eccentric side. He died when I was thirteen. Before that, he lived like a hermit at Enderly Hall. You see, my grandmother died after giving birth to twins, my father and Uncle James. She'd had a choice of saving herself or her children, and she chose her children. Apparently, my grandfather never forgave my grandmother for making that decision. Afterward, Grandfather wasn't the same, wanting nothing to do with his sons, retreating into his shell. The shell being Enderly Hall. My great-aunt moved in and raised my father and uncle. After they went away to college, she moved out and left my grandfather to his obsession—Enderly Hall.

"Grandfather was a packrat. On the few times my parents took me to visit him, I remember seeing him throw hundred-dollar bills, stock certificates and other papers into the fire for kindling. He didn't want anyone getting his money."

"Jenna, that still doesn't explain why you think your grandfather is haunting Enderly Hall," I said. Elle gave me a look that I interpreted as *don't encourage her.*

"I'm getting to that. Shortly before my grandfather's death, Social Services rendered Enderly Hall uninhabitable. Grandfather refused to leave the grounds, so my father and uncle stuck him in Shepherds Cottage. They made arrangements for grocery and drugstore deliveries, and that's where he stayed until . . ." She dabbed the corners of her eyes and continued, "They found him down on the rocks. Still in his bedclothes. The strange thing was, he had a wad of hundred-dollar bills stuffed in his mouth. I think my father suspected my uncle of fighting with Grandfather, then accidently killing him. And my uncle must have thought the same thing of my father. There was also the suspicion someone pushed him off the cliff in revenge for something he'd done. And then there was the simple explanation that he'd been crazy. Instead of burning money, he'd thought he'd eat it so my father and uncle couldn't get their hands on it."

Not so simple, I thought.

"Even in his last years, he blamed his twins on my grandmother's death. The courts looked into foul play, especially because of what had happened on Enderly's grounds a few years before Grandfather died . . ." She paused dramatically, looking off in the direction of where the ocean would be visible if not for the fog and heavy mist.

"What happened?" I asked, knowing I could have Googled the whole thing in the time it took her to tell the story.

"You see," she said, "in his last year before his death, Grandfather had become very paranoid, posting *No Trespassing* and *Private Property* signs. A local man wandered onto the grounds and Grandfather shot him."

"Did the man die?" Elle asked.

"No, but the man spent the rest of his life paralyzed from the neck down. The Eastman Foundation took care of him until his death. Grandpa was acquitted of any wrongdoing, but following the hearing, that's when Grandfather officially went off the deep end. Soon after, he was found beneath the cliff. There was an inquiry into his death because of the bills stuffed in his mouth. The coroner ruled it accidental because of his state of mind, which had been documented by Social Services." Jenna's hand trembled as she reached for my teacup. "So, you see . . ." Another dramatic pause. "There are multiple reasons why ghosthunters are banging on Enderly's gates."

"Surely you're not scared of your grandfather's ghost?" I asked.

"Oh, not at all. It's the man he shot's ghost that has me on edge."

"You said he didn't die from his injuries," I reminded her.

"That's true, but my father said even though the man received a million dollars in the settlement, he told everyone in the Hamptons that 'The old man looked him in the eye, then pulled the trigger,' claiming it was no accident. He died four months after grandfather shot him, refusing to be put on a feeding tube."

And here I'd thought proving Stanford White had been the architect of Enderly Hall might be one mystery I could sink my teeth into that wouldn't involve dead bodies. Boy, was I wrong. What a crazy tale. I was beginning to understand why Jenna was the way she was. "But Jenna," I said, getting back to her initial accusation that her husband was trying to kill her, "why do you think it was Roland in the car? You have a prenup. What would he gain? And do you know how many silver Mercedes there are in the Hamptons?"

"Oh, I'm sure he could find some lawyer, somewhere, to nullify our agreement. You know Roland. If he wants something, he'll get it."

Jenna shivered, and Elle said, "Let's move inside by the fire."

I got up and stood by Jenna's chair. Elle grabbed Jenna's elbow and helped her up, then handed me her cane.

As we walked toward the French doors, Jenna said in a whiny voice, "And I keep seeing lights in the cottage. Roland says I'm imagining things. But I know I'm not. Unless . . . it's a ghost and that's why those ghosthunters are lurking around. That's all I need! Icing on the cake. Maybe the ghost will kill me before Roland does."

In Jenna's mind, if lights flickering in the cottage behind Enderly Hall meant there was a ghost, then maybe the car she saw in the fog had nothing to do with her husband or anyone else trying to kill her. It was just another instance of her overblown imagination.

Then again, maybe not.

Chapter 2

"Well, that wasn't the luncheon I expected," Elle said, signing her credit card receipt.

"We both know Jenna's a hypochondriac and an alarmist," I said, "but we also know that people have murdered for far less reasons than money and prestige. I'll try to spend as much time as possible with her before the cocktail party. To err on the side of safety, you should tell your detective fiancé about Jenna's concerns. Have him check into her hubby's past."

"Arthur's not a detective anymore. Remember? He's in Manhattan as a liaison between the NYPD and City Hall."

"You've never told me how he likes his new job."

"That's because he never tells me anything. It's like he's James Bond or something. I know he goes to enough public functions, hobnobbing with all the city politicos. I also know this will be another weekend I won't see him."

There was something I knew that Elle didn't. And it was a whopper. Her fiancé, Arthur Shoner, former detective for the East Hampton Town Police Department, would be coming back permanently to the East End of Long Island in three weeks' time. Three weeks from Saturday would be the large party I was throwing for Elle and Arthur in my walled garden. Arthur and I had a top-secret surprise for the party that was going to blow Elle's vintage anklet socks off. I said cheerily, "So, let's make the best of it. He tries hard to see you, unlike someone else I know." I pushed the palm of my right hand in front of her mouth to let her know Cole's and my breakup was *not* a topic for discussion.

She must have seen the hurt in my eyes because she let it drop. I'd exhausted all the ways I could think of to keep our relationship going. After Cole's business partner at Plantation Island Yachts sadly passed away, the fates had been against us. Cole was now in charge of both the North Carolina office and the one in Sydney, Australia. He'd had to cancel our big trip to Cornwall, England, where I'd had hopes of relighting the spark we'd felt the first time we'd kissed on the beach. When we'd said goodbye, we were both teary-eyed. Knowing it was for the last time. That was a month ago, and we hadn't talked, or even texted, since. I agreed with Sally in the movie *When Harry Met Sally*, you can't go back to being friends after a love affair. And another thing, long-distance relationships were impossible, especially with two pigheaded people like Cole and me. Enderly Hall's showhouse event couldn't have come at a better time. I'd been too busy in the past couple of months to take time out to feel sorry for myself.

Jenna had put me in charge of decorating the interior of Shepherds Cottage. It was a small four-room saltbox that had historical pedigree. Jenna had recited its history to me like she was a docent at a museum. The cottage had been brought over by barge from nearby Gardiners Island in the late 1800s by Jenna's great-great-grandfather, a distant relative of the Gardiners. It was then pulled by horse and flatbed wagon down Old Montauk Highway to its current location.

Gardiners Island, the oldest privately owned island in America, was also where Captain Kidd had buried a king's ransom of gold and jewels. Before Kidd could return to collect his booty, he was captured, tried in Boston and convicted of being a privateer. He was shipped to England, where he was executed. Still, I doubted his ghost would be hanging around an eighteenth-century sheepherder's shack, even if it did come from nearby Gardiners Island, where his treasure had been dug up and sent back to the King of England's coffers.

Shepherds Cottage was perched on a bluff behind Enderly Hall, and I had to wonder if that was the same bluff where Jenna's grandfather fell to his death with Ben Franklins stuffed in his mouth. When I'd first viewed the cottage, it had been completely empty, except for one piece of furniture. No signs of Grandpa or his ghost. Or the ghost of the poor guy Grandpa had shot.

Along with furnishing Shepherds Cottage, Jenna had thrown me the gold-plated bone of letting me decorate Enderly Hall's sweeping verandas and porches, along with the gazebo and the pavilion that topped the stairs leading down to the ocean.

Jenna knew I had a small space and porch fetish.

Who didn't?

"Where'd you just go?" Elle asked, nudging me on the arm. "Sorry about you and Cole. But I truly think it will turn out for the best. And I promise not to bring him up unless you do."

"Thanks, buddy," I said wistfully, feeling slightly sorry for myself. Not my usual M.O. "I wasn't thinking of Cole, just the *Twilight Zone* episode we just saw Jenna starring in."

We both stood and Elle pocketed her credit card, then we moved toward the exit.

"Promise I'll get the next check," I said, holding open the door for her.

"Sounds good," Elle answered, even though I knew she'd never let me pay her back. I tried to make up for her generosity by leaving little anonymous vintage presents on the doorstep of her Sag Harbor shop, Mabel and Elle's Curiosities. Or I'd pay her back by inviting her to my cottage for dinner, ordering in something wonderful from the myriad top-rated local restaurants. I wasn't a fan of cooking like my gourmet home-chef retired-cop father was, but I was a fan of eating.

"Care to come with me to Grimes House Antiques?" I asked, joining her on the deck. My hair immediately sprang into action from the humidity. "Rita has something Jenna's been looking for to complete Shepherds Cottage for the showhouse."

"I'd love to," she said without hesitation.

I grabbed the handrail and cautiously followed her down the steps into the parking lot, not wanting to twist my ankle like Jenna had.

"Rita and I have been swapping things to sell in our shops. I give her some antique pieces and she gives me some vintage items."

"She must make a bundle with those high price tags of hers," I said, waiting for her to unlock the door to her early-model aqua pickup. "Rita's a sly entrepreneur when it comes to her antiques."

In season, Grimes House Antiques was a good place to spy celebrities looking to furnish their summer homes. They had no qualms about paying Rita's prices. I, on the other hand, had only been able to afford a handful of items. Small items.

"Don't worry about me getting ripped off," Elle said once we were in the truck. "Rita's from the old school, she thinks things that aren't over a hundred years old are junk. Little does she know this entrepreneur" — Elle pointed to her chest and the array of vintage brooches displayed on her sweater — "makes a pretty penny on what Rita gives me in our trades."

I laughed. "I'm just curious. How much of what she gives you do you sell? And how much do you keep for yourself?"

"I'll have you know that the last basket of stuff she sent went right to the set of *Mr. & Mrs. Winslow*'s head costume designer.

"Touché!" *Mr. & Mr. Winslow* was a mystery miniseries being filmed in nearby Bridgehampton for a premium television network. Elle and I had been called in last December to help the set designer recreate the late-1930s time period. The premise for the series was similar to Dashiell Hammett's Thin Man detective movies starring Nick and Nora Charles. In this case the characters were named Jack and Lara Winslow. And instead of a wire fox terrier named Asta, the Winslows' dog was a Scottie named Whiskey.

After we put on our seat belts, Elle pulled onto a hazy Old Montauk Highway, the curvy, hilly road that ran alongside the Atlantic. The same highway where Jenna claimed to have gotten run off the road by her husband in a murder attempt. I waited to speak until after Elle turned west onto flat Route 27. "So, what's your gut feeling about what Jenna told us?"

Elle took her right hand off the steering wheel and ran it through her glossy shoulder-length dark hair. "I think she's exaggerating."

"Yikes, if that's coming from you, my scaredy-cat friend, I tend to agree." Like Jenna, Elle had a tendency to be a worrywart. She was also someone who had your back in do-or-die situations. Of which I'd had my fair share since moving to the East End of Long Island.

She turned to me. "*Scaredy cat?* What are you? In the first grade?"

"Eyes on the road, it's still misty."

"Don't change the subject. Just because I don't stick my neck out at every opportunity and butt into things that have nothing to do with me. Oh, and get involved in murder investigations instead of letting the authorities, like Arthur, handle it. Doesn't mean I'm a timid mouse."

"More like a steady mountain goat, I would say."

"You're right. I'm cautious. It's an asset. I don't have a hero complex like someone I know."

"Hero complex?" I asked incredulously. "That's what you think I have? I beg to differ. I can't help it if I'm a chip off the old block. Curiosity runs in my genes."

"I know, blah, blah, blah. That excuse only goes so far. Big whoop, you share the same genes with your retired homicide detective father. I suppose when Arthur and I have kids, they'll all be poking their noses where they don't belong and find themselves in dangerous situations." She covered her mouth with her hand at the thought, the diamonds in her antique engagement ring sparkling in all their splendor.

"Geez," I said, "next time I'll think before I mention my genetics."

"Sounds good," she said sternly, then forced a smile.

It seemed I had struck a nerve. "I was just teasing, buddy." I reached over and patted her hand.

"Well, lately I'm not in a very teasing mood," she said. "At this point, I'm not even sure Arthur will make it to our engagement party. Which would be a shame, seeing how much planning you've been putting into it. It's not like you don't have other things on your plate, like your Cottages by the Sea clients and working on the showhouse. Not to mention, if needed, we're both on call to go to the set of *Mr. & Mrs. Winslow*." She took her hand and affectionally patted mine, like I'd done to hers.

There wasn't anything in the universe to break our bond of friendship. I'd just have to move cautiously until the party. "Hey, I'm just doing the outdoor spaces at Enderly Hall and a small, teensy cottage. I have plenty of time to plan my best friend's engagement party. Back to Jenna," I said, "if she didn't have that prenup, I might give her theory some credence."

"I agree," Elle said thoughtfully. "I think Jenna is more upset about the thought of selling Enderly Hall than worrying if her husband was behind the wheel of that car. With that story she just told us about her grandfather, no wonder she seems so high-strung."

Elle slowed to go through the small town of Amagansett. It seemed the miserable weather hadn't kept anyone from visiting the East End Farm Stand, as cars were parked on both sides of the road. As we passed Ocean Surf Coffee, a long line snaked its way out the door of the white shingled cottage. The line wasn't just for their coffee. Each table came with a pan of fresh-from-the-oven, gooey, on-the-house cinnamon rolls. I rolled down my window for a heady whiff of coffee and cinnamon layered with salty sea air.

Breaking me from my sensory nirvana, Elle asked, "Did you notice the color of the car we passed a little while ago on Old Montauk Highway?"

"What car?"

"I rest my case. Two days ago, the fog was just as thick as it is today. All you can make out are dim headlights, not the color, make, and model of a car. I'm betting Jenna just got scared by a passing car that was similar to her husband's."

I agreed, but there was still that niggling seed of uncertainty Jenna might be in danger. If I knew Elle, which I did, I was sure she had her own worries too.

After we left Amagansett, a drizzling rain misted the truck's windshield. Even though Elle and I thought Jenna's claim that her husband was trying to kill her was probably pure fiction, dark thoughts swirled in my head like the fog blanketing the view of the dunes out the car window. I glanced at Elle, who was gnawing at her bottom lip, a sign that something was bothering her. I told myself as soon as I delivered the blanket chest to Shepherds Cottage, I would go to the main house and check on Jenna.

For security purposes, until the showhouse closed, Jenna and Roland had moved out of their beach house rental in Amagansett and were staying in Enderly Hall's large attic. Vicki, the interior decorator and Roland's former stepdaughter, was now staying in the rental until the showhouse closed. Jenna, who basically loved everyone, had a few issues with Vicki. After meeting Vicki over the past month, I could see why.

"So, what do you think about the paranormal investigators lurking beyond the gates at Enderly Hall?" Elle asked as we passed the Hooker Mill Windmill, telling us we were entering East Hampton.

"That's one thing we know Jenna believes in," I said, "ghosts."

"Maybe we shouldn't sell those ghosthunters short. Have you ever watched any of those paranormal shows on TV? They have all this modern digital equipment that can sniff out a ghost in no time. They use soundwaves or lasers, or something along those lines."

I gave her *the look*. "No, I haven't watched any. You should have seen Jenna during last year's Montauk Point Lighthouse Week. After the caretaker told us the tale about Abigail, the lighthouse's resident ghost, who supposedly also haunts Turtle Hill Bluff, I thought Jenna was going to faint. I had to run down one hundred and thirty-seven steps to the museum gift shop and fetch her a bottle of water, then run back up another hundred and thirty-seven more to give it to her. At that point, I'm the one who needed the water. As for Captain Kidd haunting Shepherds Cottage, Jenna told me she's seen lights flickering inside when she and Roland were working at the main house. And now we know the story about her grandfather."

"Don't forget the guy her grandfather shot," Elle added.

"All these ghost stories should help ticket sales for the showhouse. However, I'm not really worried about ghosts. I'm worried more about flesh-and-blood husbands."

"Sag Harbor has their own legends and ghosts. But there's something about a lighthouse ghost that's so appealing. Picturing Jenna's dead grandfather—with money stuffed in his mouth—not so much. Tell me about Montauk's Abigail," she said as we entered the charming village of East Hampton with its white clapboard shops and New England feel.

"You know what," I said, "let's wait and go on the lighthouse tour together. As part of the tour, the caretaker will tell you all about it."

"What the heck!" Elle screeched, slamming on the brakes.

A huge white dog, barely visible in the mist and fog, bounded in front of the pickup. Our heads jerked forward, then backward. Our seat belts saved us from cracking our heads against the steering wheel and dashboard.

"I could have killed it!" Elle murmured, visibly shaken. "Was that a sign? Maybe we should take Jenna more seriously. I've changed my mind. I'm going to pull over and put a call into Arthur. How do we always seem to get in these situations?"

Her guess was as good as mine. I knew one thing: I was shaking harder than my fat cat Jo after she saw a mouse. Even I couldn't be one hundred percent sure whether what had passed in front of the truck was a real dog or some ghostly canine specter out of the pages of a Stephen King novel. And coming from me, who never had a one-on-one encounter with a ghost, that was saying a lot.

Now, who had the overactive imagination?

Chapter 3

"Don't worry, if it starts to rain, you know me, I have plenty of tarps to protect the blanket chest," Elle said, opening the door to Grimes House Antiques.

Elle took a couple steps then stopped short. I stumbled into her, hitting my chin on the top of her head. "What the heck!" I yelped, almost decapitating my tongue. Elle's phone clattered to the floor. As she lurched forward to grab it, she lost her footing. I grabbed her by the hood of her jacket to keep her from smashing into a mahogany tea cart topped with a full service of blue and white china. Based on all the small placard signs the owner had spaced around the shop, *You break it, you buy it!*, it was a good thing I'd saved Elle from *buying it*.

Elle didn't feel the same way. "Why'd you do that!" she said, choking, her hand at her neck.

"I saved you from disaster. Next time, give a girl a warning before you put the brakes on to read your phone."

Elle picked up her phone and whispered something under her breath. I pointed to my ear to remind her to speak louder, which she did. "Arthur answered. Said he'll look into things with Roland Cahill. He's also contacting someone about the ghosthunters hanging outside Enderly Hall's gates."

"Great," I said with little enthusiasm.

"Meg Barrett, you sound disappointed. Jenna has enough to deal with."

"I'm not disappointed," I said. "I'm happy Arthur is putting Roland Cahill on his radar, but you've got my interest piqued about how those ghosthunters go about their otherworldly investigations."

"Are you serious? We don't want anyone hanging around Enderly to add to Jenna's stress."

"Don't get your poodle skirt in a bunch."

"However, I am glad you might be open-minded to the idea," she added.

"I'm not open-minded, just curious about their equipment and claims of scientific proof." I put quotation marks in the air around *scientific proof.*

"One day, Meg Barrett, you'll have to admit, not everything's in black and white."

"Yes, Mother. Oh, I believe in gray. But I believe that evil only comes from human beings, not ghosts, spells, or pirates' curses."

The shop owner, Rita Grimes, stood behind an antique wood-and-glass general store counter to the right of the door. Instead of an old brass cash register, as expected in the quaint circa-1840s shop that had once been a pharmacy, Rita was tapping at a modern touchscreen monitor without even looking at it. Which told me that she'd been listening to our conversation.

"Hey, Rita," Elle called out. "How's biz?"

"Hello, Ms. Warner," Rita said.

What was I? Chopped liver? Rita gave me a dismissive look, her round tortoiseshell glasses magnifying her brown, almost-black eyes. As usual, Rita's thin lips were superglued into a frown as she walked toward us.

Once I'd made the mistake of trying to bargain with her over a brass spyglass for one of my Cottages by the Sea clients. That would never happen again. Rita had snatched the spyglass out of my hand and pushed me out the door. Later, I smoothed things over by bringing her a few items I'd scored at an estate sale in Bridgehampton. With the cash she'd given me, I was able to purchase the spyglass *at full price*. Since then, I think she tolerated me. Now, looking over at Elle and Rita exchanging Hamptons double-cheek air kisses, I knew Rita and I would never be besties. But a girl could always hope.

After they broke away from their little lovefest, Rita pointed and said, "There it is. A New England pine blanket chest."

I walked over to a small alcove and ran my hand over the smooth wood. "It's perfect. Any chance you'll tell me what Jenna paid for it?"

Putting her hands on her small hips, Rita shook her head in the negative. Her dark hair was sprinkled with threads of gray and pulled back in a tight no-nonsense bun. Her no-nonsense bun matched her no-nonsense personality. Not usually the chatty type, she surprised me when she said, "I overheard you talking about ghosthunters. Do you believe a whole bunch of them, dragging all kinds of equipment, came in here looking for any antiques relating to East Hampton's Witch, Goody Garlick? Like I would keep something from 1642 in my shop. I sent them to the East Hampton Library."

Elle laughed. "Goody Garlick? What kind of name is that?"

"Goody was a generic name used by colonists when identifying married women; first names were rarely used when addressing the commoner. It's short for Goodwife. The story goes that the daughter of East Hampton's founding father, Lion Gardiner, delirious on her deathbed, accused Goody Garlick of putting a spell on her and making her ill. Goody was sent to a witch tribunal in Connecticut, because at the time East Hampton was part of Connecticut. Goody's witch trial was decades older than any from Salem. Hence, she was thought to be one of the first accused witches in American history."

"What happened to her?" Elle asked.

"Oh, they let her go," Rita said.

"So, what did you tell the paranormal investigators?" I asked, already knowing the history of Goodwife Garlick.

"Well, Ms. Barrett, I told them to leave and never come back again. One guy had some machine hanging from a strap around his neck and was waving a wired wand over items at the back of the store. He stopped at an old yarn winder. The machine gave off clicking noises like a metal detector. You'd be surprised at how many people think antiques have some sort of supernatural connection to their deceased owners. When my elite clientele and their decorators step inside my shop, they demand privacy. I don't need anyone scaring them away."

I opened my mouth to ask Rita if she'd ever felt anything unusual with any of her pieces. She must have read my mind because she snapped, "You better get that piece out of here before it starts raining. I don't think Ms. Eastman will be pleased if that happens. Especially knowing what she paid for it." With that, Rita turned and went into the back room.

When she was sure Rita was out of earshot, Elle said, "I wanted to hear the rest of the witch story."

"I can finish it for you, but it'll have to be later. We better get this into the truck." I didn't want to let on to Rita that I probably knew more about the story than she did. In my research of Shepherds Cottage, I'd uncovered a lot of historical documents relating to the

Gardiner family, Captain Kidd, and Goodwife Garlick. Rita had been right on one score—the East Hampton Library was a treasure trove of information.

We each took a side and carried the chest toward the front door.

"Tell me the rest of it when we get in the truck," Elle said. "Sag Harbor had their own share of ghost stories, as you found out when you worked at the Bibliophile Bed and Breakfast, but I never heard of any witch stories."

I went to open the door to the street just as Rita came toward us from the back. She was taking baby steps and carrying a huge black iron cauldron. A witch's cauldron? What were the chances? "Ms. Eastman called, she said you were looking for a cauldron for the hearth at Shepherds Cottage. Tell her she can stop by anytime to settle up."

We lowered the chest to the floor and I took the dirty black thing from her arms, my knees buckling from its weight. Rita was stronger than she looked.

"Oh, and by the way," Rita said, "a word of warning about Roland Cahill. My number-one best customer told me he was the worst contractor this side of Manhattan, and that there were multiple malpractice lawsuits against him, something to do with asbestos or lead poisoning. I can't remember which. I don't know how he got to be a partner in Mr. Klein's architectural firm. Rumor has it they can't stand each other." Rita turned to Elle. "I'm telling you this because I care about Ms. Eastman, and I know you're friends. The Eastmans have been in the Hamptons since the eighteenth century. I knew her grandfather before he went, uh . . . wherever he went in that mind of his for all those years." Rita looked like she wanted to say more but held back.

"Then you must know the story about his death at Enderly Hall," I piped in.

"I don't gossip, Ms. Barrett," Rita said, even though that was exactly what she'd just been doing. She spun around, added a "Humph," then strode toward her office at the back of the shop.

"Was it something I said?" I asked Elle, who was examining a piece of old mercury glass. "Let's get outta here, before she takes back the blanket chest."

Elle nodded toward the cauldron in my arms. "Why don't you

throw that in the back of the truck. I'll wait here. Then we can carry the blanket chest together. If it's drizzling, bring the blue tarp from the storage box."

I shifted from one foot to the other, praying I wouldn't need back surgery. "Okay, boss," I said as she opened the shop's door. "I'll just *toss* this five-ton thing into the back of your truck."

Elle didn't smile. I could tell she was thinking about what Rita had said about Jenna's husband. Just because he was a shoddy contractor didn't mean he was out to kill his wife.

Did it?

Chapter 4

The rain held off, but it was still misty. Even though it was only two in the afternoon, the sky was as dark as if it was nightfall. When I finally reached Elle's pickup, I worried the stitch in my side might be the start of a hernia. I quickly reached over the tailgate and lowered the cauldron onto the bed of the truck. The truck bucked from the weight. The I climbed onto the pickup's running board and reached over to open the storage box. I removed the blue tarp, padded blanket and a couple of bungee cords. I didn't know exactly what Jenna had paid for the blanket chest, but it must have been a lot. Enough to make it worth protecting.

I took my time as I walked back to Grimes House, a reward for carrying the cursed cauldron. As I passed East Hampton Bookworks, I was reminded that I had to buy the next book for the Dead Poets Society Book Club. We were reading a biography on Walt Whitman, and I felt a tiny flutter in my stomach at the thought that I was holding the next meeting. Normally, it wouldn't have been such a big deal because I'd finally finished getting the interior of my cottage exactly as I'd dreamed it would be. The problem with having the club meet at my place was it meant I had to supply the food and drink. The drink wasn't an issue, but the food was. I wasn't a cook by anyone's stretch of the imagination. My gourmet home-chef father had been coaching me via video chat on how to make his tomato basil salmon. The recipe called for only five ingredients. Four too many, in my opinion. I wasn't confident of my ability to pull it off. Good thing I had Montauk's Pizza Village on speed dial.

Ten minutes later, with the blanket chest swaddled between us, Elle and I walked in the direction of where the pickup was parked. It wasn't surprising we hadn't gotten a parking spot in front of Grimes House Antiques. Even off-season, East Hampton was the most popular of the Hamptons, with its tree-lined shaded streets and designer clothing, jewelry, and home goods shops, not to mention Michelin-star restaurants, coffee bistros, and gourmet markets.

I loved East Hampton, and the other Hamptons, but I'd take my sleepy hamlet of Montauk over them any day.

When we were in front of East Hampton Bookworks, my heel caught a raised section of the sidewalk. My feet give way, and before

I could hit pavement, someone's strong arms caught me from behind.

A male voice whispered into my right hearing aid, "Our greatest glory is not in never falling, but in rising every time we fall."

I recognized that voice. Strangely, in his arms, I felt as comfortable as I knew I would.

"Keats? Byron?" I asked without turning my head

"No. Confucius," Patrick Seaton said, laughing. "Are you okay?"

Elle and I lowered the blanket chest to the sidewalk. I turned to face not only Montauk's most famous recluse author but also my former neighbor and current poetry pen pal in the sand. "I'm fine, thanks to you."

Standing beside Patrick with an amused grin on her face was Patrick's book publicist. "Wow, that was like something out of a Hallmark movie," Ashley Drake said through glossy lips that were the perfect shade of peach. "Patrick to the rescue." She smiled in amusement, not jealousy. I'd only met her once at a New Year's Eve party and had immediately liked her. In all honesty, I wished I hadn't. Ever since moving to Montauk, when I first found melancholy verses of poetry etched in the sand next to my rental cottage, I'd felt a kinship with Patrick Seaton that bordered on attraction. But then, there had always been Cole . . .

Patrick was a *New York Times* bestselling author of corporate thrillers. After a drunk driver killed his young wife and child, he moved to Montauk and lived in a solitary cottage on a cliff above the ocean. Based on our few meetings, the books he'd written, and the lines of poetry he left in the sand, I thought I had some insight into his soul. I recalled when I used to watch him walking the beach in front of my old cottage rental, head down, looking inconsolable.

Recently, I'd seen a change in the way he carried himself and in his choice of words he'd left in the sand. The verses were more upbeat, bordering on sunny and downright positive. I wondered if Ashley Drake had anything to do with it.

Admittedly, he and not Claire, my next-door neighbor, friend, and a renowned poet, was the reason I joined the Dead Poets Society Book Club. But I would never tell Claire that little fact. It was too soon to think of anything romantic where Patrick was concerned. I was *definitely* on the rebound. However, there was a connection between Patrick and me that sizzled in the air whenever we met. I just didn't know if he and Ashley felt that same connection.

"Mr. Seaton!" Elle said. "Thank heavens you were there to catch Meg."

"Call me Patrick, please," he said, running his long-fingered hands through his tousled dirty blond hair. The color of his eyes changed with his surroundings. Sometimes they were blue, sometimes green. Or, like today, a shade that matched the fog-drenched sky.

Elle had met Patrick for the first time at Claire's New Year's Eve party, then again at the wrap party for the pilot episode of *Mr. & Mrs. Winslow*. When Elle had found out last December that Patrick was the screenwriter for *Mr. & Mrs. Winslow*, she'd said, "Wow! What are the chances?" Insinuating that Patrick and I were star-crossed lovers.

It seemed the universe did keep bringing us together.

I glanced over at Elle's face. I could tell she was oiling her fixer-upper gears, and I wasn't referring to vintage furniture fixing up. Now that she'd hit the matrimony trail, she was determined to drag me along with her.

"Megan," Ashley said, "I'm so happy we, or should I say Patrick, literally ran into you. I've finally found a cottage in Montauk that I would love to have your company decorate. I'd adore it if you'd come by before I sign the papers at Sand and Sun Realty with your wonderful friend Barb. By the way, thank you for that. It's not on the ocean like Patrick's"—she smiled at him—"it's on Lake Montauk and there's a hill view of both the ocean and the sound." She waved her left hand in the air and I noticed an unusual ring on her finger. *Her ring finger.* An exquisite ring. A large amber cabochon topped a gold band resembling a filigree coral reef. I'd never seen anything like it. Had Patrick given it to her?

It was none of my business, but my heart sank just the same. I realized the crux of my problem. I was mourning Cole one minute, then attracted to Patrick the next. I mentally pinched myself. I loved my solitary life. Who needed a guy to complicate things, tell you what to do, promise things and never come through. *I am woman, hear me roar!* Then I looked over at Patrick and all my brain came up with was a weak *meow*.

"Uh, sure, Ashley," I said with forced enthusiasm. "How about I come by next week? My hands are quite full with the showhouse."

"Showhouse?" Ashley asked, raising a perfect brow and looking over at Patrick. "The new Montauk Designer Showhouse?"

In mama bear mode, Elle said proudly, "Meg's doing all the exterior spaces at Enderly Hall and the interior of Shepherds Cottage."

"How perfect," Ashley chirped. "I heard about the Stanford White cottage on Hamptons TV. Even managed to get an invite to the cocktail party, didn't we, Patrick?"

"Not that I'm aware of," he said.

Ashley put her hand on his arm. "Patrick hates when I drag him to these Hamptons events. But if he wants to sell his next book, we have to hit the publicity trail. Whether he likes it or not." Then she turned to Elle. "I'm sorry, have we met?" She extended her hand, "Ashley Drake."

Elle seemed starstruck. "Yes, we met briefly last New Year's Eve at Claire's."

"Of course," Ashley said, adding a huge white-toothed grin, "now I remember." Not even the fog could diminish her beauty; hazel eyes sparked under thick dark lashes, pink flushed her cheeks and a few stray sections of glossy dark brown hair escaped a loose chignon, giving her a tousled, just-got-out-of-bed look. I glanced at my reflection in the plate glass window of Bookworks. My shoulder-length blonde hair was in tight ringlets from the humidity, springing out horizontally. Instead of a just-got-out-of-bed look, my hair resembled Frankenstein's bride's after waking from the dead and getting zapped with a few bolts of lightning.

Ashley winked at Elle. "If we let these poetry geeks go on and on about their dead poets, we could be here all day. And I think it's starting to drizzle."

"You're right," Elle said.

Patrick handed Ashely a bag from Bookworks and bent to pick up the blanket chest.

"Let me get the other end," I said.

He didn't protest. "I'll walk backward. Just give me a warning if I'm going to bump into anything."

"Promise. I've got your back. Like you had mine." After my

words came out, I giggled. A schoolgirl's giggle. An embarrassing giggle.

"This sucker is heavy," he said as we started walking, "you have a body in here?"

"Nope. Just an antique blanket chest for Shepherds Cottage."

"Do you know the history of Shepherds Cottage?" he asked.

"As much as I could find out."

I thought he was going to mention the cottage's connection to Gardiners Island and Captain Kidd or Witch Goody Garlick. Instead he said, "I've been told Walt Whitman stayed in Shepherds Cottage when he was invited onto Gardiners Island in the early 1850s."

"Really? Long Island's very own poet laureate? This month's dead poet? I had no idea. Isn't that around the time he wrote *Leaves of Grass*? 'Resist much, Obey little.'"

"Is that your credo?" he asked, his face blurred in the mist but still extremely handsome.

"Hmmm, kind of. I try."

Elle and Ashley were following behind, my best friend singing my praises and telling Ashley how she wouldn't be sorry she'd decided to hire Cottages by the Sea to decorate her new place. I didn't hold an interior design degree or belong to any top-notch guild, but I still considered myself an interior decorator, drawing on my years of experience at *American Home and Garden* magazine, an unhealthy obsession with home décor magazines and blogs, along with a passion for creating cozy nests using one-of-a-kind vintage décor.

"Tree!" I called out to Patrick.

"Tree?"

Bam! The corner of the blanket chest hit the trunk of an elm. Patrick didn't lose his grip, but I whiplashed backward, then forward, the wind knocked out of my lungs from where chest met chest.

"Oh, that tree," he said, laughing. "You okay?"

That was the second time in a few minutes that he'd asked me that. After I righted myself, I apologized for not giving him a better warning, blaming it on the fog. As we resumed walking, a crack of thunder sounded.

There was no time for anything but hurrying to Elle's truck before the deluge hit.

A few minutes later, after quick farewells to Patrick and air kisses from Ashley, we put the chest in the bed of Elle's truck and hit the road.

By the time we reached Amagansett, the rain had stopped. The sky was still hazy but brighter than what we'd left behind in East Hampton.

"Well, that was an interesting encounter," Elle said. "What do you think? Any chance you and Patrick might become more than just pen pals in the sand."

"Eyes on the road. Don't want to run over any ghostly white dogs."

"You're incorrigible. Are you worried Ashley and Patrick are dating? Even if they were, Ashley's not his type. You are."

"Did you see that ring on her finger?"

"Pshaw. It didn't look like an engagement ring. Very unusual though. Exotic."

I glanced out the window thinking of Patrick and Ashley. And Cole. "Elle! Pull over!"

"What! Why?"

"Just park. We just passed Jenna's husband, Roland Cahill in front of the Cantina with his back facing the street. He was gesturing widely and angrily to someone in front of him."

From years of putting up with my *antics*, I was happy Elle did what she was told and stopped the pickup.

"Look," I said, "it's Kuri he's talking to. I wonder what's going on?"

"Who?"

"Kuri Shui, one the decorators for the showhouse. She also works at Klein and Associates with Roland. Jenna says she's an amazing interior designer with tons of credentials. Roland's not happy with her aesthetic. Let's mosey over and check it out."

"Mosey? What about the blanket chest?" Elle asked. "It might start raining again."

"It's safe. Plus, it's lasted a couple centuries, and it's wrapped well. A few more minutes or drops of rain won't hurt it. Stop being a killjoy."

Elle put her foot on the gas and coasted into a spot in front of Hampton Chutney. "I don't know if this is the right thing to do. You and I both agreed that we thought Jenna was exaggerating about Roland trying to kill her. What's the point of stalking him?"

"We aren't stalking. The point is, she's our friend. In case we're wrong, we need to keep an eye on him. Even Rita thinks he's a bad egg. I never cared for the guy, but for Jenna's sake I've been tolerating him while working on the showhouse. Oh, the stories I could tell . . ."

"Tell me. Tell me," she said, clapping her hands like a toddler. "I need something to keep my mind off my fiancé's minimalist texts. I ask him what he's up to and he always replies with stock two- or three-word answers. If I hear another *I'm fine. All's good. Call you later. Love you,* I'm gonna scream."

"The last one wasn't bad."

"I want to hear about Roland. I only know the good things Jenna has told me. Up until today, that is."

"I'll tell you after we check out the scene across the street. If you don't want to come, that's cool. You can wait here."

"I'm coming. You know you need me as your wingwoman. People tend to trust me when I tell a fib. You, on the other hand, they seem to steer away from."

"Must be your trusting Bambi eyes and freckles."

"Funny. More likely it has to do with your Hamptons rep of always finding dead bodies."

We looked at each other in recognition that Jenna Eastman might be our next dead body. Not if I had anything to do with it, I thought, glancing back toward the street. "Look, Roland has a hold of Kuri's wrist." I watched Kuri pull away. Then she spat some words I couldn't make out by lipreading. It must have been something along the lines of *Get your huge mitts off my delicate wrist or else.*

Before Elle could protest, I leaped from the truck and bounded toward the pair. Behind me, I heard the driver's door to the pickup slam and Elle shout, "Wait!"

Now she'd done it. Both Roland and Kuri looked toward us.

So much for sneaking up on them.

Chapter 5

"Ms. Barrett, fancy meeting you here. Done with the cottage and outdoor spaces already? We only have one more day until the cocktail party." Roland Cahill stuck out his wide chest cock-a-doodle-do style. "And in my opinion, everyone except Freya seems too laid-back about it. Including my wife." Roland looked down his long nose at Kuri, apparently including her in his chastising.

Today he was dressed in his stock outfit of stonewashed jeans, black loafers, no socks, and a white open-collar shirt under a navy blazer. He reeked of expensive cologne. I guessed he was about six foot one, Patrick Seaton's height. But that was where their similarities ended. Roland probably had fifty or more pounds on Patrick. His white hair was buzzed close to his scalp, military fashion, and he wore a pair of black Ray-Bans on top of his head. There hadn't been any sun in days. When he turned his head toward me, I saw the reason for the glasses. Roland had a black eye. Well, more of an eggplant-colored eye. Day two of a good shiner.

Who walloped him? Jenna? A disgruntled client?

Roland placed his large hand on my shoulder and said, "I've been meaning to talk to you about the way you arranged the sleeping porch . . ." Here it came. I moved back a step and his hand dropped to his side. "I'm happy with what you've done."

Say what? "Uh, thanks," I said cautiously.

"Actually," he said, "Freya pointed out how much she loves your choices for all our exterior spaces. Maybe you should thank her. It might help to get your name known in the Hamptons. Play your cards right and she might put you on her show, *Hamptons Home and Garden*. When she contacted me about being on the team for the showhouse, she promised to spread the word about my contracting services." He leaned in close, as if to whisper, then said in a super-loud voice that made me jump from the amplified sound in my hearing aids, "She also hinted she would arrange a meeting with a certain celebrity acquaintance who is looking to do a teardown of his 1920s cottage in East Hampton. I'm not allowed to disclose his name, but . . . I'll give you a hint. His last name rhymes with *sit*."

"And his first name," I asked, taking the bait.

"Hmm, that might give it away. Oh, what does it matter. His first name rhymes with *sad*."

Sad Sit. As far as I knew, the megastar actor he was alluding to didn't hang out much in the Hamptons. Another sterling quality of Roland's, he was a name-dropper. I'd bet it took everything he had not to disclose the star's name. You'd think just the fact his wife was worth at least as much as the person he alluded to would make Roland less of a wannabe. Being a yearlong resident, I was cognizant of all the star-studded comings and goings by reading our local papers, especially *Dave's Papers*. I liked a good celeb sighting as much as the next guy, reminding me of the time I was paying for my produce at the East Hampton Farmers Market and looked over to see . . .

"I'm sure I'll be getting lots of star clients now that I'm with the most prestigious architectural firm in the Hamptons, Klein and Associates," Roland boasted. "Right, Kuri?"

"Oh, I wouldn't be so sure about that, Mr. Cahill," Kuri said, clenching her fists. Her black hair, stick-straight and angled to the shoulder, and her blunt-cut bangs complimented her small-featured face, giving her an exotic appearance. "I'm going to have a talk with Nate, then the firm's lawyer, about your earlier, inappropriate behavior." She began rubbing the red area on her wrist from where Roland had held it. Maybe Kuri was the black eye deliverer? If she wasn't, by the look on her face she might go after the other eye.

"You talk to Nate, then maybe I'll have a little discussion with your husband about *your* inappropriate behavior, Mrs. Shui."

Roland's threat seemed to quiet Kuri. Then he turned to Elle and asked brusquely, "Who are you?"

"Elle Warner. I worked with Jenna at *American Home and Garden* magazine."

My dander was up, and I took a step toward him. "She also owns Mabel and Elle's Curiosities in Sag Harbor, the same place Jenna found many items for the showhouse. I'm sure without Elle and her shop the showhouse wouldn't be a success."

He snorted dismissively. "How could it not be a success? The furniture and most of the accessories were stored in the attic, and they came straight from Stanford White's warehouse. I'm sure, Ms. Warner, you've helped Jenna with a few pieces, but I don't think you can take the credit for the success of the showhouse. That goes to Stanford White."

Jerk. "And Jenna and the designers, and Elle," I added.

He softened a little in his response. "You forgot to add my name to the list. If it wasn't for me and my construction team and making sure everyone is on task . . ."

"And Nate's architectural plans," Kuri added.

Roland shrugged his shoulders. "There's a difference between drawing up pretty renderings and actually doing the brick-and-mortar physical work."

It was a fact that Roland hadn't done any physical work at Enderly. He'd hired outside contractors to do the repairs, including my go-to team of Duke and Duke Jr. They'd renovated the pavilion at the top of the cliff, along with erecting a new gazebo based on Nate Klein's architectural plans.

There was an awkward silence while Kuri and Roland exchanged dagger eyes. I broke it with, "We had lunch today with Jenna. She told us about her accident." I wanted to warn him that we had our eyes on him.

Roland turned his head in my direction, then refused to meet my gaze. "What accident?" he asked a little too innocently. "Oh, that. I think Jenna has overexaggerated what happened. You know how she is. But I'm keeping an eye on her, don't you worry." He took his phone from his blazer pocket and tapped the screen. "Looks like she's back at Enderly. Snug as a bug in a Persian rug," he said, laughing at his own pun.

Not so safe and sound, I thought. Especially if what she said was true, that he was driving the car that caused her to jump to the side of the road. "We better get back to Enderly ourselves," I said. "I have a few things to add to Shepherds cottage, then a little finessing in the morning and I'll be ready for tomorrow's opening-night cocktail party."

"Well, at least someone is on task." Roland looked at Kuri. "And you will be too, won't you, dear, after you implement the changes I've dictated." Roland looked at me. "Ms. Barrett, you have the most amazing blue eyes. With your fair looks and blonde hair, I bet you have some Scandinavian blood in you. My mother was Norwegian. Add a few pounds in the right places and . . ."

Luckily, just as I was getting ready to slap him, Kuri broke in, "I told you, I'm not changing anything. Jenna and Nate agree. And I'm not your *dear*."

"I know what needs to be done. Nathaniel has no clue."

I wanted to say, *What do you know about interior decorating, you're a contractor?* Instead I said, "Stanford White was not only an architect like Mr. Klein but also an interior decorator. He traveled all over the world collecting one-of-a-kind objects to furnish his Gilded Age clients' homes. Rosecliff in Newport, Rhode Island, is only one example."

Roland scowled at my history lesson, then added a rebuttal. "I'll have you know that in my career I've staged many model homes."

Kuri stepped between me and Roland. She looked Jenna's husband up and down, totally unafraid of his imposing stature. Her dark brown eyes showed fury, not fear. "Jenna also agrees with my aesthetic. She's shown me photos from the early 1900s of my assigned rooms and I've recreated them to her specifications, even adding some contemporary touches. She also told me only this morning that I need to listen to her directives, not yours. And staging small, two-bedroom tract houses and tiny condos is not the same as what I do for Klein and Associates. Remember, I'm not a decorator, *I'm a designer.* There's a big difference between the two."

Roland's ruddy round face got even ruddier. "I know the difference. You design the space with built-ins and furniture placement. But what we need for the showhouse is a decorator. The space has already been *designed* by Stanford White himself. Oh, I'll have a word with my wife," he said through gritted teeth, "and perhaps someone else you might not want me to contact. Better get going, Kuri. I'm doing a walk-through tomorrow and I better not—"

A young man in a black hoodie who I hadn't even noticed approach us tapped Roland on the shoulder. "Sir, I think you dropped something." He held a white envelope in his hand. "That's if you're Roland Cahill?"

"Yes, I'm Roland Cahill, but I . . ."

The guy in the hoodie shoved the envelope into his hand. "Then Roland Cahill, you've been served."

I smiled inwardly at the stunned look on his face, remembering that Rita Grimes had told us her number-one best customer (I would never be in that honored slot, Jenna maybe) said Roland's had numerous past lawsuits. The guy was really turning out to be jerk.

I just hoped he didn't turn into a murderer.

Chapter 6

The ornate iron gates were closed as we approached Enderly Hall; the tips of the arrow-shaped spires were lost in the fog and mist. I passed Elle my key fob with the attached remote Jenna had given me to open the gates. Elle slowed the pickup to a crawl, then stopped under the stone and crushed-shell-covered archway that housed a silver security keypad. Holding the remote, she raised her hand and aimed it in the direction of the keypad.

"Wait! Hold on a minute," I shouted.

Elle lowered her arm. "What is it now?"

"There's someone, or something, lurking behind those bushes." It wasn't Roland waiting to attack his wife because when we'd left Amagansett, he was still on the street talking to someone on his phone. I'd assumed his lawyer.

"I'm getting out."

"Meg, don't be foolish. Let's just get inside the gate and let Jenna and Roland deal with them."

"If we open the gates, whoever they are can slip inside. And remember, Jenna claims Roland wants to kill her. What if instead he hired someone to do it for him?"

Before she could protest, I opened the door and charged in the direction of the shadowy figure I'd seen. For a lack of better words, I called out, "Who goes there?"

Through the bushes red and green lights blinked back at me. The lights moved to the left, then slightly to the right.

"I know someone's there," I warned, stepping closer. "Whatever those lights are, they're giving you away."

The shrubbery parted and a man stepped forward.

Wonder Woman–style, I put my hands on my hips and said with my sternest voice, "This is private property. Vacate or we will call the police."

He didn't answer, his face expressionless. The same couldn't be said for all the gadgets hanging from straps around his neck. He stood about six-three, with short spiked, dark, almost black hair that matched his oversized black-framed glasses. He seemed as solid as the oak he was standing next to. For all my bravado, there was no way I would mess with him. Let Roland get him to leave.

34

Trying a different tactic, I said with a laugh, "You look like a lit Christmas tree. What's all that stuff for?"

He didn't answer. Instead he reached in his pocket, took out something and handed it to me, a business card that I could barely make out in the fog: *Mac Zagan, Certified Scientific Paranormal Investigator* with a phone number and web address.

It seemed I wouldn't have to go surfing TV channels for paranormal reality shows. I had my own personal ghosthunter right in front of me. I dug in my shoulder bag and handed him my card.

He read, "*Meg Barrett, Cottages by the Sea Interior Decorating.* Ever worked on a haunted cottage? This area of Long Island has been around for centuries."

I opened my mouth to say *No ghosts, just a couple of skeletons and dead bodies,* when a low voice filtered toward us from behind the murky foliage. I missed what had been said, but then a young guy with long beach-blond hair, who looked like he'd be more comfortable surfing a mile down the road at Ditch Plains Beach than investigating the paranormal, stepped into view.

"Hey, Mac. Frank's arm is stuck between the bars of the wrought iron fence. He seems kind of new to this stuff. Are you sure he knows what he's doing?"

Mac's voice was deep. "No. I'm not sure. We'll get him out. You're right, I'm getting a feeling he's not cut out for this work. This is the second time he has interfered with one of our scariest, (pause) most chilling, (pause) ghost encounters, (pause) yet."

"Yeah, you mean like earlier at the Montauk Point Lighthouse. When we were down by the rocks and he claimed to have picked up infrared light anomalies of our two-hundred-year-old ghost Abigail, then slipped on a boulder and dropped your Powershot SX620 into the water?"

"He claimed (pause) that Miss Abigail, our spirit, (pause) grabbed his ankle," Mac answered.

The blond guy stepped closer to us. "The dude doesn't even know what crossing over means. Hope Sam's back soon. Where'd you get him, anyway? Craigslist?"

Either they both didn't see me standing in front of them or they thought I was an apparition. I didn't protest, the conversation was quite interesting.

Mac's face remained serious. "We must release him. I wouldn't be surprised if some specter" — he raised a thick black eyebrow then glanced my way to see if I was enjoying the show—"had grabbed him from the other side of the fence. Our EVPs have been off the charts since arriving here."

"What's an EVP?" I asked, loving the way Mac's loud voice made everything seem so intense. I had no problem hearing him.

"Electronic Voice Phenomena," he answered. "We must go to him at once. You have a lot of unexplained light anomalies and shadow figures going on behind those gates, Ms. . . ."

"Barrett, Meg," I answered. "I'll come with you. I was in a similar situation once." Before he could protest, I entered the wooded area that followed the front of Enderly Hall. It wasn't raining, but the air was thick with moisture, the temperature dropping by the second.

The surfer-looking dude took over the lead, stopping about five hundred feet from the front gate. A figure dressed in all black, who I assumed was the dunderhead Frank, was crouched near the wrought iron fence. His right arm, to above his elbow, was stuck between the rails of the fence.

Mac looked down at him and shook his head in annoyance. "Unless you tell me some entity yanked on your arm and that's the reason my ten-thousand-dollar EVP meter is lying on the damp ground on the other side of the fence, then I'll make you pay for any damages." Mac bent next to him, grabbed Frank's upper arm and yanked.

"Ow!" Frank howled, then he followed with a doozy of a curse word.

"You'll dislocate his shoulder," I said, reaching in my pocket for my trusty tube of Burt's Bee's Beeswax Lip Balm. "Allow me." Mac got up and I crouched next to Frank.

I guessed Frank was in his fifties, but it was hard to tell in the gloom. He was thin as a rail—well, maybe not, or he would have been able to remove his arm. Stringy dark hair escaped from under his Yankees baseball cap.

"Does anyone have scissors or a pocketknife?" I asked.

"What the hell are you doing!" Frank said in a gruff and, I thought, very unappreciative voice.

A pair of scissors were put in my outstretched hand and I went to work cutting through Frank's lightweight jacket and shirtsleeve. I reached the fingers of my left hand through the space between the bars and tugged on the fabric, leaving the trapped part of his arm bare. Then I took the cap off my lip balm and greased his arm on both sides, along with the two bars surrounding it. "Okay, you can tug on his upper arm."

Mac did as he was told, and voilà! Frank's arm came free. He collapsed on the damp ground and looked up at us. "My electrocardiogram was going off, so I stuck it through the gate for a closer reading. I swear, Mac, some spirit knocked it from my hand."

"Electrocardiogram?" Mac didn't bother hiding his annoyance. "Were you searching for the spirit's (pause) heartbeat? They don't have one. It's a digital voice recorder, used to conduct EVP sessions. We've been over this. EVP, Electronic (pause) Voice (pause) Phenomena. Mr. Holden, you said you've been on many ghost adventures. I don't think that's the case."

I was about to volunteer to go retrieve the EVP machine, curious about any disembodied voices it might have picked up, when I heard a male voice behind us: "Everyone stay where you are. And back away from Ms. Barrett."

Chapter 7

After an East Hampton Town Police officer sent Mac and his abnormal paranormals away, I got back in the pickup and asked Elle, "Why'd you send for the cops? I was just learning how those ghosthunters work."

She looked at me. "Are you serious? Tell me you're kidding. You disappear with some big guy who steps out of the shrubbery like Frankenstein's monster and I don't see you for ten minutes. What did you think I would do?"

"I was fine."

"Well, next time shoot me a text or something. Jeez."

"Understood. Sorry." I explained to her what went down, ending with, "And the officer wouldn't even let Mac retrieve his lost EVP, saying it had fallen on private property." I didn't tell Elle what an EVP was, or that as soon as she headed home for Sag Harbor, I planned to search for it myself.

Once again, I handed her my key fob. She aimed the controller at the keypad and pulled the truck through the gates.

Even in the doom and gloom, Enderly Hall looked welcoming in its whiteness. The architecture of the main house was a cross between Greek Revival, Colonial, New England Shingle, and Georgian, with a touch of Antebellum that was all cobbled together under a fish-scale roof. It had a pleasing cohesiveness. The combination of styles made me believe that Stanford White had been Enderly Hall's architect. He was known for mixing centuries and traveling the world for inspiration. A wide eight-column front veranda wrapped around both sides of the mansion. I'd painted all the veranda's wood floorboards a pale dove gray, added rugs, wicker furniture, tons of potted ferns and even a few small trees in baskets.

Whether it was Stanford White who designed Enderly Hall or someone else, it was an amazing structure. The icing on the cake was a circular cupola enclosed with eight six-foot windows and a circular balcony affording views of the lighthouse, ocean, and Block Island Sound.

Once through the gates, I directed Elle onto the dirt road that led to Shepherds Cottage. She parked near the only door and we unloaded the blanket chest.

After we climbed the wood steps and placed the blanket chest on the porch's plank floor, Elle asked, "Wait! Did you hear that?"

"No?"

"Sounds like something, or someone, was crashing through the wooded area behind the cottage."

"Probably a human, or a ghost, most likely a deer," I said, removing my keys from the handbag slung across my torso.

She laughed. "Definitely ghost."

I inserted the key into the padlock on the door to the cottage, but the lock swung open without a twist of my key. "What the hey . . . I locked this myself. As far as I know, I have the only key."

"You probably forgot, or Jenna has a spare," Elle said, not too convincingly.

Elle remained at the door and I went back to the truck to get the cauldron. A thick ocean mist hung like a curtain beyond the bluff, blocking breathtaking ocean views. This close to the lighthouse, gorgeous sandy beaches had been replaced with boulders and smooth stones. Some called this part of the shoreline the Montauk Moors, the terrain found in novels like *Wuthering Heights* or *Jane Eyre*. I loved living in my oceanside community, but a few wrong steps on a foggy night and I could find myself tumbling to the rocks below.

My thoughts went to Jenna's grandfather and how he'd been found exactly that way. Then I thought of Jenna's accident with the car—dense fog might have been a factor. As for her grandfather's death, he may have simply wandered off, lost his bearings and dropped to the beach. But what about the hundred-dollar bills that were stuffed in his mouth? Surely that was a warning of some kind. Something you might see on an episode of *The Sopranos*. Jenna said he'd lost his mind, which would also explain things.

I shook off my morose thoughts and went to grab the cauldron.

"Meg."

I jumped at least a foot and turned to face Elle.

She laughed. "What's wrong, did you think I was a ghost? Or ghosthunter? We have so many to choose from. Next time think before you run off with strange men."

"I wasn't worried you were a ghost, but you've gotta give a girl a warning if you're sneaking up behind her. Especially a girl with a hearing loss."

"Sorry. I called your name a few times but you were staring weirdly off in space. With your blonde wavy hair and that long white raincoat, I almost took you for Abigail, the Montauk Point Lighthouse ghost you told me about."

I laughed. "I think I'm more spooked by that husband of Jenna's, not any local ghosts or strange men. Roland Cahill's a piece of work, isn't he? I'm dying to know what was in that subpoena he got."

"My impression is he's very self-absorbed," she said, shivering. "He didn't even remember meeting me at his wedding. Seems a completely different person than the one I saw that night. Always doting on Jenna, never leaving her side. That must be the man Jenna fell in love with. I'm thrilled I called Arthur to look into him. I wonder if we should also have a talk with Morgana. She's the one who sent the officer to save you."

Officer Morgana Moss had been promoted from the front desk of the tiny Montauk substation of the East Hampton Town Police Department to a full-fledged Town of East Hampton officer. She was also the sister-in-law of my Realtor and good friend, Barb.

"Why didn't you tell her about Jenna's fears?" I asked. "If I talk to her, she'll try to pawn off one of those adorable pups on me." Morgana bred Maltipoos—Maltese/poodle mixes—and had been after me since the first day I met her to take one. I had a feeling my fat cat should remain an only child, not only for her sake but for the sake of any other poor pet I tried to bring into the household.

"Thought you would be better at explaining things. Plus, at the time, I thought your life was in danger. I'll keep my fiancé in the loop. You can tell Morgana."

I shrugged my shoulders. "As you wish. I'll stop by after I leave here. Any subpoena would be a matter of public record. Maybe she could help us with that too."

"FYI, Barb told me Morgana is pup-free for the time being. Taking a break from breeding to focus on her new position."

"That's a relief," I said, nodding my head toward the cauldron. "Let's get this inside, I'm looking forward to getting out of here and warming these old bones in front of a fire. My fire."

"That sounds good. Let me help you."

We grabbed hold of the cauldron's handle Jack and Jill–style, then walked to the cottage and went inside.

After we placed the cauldron on the wrought iron hook inside the cavernous brick fireplace, Elle surveyed the space and whistled. "What an amazing job you've done with everything!" Before coming to *American Home and Garden* as my Antiques and Collectibles editor, Elle had worked as an appraiser at Sotheby's Auction House in their Americana division. Not letting her talents go to waste, she was occasionally called in to appraise the value of antiques and art for First Fidelity Mutual's mega-wealthy Hamptons clients, sometimes letting me tag along as her paid assistant.

"With your guidance and counsel, of course." I glanced around the main room to see if anything was missing. Nothing was missing, but I knew the drawer under the primitive server had been closed when I'd left this morning. I also noticed the slight odor of pipe tobacco.

"Was most of the furniture here when you came in?" Elle asked, walking over to the pine sideboard topped with a double-tiered rack lined with pewter plates and tankards.

"No. There was only one piece here when I started. I guess it makes sense, if Jenna's grandfather was a hoarder. They would have had to empty the place out. Have you ever seen one of those hoarder shows? They're awful."

"I agree, we all need a little dignity when living with our idiosyncrasies. We don't need our neuroses plastered all over the boob tube. One look at my carriage house and a shrink might think the same thing about us."

I turned and looked at her. "Boob tube?"

"One of Auntie Mabel's sayings." Elle picked up a mustard-colored pie bird from the sideboard's shelf and cradled it in her hands, then returned it to the shelf. "When Thomas Eastman had to move in here, maybe he brought the Stanford White papers with him."

"Now you're starting to think like a detective. Arthur will be proud when I tell him."

"Doubtful. I've been warned not to get involved in any of your hijinks," she said, then trailed her fingertips across the small rectangular farm table I'd just oiled. "I'm to be on my best behavior while he's working in Manhattan and not let Ms. Barrett get me in any trouble. And you know what he means by trouble."

"Nothing going on had to do with me or you . . ."

"Yet. Oh, there's still time for hijinks, I'm sure. But you have done a wonderful job with the interior of the cottage. Everything looks so authentic for the time period."

I beamed at the compliment. "After the designer showhouse, Jenna plans on keeping Shepherds Cottage open to the public, making it a stop for school field trips. Jenna really cares about her family estate."

"At the thought of Roland selling Enderly Hall and Shepherds Cottage, I think Jenna's justified in her anger. I'll bet a hundred bucks Roland doesn't tell her about that subpoena. You should tell her," Elle said, walking over to a primitive yarn winder.

"I should? I'm working here. You tell her. Her husband can't convince Jenna to fire you."

"She would never do that. And I have a feeling his bluster is worse than his bite."

"I'm not so sure. Did you see Kuri's wrist?"

"Enough of this depressing talk," she said, clapping her hands. "Let me enjoy looking around, then I need to scat."

"Yes, ma'am. The space is so tiny, your tour should take about five minutes. I don't know how they did it back then. I would be claustrophobic. Here's the main room, obviously," I said.

In the main room was a primitive handmade wood table and rush seat ladderback chairs. A pine corner cupboard displayed white ironstone and an assortment of wood butter molds. Next to the cupboard was a New England spice chest that I knew wasn't a reproduction, because Jenna had purchased it at an auction from Christie's in Manhattan. The final piece of furniture next to the yarn winder was a pine dry sink. I'd placed an antique crock sporting a New York pottery maker's mark in the dry sink. Inside the crock, I'd added a lush Boston fern, wanting to add a touch of green to enliven the low-ceilinged, cramped space. The plant was the only thing that differed from what you might find in an original late-1600s sheepherder's cottage.

Elle walked next to the dry sink. She held up the crock to read the maker's mark. "Wow, where did this come from?"

"Jenna found it at a shop in Bridgehampton. Paid five hundred for it."

She turned it around in her hands, then searched the bottom. "Don't tell her, but it's a fake. A good fake."

"It fooled me," I said, disappointed. "But you're right, Jenna has enough going on. And most everything from the time period Shepherds Cottage was first built is long gone anyway, and completely unaffordable.

"Jenna's vision was to recreate how the interior might have looked in 1699, the same time period of Captain Kidd's historic landing on Gardiners Island, where he'd buried his treasure. It's said that he warned the Gardiner family that if they touched it, they would pay the highest price. Only it was Kidd who'd paid the highest price."

"You've gotta love a good treasure story," Elle said.

"Exactly." I bent down to grab one side of the blanket chest. "Can you help me bring this to the bedroom?"

"Of course," she said, reaching for the other end.

Ten steps later, we went through the open doorway to the bedroom. At five foot seven, my head barely cleared the top of the threshold. I'd read somewhere that the average height of a man in the seventeenth century was around five foot four, which explained the cottage's low ceilings.

We centered the chest in front of the bed.

"Pretty snazzy for a sheepherder's cottage," Elle said, referring to the fourposter bed that took up most of the room.

"Tell me about it," I moaned. "I only had enough room left for a candlestand table and that small dresser that I got from your shop. The bed's the only piece of furniture that came with the cottage from when it was delivered in 1900 from Gardiners Island. Jenna said it originally came from the Gardiners' manor house. How it ended up in Shepherds Cottage is a mystery. I got rid of the mattress and added a cotton feather topper from a catalog. It's not like anyone will be sleeping on it."

"Especially if the cottage is haunted. The bed's beautiful. The hand-carved spindle posters and legs were made on a lathe, quality craftsmanship for the time period," Elle recited in her Sotheby's voice.

"Instead of slats to hold the mattress there are ropes. I even found an old key tied to the frame. Not sure what that's for."

"That's one mystery I can solve," Elle said. "The key is to tighten the ropes if the mattress starts to sag."

"Of course. I should have thought of that."

"You're learning, my little Americana grasshopper," she said, smiling. "Seriously, you've done a magnificent job."

I was pleased by her compliment as I took two folded quilts from the end of the bed and placed them in the blanket chest, letting the corner of one peek out before closing it.

A few minutes later, after I showed her the other small room, Elle said, "Well done, Meg Barrett. And you didn't even need help from little ole me."

"Good thing I let you drag me to Colonial Williamsburg that time," I teased.

She laughed. "You mean the time you didn't want us to veer off the Virginia junk-pickin' trail in order to see some *boring*, fake colonial village. The same place where I had to physically pull you away from the blacksmith's shop, where there was that muscular reenactor, all shirtless and oozing muscles, wearing a leather apron, and who you said looked like, if I might quote you, *the dark, brooding actor who had played Ross Poldark on PBS?*"

I grinned. "Not true. I wasn't interested in him; just how to form a horseshoe the old-fashioned way."

"Horseshoe, my . . ."

"Okay, okay." I threw my hands in the air. "I surrender. You win. Colonial Williamsburg was an amazing experience."

Elle headed for the doorway. "Unless you need me," she said, reaching in her handbag and removing her keys, "I better head back to Sag Harbor. Maurice has his little league game to coach, although I don't know how those boys will be able to see each other in this fog." Maurice was Elle's full-time salesperson at Mabel and Elle's Curiosities. "And I have a pine breakfront to wax," she added. "Wait until I show you the before and after pics. Maurice has been putting things on a photo app with their price and selling them before they can even make it from the carriage house to the shop," she said, grinning.

"Hey, I'd like a preview of your treasures before you send them out to the masses."

"I think you have enough of your own fixer-uppers in the carriage house. It seems your assigned half is piled high with projects. But yes, I will give you a heads-up. Only because you're planning my engagement party, bestie." She gave me a quick hug and I followed her back into the main room.

Putting her hands on her hips, Elle did another scan of the room. "How perfect is that cauldron from Grimes House? A perfect pairing, along with that crude broomstick leaning against the hearth. Now all you need is a docent dressed as the witch from Hansel and Gretel to tell the tale of Goody Garlick." She glanced at her wristwatch. "Hey, you said you'd tell me about her."

"A quick synopsis. Once upon a time, Goody Garlick's husband worked on Gardiners Island. Lion Gardiner, owner of the island and founding father of East Hampton, also the father of the woman who accused Goody of witchcraft, knew his daughter was out of her mind from an illness when she accused Goody of witchcraft. After Goodwife Garlick was exonerated, Lion Gardiner took care of both Goody and her husband until their deaths. I'm pretty sure the Garlicks lived in East Hampton, though, not in Shepherds Cottage, but the romanticist in me likes to think they did. It's a much better picture than Jenna's unsound grandfather living in here. Maybe I should let my paranormal investigator buddy Mac inside, so he can use some of his gadgets to look for trapped spirits needing to pass over to the other side." I hummed my version of the *Twilight Zone* theme song.

"Now I have the heebie-geebies," Elle moaned, wrapping her arms around herself. "Let's continue the ghost discussion when we go to the lighthouse. Now that the ghosthunter crew has been evicted from Enderly, I bet they mosey down the highway to the lighthouse to visit your Abigail."

"You mean Montauk's Abigail," I said as she blew me a kiss, then went out the open door.

I called after her, "Be careful driving in this ungodly weather." All I could see as she walked away were her vintage red high-top Keds. "Text me when you get there."

She called back, "You're not usually a worrier. What's got you so mushy and motherly?"

"Mushy? Me? Motherly? Never. Now scat!"

I closed the door against the cold and damp, then glanced around the interior of the cottage. Suddenly I felt isolated. *What was up?*

I'd never been one with any psychic tendencies. Did I detect a premonition of doom?

Maybe. No. Just a long day.

I tried to shake it off like a dog drying off after a dip in the ocean. But couldn't.

Chapter 8

Satisfied the cottage was good to go, I padlocked the only door, then followed the path toward the main house. Earlier, after looking at the tracking app on his phone, Roland had told us that Jenna was at Enderly. When Elle and I pulled up, we hadn't seen her navy Range Rover, just Vicki's pink minivan with her Veronica's Interiors logo, a black Infiniti sedan, Freya's BMW, and my Woody Wagoneer.

The air carried with it a chill that belonged to November, not May. Halfway to the main house, I looked to my left and saw movement inside the gazebo. Through the haze, like something from a romance movie, I saw the silhouettes of two people in an embrace. I crept closer, not because I was a voyeur, more that I was positive one of the figures was Jenna. If the other person was Roland, then apparently they'd made up.

Only the man wasn't Roland. It was the architect Nate Klein, Roland's new partner, the owner of Klein and Associates, and Kuri's boss.

Was Nate just comforting Jenna? Perhaps she'd told him her suspicions that Roland was trying to kill her. Or were they an item?

Not wanting to get caught spying, I turned and walked toward the main house. Out of the fog, I saw Vicki appear. She called out, "Hello. Who's there? This fog is ridiculous."

"Meg. Meg Barrett," I answered when she was only a few feet in front of me.

"Hard to tell what's what in this crappy weather," she said in a loud voice. "I saw that Nate's, I mean, Mr. Klein's car is parked in the circle. I need to ask him a question about the back parlor, to see if my choices match the architecture of the room. My jackass of a former stepfather isn't happy with my choices. If Mother was alive, she'd never let him talk to me like that."

Jenna had told me that Vicki's deceased mother had only been married to Roland for a short time, and when she'd been alive, Veronica's Interiors had been a top Manhattan interior design company, which was no longer the case.

"I've forgotten, Meg, what's your role here?" Vicki asked, barely taking a breath between words. She was wearing a pale pink trench coat with its collar up, a fuchsia scarf at her neck. The few times I'd seen her at Enderly, she'd always worn some shade of pink.

Feeling protective of Jenna's privacy, I wanted to keep Vicki from seeing her with Nate. I stepped closer, giving her no choice but to take a step back. "I'm the local decorator," I said. "Cottages by the Sea. Remember? I gave you my card."

"Of course, you're Jenna's little friend. The girl who's furnishing that lean-to shack over yonder." She waved her heavily gold-braceleted wrist in the direction of Shepherds Cottage.

I kept my temper about the lean-to comment.

Her long wavy chestnut hair was accented with copper highlights and pouffed and teased at the back of her crown, styled like an aging country western singer. Sweeping bangs covered half of her right eye. The color and texture of her hair seemed almost too beautiful to be real. But then again, Vicki lived in Manhattan. If you didn't have a budget, like some, including me, you could find that special salon that would spray your hair with gold dust and chipped diamonds. But now that I thought about it, Jenna had told me that Veronica's Interiors was nearing bankruptcy. Roland convinced Jenna to hire Vicki as one of the decorators. Maybe the man did have a soft spot in his soul that I'd somehow missed?

"I know they call Montauk 'The End' because of its location," Vicki said, glancing toward the gazebo.

"Yes, the easternmost tip of Long Island."

"Well, I think it's isolating, and not as exciting as where I live in the Village. And what do they have in this one-horse town, about ten shops? Amagansett's even worse."

"But you're staying on beachfront property, only steps from the ocean. It must be heavenly." I knew the Amagansett cottage she was staying in was nothing to grumble about. But then, Vicki seemed a pro at complaining.

"Who would know with all this crappy weather," she said, flipping her hair off her shoulder. "I'm just happy Roland has moved here permanently and won't be interfering with my company anymore. Why my mother named him as chief operating officer when she was alive, I'll never understand. Are you a member of ASID? I don't remember seeing you at any of our Manhattan functions."

"No. I don't get to Manhattan much. I prefer to stay in Montauk." ASID stood for American Society of Interior Designers. I didn't correct her that I was doing more than just the cottage for the showhouse, and even though it was none of my business, the fact Roland had been chief operating officer of his dead ex-wife's design company gave me a moment of pause. It sure bothered Vicki. I wondered if it bothered Jenna.

"You do know that Roland only married Jenna for her money," Vicki said. "My mother was his one true love. Too bad Mother hadn't felt the same way." She smiled an evil grin. "Well? Have you seen him? Nate Klein?"

"No. Sorry."

She turned and started toward the gazebo. I grabbed her elbow and spun her around to face the back of Enderly Hall. She tried to pull away, but I kept hold and said, "Safety in numbers. We don't want to trip on something and not be on hand for tomorrow's cocktail party."

Vicki laughed. "You mean, and fall like Jenna did? She's the clumsiest person I've ever met. I don't know what Roland sees in her. She doesn't hold a candle, design-wise or beauty-wise, to my mother. Did you know, before her death, for five years in a row, Veronica's Interiors was voted by *Architectural Digest* as one of the top ten interior decorating firms in the country? My mother's great-aunt was Sister Harris. Design runs in our genes."

Since taking over her deceased mother's firm, I hadn't seen one mention of Vicki's or Veronica's Interiors in any home décor magazine. And I read them all. "That's amazing. I'd love to see what you've accomplished inside."

She stopped suddenly. "Do you think Nate's checking things out at the gazebo? Don't you think it turned out amazing? You know he was not only the architect for the restoration of Enderly Hall but also for another Stanford White house in Montauk. Resurrecting it from the ashes after it burned down."

"No, I didn't know that, but I do know he isn't at the gazebo because I just delivered cushions for the benches that circle the interior." A small white lie. I'd finished the gazebo décor two days ago.

"Oh, Jenna gave you the gazebo and the beach pavilion to

decorate. I need to have a chat with her. I only got two lousy rooms to work on." She stuck out her bottom lip. "And they certainly aren't the cream of the crop, like that decorator nobody Freya Rittenhouse's rooms. The woman's not even a designer. But I have to play nice with her because of her Hamptons TV show. It's not Freya's fault anyway, I blame Jenna. She's holding Roland's relationship with my mother against me. Now I have proof. Giving the best spaces to not one but two unlicensed locals."

I bit the inside of my cheek to keep from pushing Vicki headfirst into one of the thorny hedges lining the walkway.

When we reached the back veranda, Vicki stopped and looked in the direction of the ocean. She squealed, "Nate! Oh, Nate, there you are. I have a design question for you."

Nate Klein appeared through the mist like some handsome raven-haired duke from a Regency novel. He pivoted his tall, lean body as if to avoid us, then must have realized Vicki would chase after him no matter which way he turned.

I was just relieved he wasn't with Jenna.

Nate nodded at me, then gave Vicki a short, clipped reply: "Can't, Vicki. Need a word with Roland." Then he turned toward the side path leading to the front of the house.

Again, I wondered if Jenna had shared with him that she thought her husband was trying to kill her. Was Nate a confidant or a lover?

"You know he's single," Vicki said, as if reading my mind. "I don't know how Roland managed to worm his way into the firm. If I know Roland, he's blackmailing Nate with something."

The wind from the north picked up and with it came droplets of rain, reminding me I had a cozy cottage and fat cat waiting for me less than a mile down the shoreline. I took a step toward the path Nate had just taken.

Vicki grabbed my arm. "Well?"

I looked at her blankly.

"You said you wanted to see my rooms. I think you'll be surprised and maybe learn a thing or two about design. Come on, let's go. It's nasty out here. My hair's gonna frizz just like yours. Hey, do you mind videoing me when I show you my rooms? I want to post it on my blog." She pulled a pink iPad from her shoulder bag and handed it to me. I had no choice but to follow her up the rear veranda's steps.

"Did you decorate this porch?" she asked.

"Yes, all the outdoor spaces," I said, happy about the way everything had turned out. The rear veranda was the same length as the front, the furniture similar, only I'd added four white slat rocking chairs, perfect for viewing the ocean on a warm summer evening, and a round table and four chairs to play cards or chess on. Vintage McCoy pottery urns, hanging pots and jardinières were scattered across its width, all in the same pastel teal hue and all sporting lacy ferns. Flowering shrubbery met the white railing.

She held the door open and said, scanning the space, "Simple. Not horrid."

Not horrid?

• • •

Twenty minutes later, she was right. I had been surprised at her rooms. I was surprised Jenna let her set foot in Enderly Hall. At least Jenna knew what she was doing by giving her only a back parlor and a rear bedroom suite to decorate. Luckily, the furniture wasn't brought in by Veronica Interiors, it had come from Enderly's attic, where Jenna had said her father and uncle had put all the valuable pieces when their father started his decline into madness.

Vicki's spaces were filled with garish neon-colored accessories, along with rugs that looked like they'd spent a couple centuries being gnawed on by moths and creepy crawlers. Vicki had described the rugs as timeworn, but they were more like *worm*worn. The good news was, after the showhouse closed, it would be easy for Jenna to get rid of the accessories and floor coverings.

Originally, Jenna had asked me to decorate the library and study for the showhouse. Because of my commitment to Elle's engagement party, plus getting things together for a client who would be coming out after Memorial Day to see my progress, I'd had to decline. I was trying to keep things simple since moving to Montauk. If I didn't, I might as well be back in Manhattan with the rat race, and the biggest rat of all, my ex-fiancé and boss at *American Home and Garden*, Michael.

51

After I had fake *oohed* and *aahed* at Vicki's exquisite taste, followed by a few—more like a baker's dozen—of her interior decorating lessons, I was able to escape via the servants' back stairway.

Once on the main floor I took the narrow hallway toward one of the rear exits.

"Meg, you all set for tomorrow night?" Freya Rittenhouse called out, coming toward me from the direction of the kitchen. Her silky blonde hair brushed her shoulders, and her face had a healthy glow to it that made her look like she'd just come from an exhilarating horseback ride on the beach. In other words, she looked like most of the women in their forties who were pictured at charity events in the Who's Who newspaper, *Dave's Hamptons*. She wore the usual Hamptons preppy uniform, consisting of an untucked white dress shirt, slim black ankle-length pants and black ballet flats. Completing the look were two simple pearl stud earrings and a single strand of pearls that hit just below her collarbone. Freya's dewy face showed little makeup, just a touch of color to her lips and mascara, no eyeshadow. When I'd watched her local *Hamptons Home and Garden* talk show, I got the impression she didn't laugh a lot, was always serious and intent as she quizzed her interviewee or gave tours of local Hamptons estates.

"I still have a few last-minute things to arrange," I said, "and I'm expecting more flowers and plants to be delivered. Though, Shepherds Cottage is ready."

"You've accomplished an amazing job on the exterior spaces. I even peeked into the window of Shepherds Cottage. I love everything inside. I'm a big primitive antique collector. I practically live at Grimes House Antiques in Bridgehampton. Have you ever been?"

"Funny you should say that. The truly primitive Americana items in Shepherds Cottage came from Rita's shop. She's quite a character, don't you think?"

"She certainly is. But she is also trustworthy and knows her stuff. Half my home is furnished with things from her shop. Rita calls me her number-one best customer. You'll have to come by and see my home on Egypt Lane."

It seemed like everyone had a good relationship with Rita Grimes except me. "Wow. I would love to." Egypt Lane was the same street in East Hampton where Martha Stewart had a house — well, a mansion. You couldn't get more exclusive.

"I especially love what you've done in the gazebo and pavilion," she said. "I've asked Nate Klein if perhaps he could draw up plans for similar structures for my property. They look like they were built the same year Enderly Hall was. My home is even older. From 1885."

"That's the same year my friend Elle Warner's Victorian Captain's house was built in Sag Harbor. If you love antiques, you'd love her shop, Mabel and Elle's Curiosities."

"I've heard about it. Have been meaning to check it out, but with my TV show and taking care of my sister, who's been developmentally disabled since she was a toddler, there aren't enough hours in the day. In fact, I feel guilty spending all the time I have here. She has a good caretaker though; Rosie is the best. I couldn't do it without her."

"Let me know when you want to see Mabel and Elle's. I'll make sure you'll be the only one inside." Secretly, I was thinking a little television exposure couldn't hurt Mabel and Elle's, not that Elle needed the money. I just wanted the world, or at least the Hamptons, to see what a wonderful job Elle and her assistant, Maurice, had done with the shop.

"Sounds good. How about when the crew gets here tomorrow, we can do an outdoor tour for *Hamptons Home and Garden* of the spectacular job you've done? That's if this fog ever lifts." Even though she smiled, I could tell it didn't come easy. When she talked, her dark blue eyes never left my face.

"Thanks for the praise," I said. "But it's easy to furnish and accessorize with the ocean as your backdrop. I just took a peek and love what you've done in the great room."

"I had a lot of help from Jenna and my TV crew. We're set to go live for a short segment at the cocktail party. It should be fun." Then she said, "I better run, I have to get home to Emma and relieve her caregiver. I see you wear hearing aids; my sister has cochlear implants. It has really made a difference on how she relates to those around her, especially me. Sometimes I get a glimpse of the old Emma when she's sitting outdoors, listening to the birds and drawing in her marker coloring books. If only . . ." Tears welled, then she clenched both her jaw and her hands in anger. "She didn't have to turn out this way."

I waited a couple beats, and when I saw she wouldn't explain, I said, "I was told years ago that cochlear implants wouldn't improve my hearing loss."

Freya recovered her composure as if she was facing a camera and someone had said *You're on.* "The same for Emma when we first looked into cochlear implants twenty years ago, but the technology is so advanced now."

"Something to think about," I said.

"Well, I better run. See you tomorrow for the big reveal."

"Looking forward to it," I said as she walked toward the front door.

A few minutes later, when I trotted down Enderly's steps after adjusting a few minor details on the front wraparound veranda, I didn't see any sign of Jenna or her irritating husband.

Free at last. I looked forward to getting home to my fat cat Jo, building a fire, and hunkering down with some poetry by Walt Whitman. At the thought of Whitman, Patrick Seaton's warm smile came to mind. I thought back to his last quote that I'd found in front of the nature preserve:

> *Long, barren silence, square with my desire;*
> *To sit without emotion, hope, or aim,*
> *In the loved presence of my cottage-fire.*
> WW

Patrick and I had come to an understanding—instead of writing out the author's name, we'd begun using only their initials. I'd spent one lazy Sunday going through a few of my late-nineteenth-century quotation books, writing down initials, then I made a copy and handed it to Patrick at the last Dead Poets Society Book Club meeting. Patrick had given me a knowing smile and a wink, understanding what I'd done. For the last quote, I'd known WW stood for William Wordsworth, not Walt Whitman, because I'd memorized Wordsworth's short poem "Personal Talk" by heart. Its simple lines were what I aspired to create in my serene Montauk life. As, I'm sure, had Patrick or he wouldn't have chosen it.

Lost in thoughts of romantic poetry, I realized I'd gone a couple hours without thinking of Cole's and my breakup. It wasn't for public knowledge, but I'd been heartbroken, still was, nothing like when I'd stopped dating Hamptons premier landscape architect Byron Hughes. Now, even though I was entertaining fantasies about Patrick, it didn't mean I would act on them. I knew better. It was time for Megan Elizabeth Barrett to be single once again and loving it. Or at least at peace with my solitary lifestyle. Patrick was a man of few words, and very modest, but I felt like I'd learned a lot about him just from the poetry he chose to pen in the sand. He seemed to be finally stepping into the light — or at least hopeful to return to the living. I couldn't imagine his pain. Cole had also suffered major losses. There I was again. Cole. Patrick. Patrick. Cole. Nobody.

Chapter 9

Roland Cahill found me digging through the underbrush. I'd been on my way to my car when I remembered that Frank the ghosthunter had never had a chance to retrieve his EVP gadget from the other side of Enderly's fence. I felt it was my duty as a nosy busybody to find it for him. Luckily, it was safely in my pocket when Roland called out, "What the hell are you doing, Ms. Barrett? You're lucky I'm not carrying Jenna's gun."

Jenna had a gun?

I quickly shot up and looked behind me. I could barely make him out in the early evening darkness and thought for a moment I'd conjured my own apparition of the man who Jenna's grandfather had shot twenty years ago. "I, um, thought I saw someone on the other side of the fence. I know Jenna doesn't want those paranormal investigators hanging around."

"That doesn't explain why you were on all fours. It doesn't matter, I've had a talk with the head of the organization anyway. I got a call that the town police were here. I'm allowing them to have free range of the grounds. I think it will help to get publicity for the showhouse."

"*You what?* Have you told Jenna?"

He glowered back at me. "I'll take care of my wife, you just worry about your job for the showhouse."

"I'm not just your employee, I'm also Jenna's friend. So, don't threaten me, buster."

He was taken aback, but only for a moment. Then he softened his tone, "What has Jenna told you about our marriage? Whatever it was, I'm sure she overexaggerated my part in it. I think she cares more about Enderly Hall than our relationship."

And you don't? I thought, shifting from one foot to the other, uncomfortable about him sharing his personal life with me.

"I want you to know, Jenna has been seeing Dr. Sorenson at my suggestion. Having to deal with the recent loss of her parents and the stress of the showhouse, she's not thinking straight. I hope, if as you say, you're a true friend, you'll encourage her to continue her therapy. Now I need to go find my wife."

He took my upper arm and pulled me toward the blacktop lane

leading to the front of the main house. His grip was firm—nothing that would leave a mark, but I shook him off anyway. Who did he think he was? The lord of the manor? It was a bully move, and I wouldn't put up with it. Jenna might be right in her suspicions about her husband.

Through gritted teeth I said, "I'd prefer you keep your hands off of me." I looked toward the circular drive in front of Enderly and saw that Nate's car was gone, and was happy that there was no chance Nate was with Jenna. Even if their meeting in the gazebo had been nothing more than a comforting embrace, I didn't want big, blustery Roland to see them together.

"You take after your friend, my wife," he said with laugh that came out more like growl. "Overexaggerating and letting your imagination run away with you. I would suggest you scurry on home and get a good night's sleep for tomorrow. You know how much this showhouse means to Jenna."

"What was in the subpoena you got in Amagansett?" I blurted out.

As I thought, he didn't answer. He just turned and strode toward the main entrance of the mansion, disappearing into the night and fog. I was torn whether to go after him or return home. I chose the latter, knowing he wouldn't be so stupid as to harm Jenna before the cocktail party. He wanted the showhouse to be a success as much as she did, especially if he was going to find some way to sell it out from under her.

Jo, here I come. Momma's had a rough day. I need a good snuggle.

My fat cat didn't snuggle.

But a girl could always hope, couldn't she?

• • •

When I got to my cottage, I found a note on the door from my neighbor Claire. It read, *Food in fridge. I know you're crushed with work on Enderly Hall. I fed Jo. Don't let her trick you that I didn't.* What she didn't say was, *I know your cooking skills are poor at best.* But I wasn't complaining, especially when I went inside and opened the refrigerator and found an asparagus and gruyere quiche and bagged organic Caesar salad.

After I changed into an old T-shirt and soft flannel lounge pants, I heated up a slice of quiche in the microwave. Okay, it was more like two servings cut into one big wedge. I made a salad, poured a glass of pinot grigio, and brought them and the quiche to my kitchen table — one of my refurbished vintage finds.

Jo followed me.

"Claire told me you've already been fed. You can't trick me."

She rubbed against my leg and looked so pathetic I tossed her a sliver of parmesan cheese from my salad. She looked at it, looked and me, then skulked away.

I finished eating, then grabbed a throw off the sofa and went out to the deck and took a seat on the two-person swing that hung under the eaves. I tried to erase the memories of the last time Cole and I sat here. The time we'd decided to call it quits. One last embrace, and then he'd left to his life without me, and mine without him.

I leaned into the swing's soft down cushions, my eyes searching the darkness for a glimpse of the ocean. Nothing. Only a milky opaqueness. I'd taken out my hearing aids and rejoiced in the silence. Now, if only I could quiet the chatter in my head. I wasn't one to wallow in sadness, so I focused on my breathing — breathe-in, breathe-out — like I did each morning when I woke and went down to the shore to sit on my favorite boulder and take solace in the steady waves.

After feeling clearer and more grounded, I toyed with the idea of walking toward Patrick Seaton's cottage, until lightning cut through the fog over the water. A crack of thunder followed. Without my hearing aids, the thunder wasn't loud, but I felt the vibration running down the chains of the swing. I was suddenly spooked. I thought about earlier and the white dog that Elle had almost hit. Shivering, I wrapped the blanket tighter, nixing the idea of walking on the beach. Not that I feared supernatural ghosts or paranormal activity, just getting zapped by lightning.

Or so I told myself.

Something jogged my memory. Paranormal activity! The EVP recorder was still in my jacket. I ran inside the cottage, thankful for the distraction. The fire still blazed, and Jo was fast asleep on my favorite reading chair. She raised her head and opened one eye because that's all she had, then closed it again. She was a beautiful specimen of a Maine coon, especially when she was sleeping.

On my way to the closet to retrieve the recorder from my jacket pocket, I noticed a light blinking on my landline phone, notifying me that I had a voice message. I doubled back, looked down at the large display, and saw an unknown number. The phone was specially equipped to transfer voice calls into text. I said, "Wonder if the EVP recorder works the same way?" I laughed at my own joke, Jo not even batting her eye.

But what I read after pushing the Play button was no laughing matter.

Meg, this is Imogine, Cole's assistant at the North Carolina office. I just wanted to let you know, before you heard it somewhere else, Cole has been out of radio frequency since a squall hit the Reliance on his way to Portugal. Search and Rescue has been deployed to his last coordinates. If by any miracle you hear from him, please contact me immediately. I would say don't be worried, and of course there's hope. You know Cole. He's been in similar situations before. Take care, and keep him in your prayers.

Robotically, I took out my cell phone and typed "Cole Spenser" in the search bar, then the name of the sailing yacht, *Reliance.*

There it was. It hadn't been a mistake. Cole was lost at sea.

Cole usually took his sweet dog Tripod with him on his voyages, but he'd told me the last time I'd seen him, the time we'd broken off our relationship, that he was leaving Tripod behind because his new chief mate, Billy, was allergic to dogs.

I had an urge to hop on a plane and fly down to Oak Island, North Carolina, and bring Tripod home with me until they located his master. Instead, I grabbed my flashlight and charged out of the cottage, stumbling twice on the steps leading down to the beach. I ran like I was being chased by a madman. Which, a year ago, I had been. Almost losing my life.

When I reached the beach in front of the nature preserve, I fell to the ground, my lungs on fire. Pushing away the wet bangs plastering my forehead and blocking my vision, I swept the flashlight across the sand until I spied a stick of driftwood. I crawled over to it then penned in the sand the first quote that came to mind:

Now would I give a thousand furlongs of sea for an acre of barren ground.

There was no need to leave the author's initials.

Patrick Seaton knew his Shakespeare.

Why I'd chosen to share my worry and words with him about Cole was something I would analyze later. For now, knowing Patrick might read them provided the only solace I could find.

He knew all about loss.

Chapter 10

Even though I hadn't had a drink the night before, I woke Saturday morning feeling like I had a hangover. When I'd returned home from the beach, I'd gotten calls from both Elle and my friend Georgia, owner of The Old Man and the Sea Books in Montauk. The news about Cole, whose family had been in East Hampton since the late 1600s, was all over the local television stations. *Lost at sea, lost at sea,* had repeated in my head all night long. Before turning in, I'd gone out to the small Juliet balcony off my upstairs bedroom and looked out toward the Atlantic, feeling like a figurehead at the bow of a ship, sending out sonar waves of positive thoughts toward the waters off Portugal.

Back inside, I had lighted a candle and said a prayer for the safety of the *Reliance* and its crew, got into bed with Jo, then tossed and turned, sleep evading me. Around one in the morning, I'd grabbed the soft eiderdown quilt from my bed, scooped up Jo and gone down to my secret room behind the bookcase in the great room and lowered Jo to the cushioned window seat that faced the lighthouse—a beacon of safety to so many over the centuries. After I'd snuggled up next to Jo, covering us both with the quilt, I'd placed my cell phone on vibrate, then shoved it under my pillow. Jo had sensed my unease because she'd inched closer to my chest. Sometime after three, her steady purring lulled me off to sleep. A fitful sleep. Fraught with nightmares and images of Cole's handsome face and cerulean blue eyes.

• • •

It was another foggy morning, adding more malaise to my splintered thoughts. Tonight was the cocktail party at Enderly. I needed to show up and double-check everything was en pointe. But I also didn't want to leave my cottage until Cole had been found safe. I called Imogine. She didn't pick up, so I left a message. I showered and dressed hurriedly, fed Jo, chugged a cup of coffee and went down to the beach. In front of the nature preserve, footprints and dogprints told me Patrick had been there. His words brought hope.

When crew and captain understand each other to
the core,
    It takes a gale and more than a gale to put their ship
ashore.

RK

RK, Rudyard Kipling, a poet in his own right and the author of *The Jungle Book*.

Patrick must have seen the news and heard about Cole, and I was sure our mutual friend and book club member, my poet laureate neighbor Claire, had filled Patrick in on Cole's and my relationship and breakup.

Before leaving the beach, I took another glance at the quote, then looked toward the direction of Patrick's cottage, half hoping I would see him and his greyhound Charlie materialize out of the mist. But they hadn't. It was time to face reality: no matter what was going on with Cole, this evening was the cocktail party and I still had things to do.

Reluctantly, I trudged back up the steps to my cottage. After checking my phone, I grabbed my handbag and the hanging bag holding my dress, shoes and jewelry for the cocktail party, then headed out to my car.

I sat for a moment before starting for Enderly Hall, only a five-minute drive. I looked at my choices: I could wallow in fear that something catastrophic had happened to Cole, or I could think positive like Imogine suggested in her voice message. I stuck out my chin and put the car in gear.

Cole would be fine; he'd weathered many storms and always came out unharmed.

Then it hit me, Patrick's quote by Kipling reminded me of something that brought more worry. Cole had a new chief mate. I knew Cole. He wouldn't hire a subpar crewmember for such a long voyage.

But what if he had?

• • •

The morning at Enderly flew by. Jenna had forgone her cane and was scurrying around like the proverbial chicken with its head cut off. I hadn't told her about Cole. I didn't want to ruin her big evening.

When I'd arrived, I'd noticed Roland was nowhere to be seen. It wasn't like him to be waiting in the wings, but I counted it as a good thing. None of the decorators, including myself, needed him breathing down our necks. Plus, Jenna was a pro when it came to interior design, proven in the way she went from decorator to decorator, adding suggestions, not demands. The antithesis of her husband's style.

By two in the afternoon, I had already done the final walk-through of my spaces for the showhouse: the front and rear wraparound verandas, a baluster-railinged porch at the top of the house, and two screened-in porches, one off the dining room, the other on the opposite side of the house, which I'd turned into a sleeping porch. The flowers and plants for the porches had arrived around ten from La Cote de la Mer Florist in East Hampton. If I had to pick one thing that I'd learned from being at *American Home and Garden* magazine, fresh flowers and plants transformed any setting from dull and lackluster to fresh and extraordinary. Even a faux green fern here and there was better than nothing. When decorating my clients' porches, I gave them as much attention to detail as I would one of their interior rooms.

Around three, over a quick cup of coffee and a stale croissant, Jenna had confided that last night she and Roland had had a knock-down, drag-out fight, mostly having to do with him allowing the paranormal investigators free range on the property. "After you told me about Shepherds Cottage being broken into, I told him he was an idiot to let those ghost conjurers roam the grounds. He knows that I believe Enderly has ghosts. However, right now I'm not afraid of ghosts, just him. Maybe he's trying to drive me crazy. Just like in those suspense books and movies where the husband makes everyone think his wife is losing her mind, only to find out he is plotting to get control of her money through a power of attorney after he sends her to the looney bin. Then Roland could sell Enderly out from under me."

I held back from correcting her that the cottage had been unlocked, not broken into. There'd been no sign of forced entry and nothing was missing. I had to stop her before she went into a downward spiral. I snapped my fingers in front of her beautiful face. "Jenna! Focus! Tonight is your dream come true. Enderly looks amazing. And so do you."

"This was my mother's Dior. Do you think the sapphire choker is too much?"

Why did she always have to second-guess her choices. "It's lovely. Perfect. This is your time to shine. Don't let anyone spoil it."

"You're right," she said, the start of a smile forming on her perfect lips. "I have to look at the big picture. And there's only one part of the picture that needs touching up. I need to check on Vicki's space." She got up from her chair and winced in pain. "Meg, be a dear and please get my handbag from the pantry. I need some ibuprofen. There's no time to hobble around. There's still so much to do. I blame Roland for this," she said, pointing to her leg. "Where is he? I begged him to do one thing. Leave my decorators alone. I didn't mean that he should be totally MIA. He needs to pay the florist and a thousand other things."

It took me a few minutes to unearth the Advil bottle from the bottom of her handbag. I took out two and brought them into the kitchen. "One or two?" I asked.

"Two," she answered without hesitation. I wasn't surprised.

"Here you go," I said, placing the pills in her hand. "Do you need me for anything?" I asked. "I have a few last-minute things to take care of." I really didn't. I just wanted to check my phone for any news about Cole and see if Imogine had returned my call.

After going to the sink for a glass of water and swallowing the Advil, Jenna limped toward the doorway leading to the formal dining room, then turned to me. "No. I'm good. Thanks for being such a good friend."

I walked over and gave her a hug. "You're skin and bones. You need one of my father's meals to fatten you up. He'll be in town Memorial Day Weekend. I'll be sure to invite you over for dinner."

"Oh, dear, do you think I'm too thin? I did notice my clothes not fitting too well. But I thought I was gaining weight, not losing."

I'd stuck my foot in it this time. I wished Jenna didn't always feel like she had to play the victim. Maybe the psychiatrist Roland had mentioned would help her. I know seeing a therapist helped me when I found my fiancé Michael in the arms of his ex-wife. If it wasn't for therapy, I probably wouldn't have left my job at *American Home and Garden* and moved to Montauk. Now I let the ocean and my walks on the beach substitute for a therapist with the same result. Serenity.

"No. You're perfect," I said. "Better than perfect. Now go finish up and we'll meet back here at five and share a glass of wine. Now, vamoose." I put my hand on the small of her back and guided her through the open doorway.

Finally, I was able to make my phone call. But it was all for naught.

There'd been no news about Cole or the *Reliance*.

Chapter 11

At five, after changing into my party clothes—or should I have said Elle's party clothes—I stepped into Enderly's massive kitchen, noticing that Jenna had made it feel both homey and elegant at the same time. An open bottle of wine stood next to an ornate sterling silver tray holding champagne flutes and wineglasses. I went to the tray and poured myself a glass of pinot noir, hoping it would calm me. I wasn't nervous about the cocktail party, I was worried about Cole. I kept checking my phone for some news on him and the *Reliance*. Nothing new came up on search. It's as if the media had given up on the story and had moved on to the next big thing. I couldn't think of anything bigger.

"Oh, I'll take one of those!" Vicki called out as she entered the kitchen. She was a vision in pink, wearing a sleeveless cocktail dress the color of Pepto-Bismol. Violet sequins had been sewn around the dress's plunging neckline, highlighting her deep cleavage. The dress was too tight for her curvy figure. Judging by its vintage feel, I'd bet it had once been her mother's. Vicki grabbed the glass of wine I'd poured for myself, then sat on a bar stool at the Carrera marble counter.

Not able to help myself, I said, "You're welcome," as I poured another glass, then turned toward her.

"Thank you. Don't you think that chandelier is a bit much for a cooks' kitchen? It belongs in the dining room. But who am I to give the queen of the castle decorating advice, I've only been at my mother's knee helping her with her sketches since I could walk."

I didn't answer her or defend Jenna. Some people weren't worth arguing with, and I could tell she was one of them. I smiled when I saw that a brown hydrangea leaf had gotten woven into the teased section of hair at the back of her head. I doubted it was a hair accessory—it wasn't pink. I decided not to tell her. Served her right.

I sat at the counter just as Freya ran in, frazzled and in a sweat. "Do you believe it? Only two hours until we open the doors for the cocktail party. I promised Jenna no television crew until nine. Before letting the cameras roll, she wanted me to get written permission from the top celebrities attending the cocktail party. I agreed." Freya also went for a glass, but instead of filling it with pinot noir she went to the sink and downed a couple glassfuls of water. Turning back to Vicki and me, she said, "I'm finally happy with my rooms. I hoped to find Jenna here. Get her stamp of approval before they open the doors for the guests."

Nate Klein came through the open doorway, a sterling ice bucket in his arms. A bottle of Moet, its neck wrapped in a linen napkin, crowned from cubes of ice. He set the bucket on the countertop and said, "I've also been looking for Jenna. I thought before we open the doors we could pop the cork to a bottle of bubbly in celebration of a job well done."

"I'll drink to that," Kuri said, entering the kitchen from the back hallway leading from the servants' stairs. "I just saw Jenna about ten minutes ago, she said she got a text from her husband to meet her at the pavilion at five. Seemed pretty upset at his timing."

Yikes, I thought, not such a good idea for the two of them to rendezvous so close to opening the doors for the party. What if Jenna's husband found out about her and Nate? Before I could decide whether I should run to Jenna's rescue or mind my own business and let them work it out, my phone vibrated. I pulled it out of my pocket and saw that Elle was calling. I was torn between answering and going to find Jenna. Then I realized she might have word of Cole. I tapped a small button on my hearing aid processor, excused myself from the kitchen and stepped into the back hallway. I heard Elle say, "Hello! Hello! They found the *Reliance*. Cole is fine. He got beached on an island off the coast of Lisbon!"

"Thank God!" I shouted, then jumped in the air in relief.

"I'll see you soon," Elle said. "Can't wait for the party. I'm wearing the perfect 1940s dress and Schiaparelli jewelry in honor of Cole's safe rescue and the showhouse. Lots to celebrate. Love you."

Before I could say I loved her back, there came a wailing from the direction of the kitchen.

That was when I heard Vicki say, "Dead? What do you mean, dead!"

Chapter 12

Jenna stood in the middle of Enderly's kitchen. Her hands were at her sides, palms upward, looking like they'd been dyed red, then coated with a dusting of sugar. They weren't a bright scarlet red, more like a dried ketchup red. Everyone crowded around her. Her howling finally settled into a soft whimper.

Nate had his arm around her shoulder, careful not to touch her hands. He asked gently, "Jen, where is he? Are you sure he's dead?" I must have missed her declaration about who was dead. But I had a good idea. The only one missing was Roland. Freya took out her phone and tapped three numbers — nine-one-one.

Jenna's lower lip quivered, and everyone sucked in a collective breath. "Yes, I'm sure," she gulped, "no one could survive a thirty-foot fall, especially the way he landed. Poor Roland . . ."

No one had noticed when I'd slunk back into the kitchen, and hopefully no one noticed when I slowly backed out. The authorities and ambulance would be here soon, and I wanted — no, needed — to see for myself what had happened to Roland. Sadly, this wouldn't be my first corpse. I just prayed it would be my last.

On the way out, I grabbed a pair of disposable booties from a box by the door leading to the rear veranda and put them over my shoes. Jenna had kept them there for everyone to wear during the installations so as not to muddy the floors, but today there was no need because all the dirty work had been done and we were dressed in party attire. I'd learned from my retired Detroit PD Homicide Detective father the importance of not contaminating a crime scene. Plus, I didn't want to ruin the vintage Gucci insignia shoes that Elle had given me to wear. They coordinated perfectly with a turquoise raw silk 1960s dress with a full skirt that made me look like Doris Day stepping out of a scene with Rock Hudson. The advantage of the dress had been its pockets, making it easy to stow my cell phone for news of Cole. Wow! Cole was safe.

The same couldn't be said for Roland Cahill.

I hurried outside, trotting toward the pavilion. I thought I heard the faint sound of sirens. Even with my hearing aids turned to their highest volume, it was hard to tell how close they were. The high-pitched frequency of a siren was where most of my hearing loss fell on a decibel graph. When I got closer to the pavilion and the steps leading to Enderly's beach, my trot turned into a full gallop. I wanted to see what happened to Roland before anyone arrived. Anyone, included Chief Pell from the Suffolk County Police homicide squad. Last January, Elle's fiancé, Detective Arthur Shoner, and I had had a falling out with the almighty Chief Pell. I'd never told Elle, but I thought it had been the chief who'd orchestrated her fiancé's transfer to Manhattan, guessing the chief was tired of Detective Shoner getting all the limelight and praise for catching a murderer or two. Or three. Or four. Chief Pell's problem with me was that I'd been involved, one way or another, in those same cases. A murder magnet was what Elle called me. The reason—at least that's what I told myself—why it was imperative that I take a quick look at the scene before he arrived. Chief Pell would never share info with me like Detective Shoner had.

When I got to the entrance of the pavilion, I paused before stepping inside. Everything seemed as I'd left it this morning when I'd waited for the garden shop to deliver the potted trees for each corner of the space. A wicker chaise lounge was angled strategically toward the lighthouse. Arranged in front of a white balustered railing, overflowing with nodding violet hydrangea heads, where two cushioned wicker rocking chairs. A glass-topped wicker side table stood between them. Butting up to the railing was a bar and bar stools. In the Hamptons, a bar was a necessity, not an extravagance.

At first glance everything seemed as I'd left it. But then I looked over at the swing built for two hanging from thick braided ropes. The two huge pillows that I'd so artfully arranged by giving them a decorator karate chop showed the imprints of two bodies. I stepped inside the space and noticed another anomaly. The white fairy lights I'd strung on the potted trees were unlit. I'd purposely left them on when I'd left the pavilion, wanting them twinkling and visible by anyone who stepped out onto the main house's veranda during the cocktail party.

What the heck? I hoped one of the bulbs weren't bad, causing all the others not to work. But that wasn't the case, because when I looked at the outlet under the railing, nothing was plugged in. Not only that, but there was no sign of the white extension cord I'd used.

Someone must have taken it. Strange, but I didn't have time to waste thinking about it.

I took out my phone and shot a few photos, then I went to the wood railing that on a clear day would have a no-holds-barred view of the Atlantic. I was cautious not to get too close, recalling Jenna saying that Roland had fallen thirty feet below. Glancing down, I felt the bile rise. Near the base of the steps ending at Enderly's rocky beach was the fuzzy outline of Roland's twisted body. I gulped a few breaths of cold, damp, salty air.

Roland was a jerk, but he didn't deserve to die like this. No one did. I needed to go down there.

I hurried to the open gate, then charged down to the steps. I wasn't worried about my fingerprints being on anything because I had an alibi. I'd gone down to the beach earlier, after finishing up the décor in the pavilion, and had sent out a feverish prayer across the ocean for Cole's safe rescue.

Roland's large body blocked the area to the left of the steps. His eyes were open, more in surprise than pain. If he was pushed, by the look in his eyes I would say he knew his attacker. Owing to the dense mist that pressed down, thick and suffocating, along with the fact anyone could have been lurking behind the large hydrangea bushes that circled the pavilion, it could have been anyone.

Adjacent to Roland's head was a small area of rocks covered in blood. That must have been where Jenna had lifted him with her hands, sand clinging to them when she did. I bent closer and saw Roland still held his cell phone in his right hand. I recalled Kuri saying Jenna had received a message from Roland to meet him at the pavilion. Knowing the drill, I didn't touch anything. The front of him seemed blood-free. Could he have just tumbled over the railing by mistake? In this weather, it was certainly possible. It was then that I saw the deep gouge circling his neck. Roland had been choked.

There was no mistaking the sirens now. I took one last glance around to see if I could find what had made the mark. The tide was coming in. There, in the early evening gloom, as the last wave receded, I saw it. My white extension cord.

Whoever killed Roland must have tossed it into the ocean, only for it to come back with the tide. I made a decision that my cop father wouldn't have been happy about. I picked up a stick, used it to wrangle the cord, then tossed the extension cord under the steps, where I knew the CSIs would find it. Tampering with evidence, Elle's fiancé would say. *Preserving evidence* was the way I looked at it.

Wisely realizing that everyone back at Enderly, including myself, would have to be questioned about his death, I didn't take any photos of Roland's body. There was also the possibly of our cell phones being confiscated. The photos I'd taken inside the pavilion were innocent enough. A candid of Roland's corpse, not so much.

I ran up the steps and bounded toward the main house, careful not to slip on the damp lawn. When I reached the gravel path leading to the rear veranda, I looked ahead. The front gates were slowly opening and a train of law enforcement and rescue vehicles nosed their way through. To the left of the gates I thought I saw movement. Something, or someone, was crouched near the hedges. Or was my mind playing tricks on me because of the fog? I stored the information away and charged up the rear steps, opened the door and silently slipped inside.

After taking off my booties, I tossed them into a brass umbrella stand by the door, then tried to make myself presentable. If that was possible. My reflection in the gold-framed convex mirror over the hall's refectory table made me wince. I looked like I belonged in a circus sideshow. Mascara ran down my cheeks. I must have been crying for Roland without knowing it. Luckily, I had a tissue in my dress pocket. My hair, which earlier had been tamed into a loose chignon and lacquered with hairspray, sprung out in all directions from the humidity on the beach. I did the best I could with what I had to work with by licking the palms of my hands then smoothing them over the Brillo pad texture of my blonde hair. Giving up, I tiptoed to the now-empty kitchen, then to the main hallway. I wanted to be safely in the others' midst when the police rang the doorbell.

As I walked up the hallway, I listened for voices. Not an easy task with a hearing loss. Luckily, the door to the library was open. I peeked in and saw that everyone except Nate was inside. Of course, what other place would everyone gather in a murder mystery but the library? If this was a game of Clue, our murder victim wasn't killed with a knife, wrench, candlestick, revolver, or lead pipe but a makeshift rope — aka a white extension cord.

Before stepping inside, I glanced down at my phone and stopped dead in my tracks. I'd almost forgotten that Cole had been found safe and alive. *Hallelujah!* There hadn't been a moment to process the good news because of Roland. I typed Cole's name into my phone's search bar. Up popped a photo of Cole in an embrace with a woman. No, it was more than an embrace — Cole was playing tonsil hockey with a stunning dark-haired female. They were standing in front of a whirring helicopter. The caption under the photo by *The East Hampton Star* read, *Hometown boy and captain of the Reliance, Cole Spenser, along with his chief mate, Billie Taylor, celebrate their rescue after being shipwrecked on a scrub island off the coast of Lisbon, Portugal.*

My phone dropped with a clatter and bounced off the hardwood floor. I wished I had killed it. I left it there for a minute, happy it had landed facedown. Though the images in the photo were burned into my memory forevermore. Then, taking a deep breath, I picked up the phone and stowed it in my pocket.

C'est la vie.

So much for Cole Spenser.

Chapter 13

I had to suck in my breath at the finished staging of Enderly's library for the showhouse. Jenna had done an amazing job. Not only was there Southern pine tongue-and-groove paneling but also ten-foot-tall built-in bookshelves made from the same pine. Most of the shelves were filled with antique leather books. On a few of the shelves Jenna had added things she'd brought down from Enderly's attic: an ivory bust of Aristotle, an old-world globe, blue-and-white china, carved jade Asian figurines, and similar unusual pieces. Everything melded well in the eclectic room. Exactly what Stanford White might have had in his own library.

Vicki was standing next to the massive fireplace. The clunky chimney piece above the mantel showed a pagan frieze, possibly inspired by Dante's *Inferno*. It might be a good idea for Jenna to keep adolescents from viewing the raunchy scene until they at least reached adulthood. Even then, it would be hard to take in without feeling your face heat, as mine had. I glanced over at Jenna, who sat in a tufted leather chair behind a wide bamboo desk, her elbows on the glass top. Her hands were in the air, still covered in dried blood and a sprinkling of sand. Someone must have wisely advised her not to wash her hands until the police arrived. I wondered who.

Kuri and Freya sat on opposite ends of a sofa with pale pastel silk embroidery in a chinoiserie design that featured exotic birds and butterflies. A couple months ago, Jenna and I had taken the Long Island Rail Road from Montauk to Penn Station to visit an exclusive fabric and upholstery shop where they specialized in recreating fabric designs based on old samples. Jenna had brought with her the biggest swatch that the moths in the attic hadn't gotten to. What I wouldn't have given to have seen the attic before Jenna went through it. But that was before she came up with the idea for the showhouse and invited me to be one of the participants.

I stopped myself from my décor musings when it hit me that not only was Jenna's husband dead — murdered — but soon the cocktail invitees would be clamoring at the gates. Elle! She was due any minute. Hurrying to Jenna's side, I bent and gave her shoulders a hard squeeze.

Jenna looked up at me through teary eyes. "Do you believe

this?" she asked, holding her blood-splattered hands toward me. All I could do was nod my head in the negative. She looked so forlorn and alone sitting behind the huge desk. No parents or grandparents. No brothers or sisters. No husband. But she had friends. Elle and I would get her through it.

And then, just as my mind pondered if Nate Klein should be added to Jenna's list of friends – *or lovers?* – he walked through the library's open doorway.

Following, more like lumbering behind Nate, was Chief Pell, dragging a man with him. The chief's large mitt had a vise-like grip around the man's wrist. Once inside the room, Pell jerked the man forward, then let go of his arm. The man stumbled, the toe of his black sneaker catching the corner of the Persian rug, and he tumbled to his knees. He kept his head down as if doing penance for a sin.

"Anyone know this guy? Found him crawling through the bushes." Chief Pell glanced around the room, his eyes stopping on me.

I sheepishly raised by hand.

"Why am I not surprised, Ms. Barrett." His voice was deep and loud. My hearing aids had no problem picking up his exasperated tone. Having a hearing loss since the age of twelve, I'd made a point of looking for visual clues to a person's countenance, locked jaw, gritted teeth, pulsing vein at the temple – Chief Pell had them all.

"His name is Frank," I answered. "He's part of the paranormal investigating team that's been hanging around Enderly Hall."

"I see. Well, we didn't see any team out there. Only him. I need to go to the scene and meet the CSIs." He reached into his trench coat, which must have been purchased at a big and tall menswear store, withdrew a small steno pad and flipped through it. "I'd like him to stay here, just in case this death turns out to be suspicious. The same goes for everyone in this room. Including you, Nate."

So, Chief Pell and Nate Klein were on a first-name basis. Good, that might help Jenna, because as I was watching the chief in action, knowing Roland had died by strangulation, not an innocent fall from a cliff, I gleaned that the dead man's widow, the one with blood on her hands, would be Suffolk County's top suspect.

Jenna might have cowered when Pell walked in, but Vicki wasn't put off by the hulking chief. "For God's sake!" she said in disgust at

Frank's appearance, "don't let him sit on any of the furniture in here." She pointed across the room. "There. Have him sit on those library steps."

The chief scowled down at Frank, who was still sitting on the floor. "You heard her."

Keeping his head to the floor, the ghosthunter crawled over to the wooden steps on wheels and sat on the top step. All he needed was a dunce hat. I felt sorry for his degradation. Chief Pell was playing the bully card, something he was an expert at.

Looking down at a notepad, the chief asked, "Is there a Mrs. Cahill here? Jenna Cahill?"

Jenna jumped up so fast her desk chair flew back. It landed with a thud that made her yelp. I put my arm around her shoulder, knowing that Chief Pell was the type of man who could easily intimidate her. But not me. I said firmly, "Jenna goes by her maiden name, Eastman."

The chief strode over to the desk, his gaze zeroing in on Jenna's hands. "Ms. Barrett, step away from Ms. Eastman immediately." I obeyed his command and skulked back to the sofa. After I sat between Freya and Kuri, we all watched Chief Pell withdraw a couple of plastic bags and twist ties from his jacket pocket and place them on the desk in front of Jenna. He instructed her to hold out her hands, then he bagged and tied them at the wrist. He answered her raw sobs with, "My apologies. We must preserve any evidence until we know what we're dealing with."

Jenna opened her mouth, but nothing came out. Tears fell freely over her high cheekbones and landed on the desk's glass top.

"Is that really necessary?" I called out, giving the chief my best evil eye.

"Yes, Ms. Barrett, it is. I thought your father was on the job. You'd think he'd have taught you a thing or two."

Now he'd done it. Nobody disses my father. "While you're at it," I said, "why don't you collect Jenna's tears for a DNA sample? Can't you call in someone to process her now? Give her the dignity of letting her wash her hands?"

The chief glared back, trumping me with his razor-sharp, almost black penetrating eyes and blinkless stare. I stared back. Due to his size, I let him win.

For now.

"Ms. Eastman," Chief Pell said in a slightly softer voice as he loomed over her, "I have here that you're the one who found your husband's body?"

I had to give it one more try. "I'm sure she'll show you where, as long as I can come along with her for support?"

"Not happening, Ms. Barrett." He glanced around the room, nodding his head in what I thought was appreciation for his surroundings. "Too bad fancy-pants Detective Shoner can't work this case. It's right up his alley. Him and his designer suits would fit right in."

I came to Detective Shoner's defense. "I heard from his fiancée that Arthur's been hanging out with the top brass at City Hall. I suppose, if ever you needed a good hand-tailored suit, it would be to wear to those nonstop upper-echelon events he goes to." Then I made a point of looking down at his scuffed shoes and pants that made it look like he was waiting for the next hurricane to flood Main Street.

His cheeks reddened, then he turned and strode abruptly toward the exit just as newbie Officer Morgana Moss came hurrying in holding two plastic Ziploc bags. One held the fifty-foot white extension cord and the other a cell phone. Roland's, I assumed.

Lucky for me, Morgana was a friend, the sister-in-law of my Realtor and buddy, Barb Moss.

Morgana gave me a wink and small smile. Then she got on her tiptoes and whispered in the chief's ear, "The victim was strangled with this cord, then pushed down the steps. The ME said the last text he made from his phone was to his wife." Morgana knew about my hearing loss and my detecting superpower of reading lips, and she'd positioned herself so that I was in full view of her mouth. *Thank you, Officer Moss!*

"Change of plans," Chief Pell said to the room. He placed his hands on his hips, then looked first at Frank the ghosthunter, then me, Vicki, Nate, Jenna and Freya. His sharp hawklike eyes rested on Kuri. "It seems we have a suspicious death on our hands."

After one collective gasp by everyone but me, he held up one of the bags. It was as if a live, poisonous albino snake was inside. "Does anyone recognize this extension cord?"

This time, I waited a couple of beats, then reluctantly raised my hand. "It looks like the one I used at the pavilion for the fairy lights."

He lifted a skeptical eyebrow. "Fairy lights?"

I searched my mind for the right words that wouldn't give me away for being at the crime scene only minutes before. "I'm only guessing it's the same, because a little while ago when glancing toward the pavilion, I saw the lights on the potted trees weren't lit. It's hard to find an outdoor cord in white that's fifty feet long. I had to special order it from Hank's Hardware. I'm sure I have the receipt somewhere." I exhaled, then sunk back into the sofa, nestled between Kuri and Freya.

Chief Pell rolled his muddy brown eyes, then moved toward the door leading to the main hallway. "Okay, Ms. Barrett, I give. Enough prattling. Officer Moss, please keep everyone inside this room. I want a statement from each one of them, a recorded statement." He narrowed his eyes at me and added, "Starting with Ms. Barrett."

He paused for a moment under the threshold to the open doorway, his six-foot-five frame filling the space. I didn't realize that I'd been grinning at the thought of him having to duck his way around Shepherds Cottage, perhaps bumping his thick head a few times on a low beam or two.

My smile faded when the chief said, "What's so funny, Ms. Barrett? I don't think Mrs. Cahill, I mean Eastman, thinks this is a laughing matter. Maybe you better go back to her side, she looks like she's about to faint."

I glanced over at Jenna and felt pinpricks of heat from the Barrett blotches as they traveled their way up my neck to my cheeks. The first time I'd met Chief Pell, he'd been professional and caring. As time went on, something changed. Perhaps the fact that since he'd been made chief, there'd been a few too many murders in the Hamptons, all solved under the auspices of Elle's fiancé, Detective Arthur Shoner, Pell's archnemesis.

Waiting until the chief exited, I went over to Jenna. She looked at me, her eyes wide and filled with fear, as if finally registering what had just happened. "Does he think I killed Roland?" she asked with a whimper.

I didn't want to lie, but before I could form my words, Jenna crumpled to the rug. Nate bounded toward us, elbowed me out of the way, then got on his knees and cradled her in his arms.

That answered the question about Nate and Jenna's relationship.

Chapter 14

Lucky me. I was the first one to be interviewed by Morgana. Unlike Chief Pell, there was real empathy in her eyes as she talked in a soothing, neutral tone. Her questions were the same ones my father might have asked in a murder investigation.

One by one, the rest of the room went to sit in a chair next to Morgana by the fireplace, where a crackling fire illuminated the room in a cozy glow. Outside the mullioned windows, twilight descended. We could have been recreating a scene from a Dicken's novel. Too bad another scene came to mind—the one of Roland Cahill's corpse and the bloody rocks beneath his head.

I wasn't sure if the position of the chair Morgana had placed next to her was planned or serendipitous. Either way, it made it easy for me to read the lips of everyone being questioned. I was also able to gauge everyone's body movements, searching for a tell that might show me they were lying. Looking for visual clues was something that came easy. Once again, thanks to my hearing loss.

Morgana didn't ask anyone, including me, if they had an alibi. She wisely knew we would have to wait until the ME came back with the time of death.

There was one thing I'd learned from reading Jenna's and Vicki's lips. They lied about their current relationship with Roland, making it sound like they were on the best of terms. Freya was a conundrum, being a consummate television interviewer on her *Hamptons Home and Garden* show. I was surprised by the tremor in her left knee. A nervous tic? I would bet she was hiding something. Nate's interview was short. He even took it upon himself to get up from his chair while Morgana was in midsentence. Kuri was the only straight shooter; she told Morgana exactly what she thought of Roland Cahill. And I admired her for it.

The last person to be interviewed was Frank the PI—not as in private eye, as in paranormal investigator. I didn't need to read Frank's lips because he'd spoken in a loud voice, saying he was going to sue the police department for harassment, apparently taking out on Morgana what he couldn't on Chief Pell, even leaning in with fists clenched and a large vein bulging from his temple that looked ready to burst. "How many times do I have to tell you!" he growled. "I was looking for my phone. I dropped it yesterday. Call Mac Zagan, he'll tell you what happened."

Morgana was new at the cop thing, and I saw her experience a fleeting loss of control as she pulled back from Frank. I got up from the sofa and went over to them. In a low voice I said, "I can vouch for him. He was here yesterday. He dropped something near the interior fencing. But wasn't it an EVP machine you dropped?"

"Yeah. Yeah, the BVP, that too." He looked at me. "Did you see my phone?"

"Uh, no."

Frank turned to Morgana. "Told you. She was there. She's my witness as to why I'm here. Plus, we're allowed to be on the grounds. I had a talk with the owner. He said we could be here. She"—he pointed up at me—"and the rest of these hoity-toity people in this room will also be a witness to the police brutality I just endured by that bully chief of yours. I'll be calling my lawyer."

I wasn't about to give the ghosthunter an alibi. I just wanted to let Morgana know that he had been on the grounds. "Just because I said you had a reason to be here doesn't put you in the clear. I'd be careful of what you are threatening, Mr. uh . . ."

"Holden," he answered in a more subdued tone.

"What's a BVP or EVP?" Morgana asked, raising an eyebrow.

"Electronic Voice Phenomena machine," I offered. "It catches spirits' voices."

"E-V-P," she repeated with a smile on her lips, then jotted down the information.

Like me, it seemed Officer Morgana Moss was a nonbeliever. I went back to the sofa. Just as I was about to sit, I felt the phone in my dress pocket vibrate, telling me I had a text. I doubted it was from Cole, and even if it was, I'd never read it. I felt my cheeks heat and told myself I wouldn't even go there. I slipped the phone out of the pocket of my dress, then sat back on the sofa, quickly glancing down at the text. It was from Elle. *Arthur just called. Said someone died. Jenna? Did he kill her? I'm outside the gates with Patrick and Ashley. They won't let us in!*

I texted back, *Roland C murdered. Will call when home.* Then I put my phone away.

"What are we supposed to do now, Officer?" Vicki asked, looking into a small compact mirror as she applied another layer of pink lipstick to her already pink lips. After smacking them together a few times, then blotting them with a tissue from her small evening bag, she continued, "Can we go? Will we still be able to open the showhouse in the morning? I know Roland would want us to continue with our plans. Not the cocktail party, of course. I suppose that wouldn't be advisable and would be a tad uncouth."

Jenna, who up until now had been in an almost catatonic state, shouted, "Victoria Fortune! Didn't you hear Chief Pell? How can you be so callous? Of course we won't be open tomorrow. Your former stepfather is dead. Murdered. Have some decency."

Go, Jenna, I thought.

Nate went to Jenna's side.

I watched Vicki follow him with her eyes, then she burst into tears. Crocodile tears. "You're so right, Jenna-a-a. It never crossed my mind that he was murdered. I thought maybe he hung himself with that extension cord because of the argument you had with him last night." Fake sob. Fake sob. "What a loss."

"How dare you!" Jenna shouted. "Roland would never kill himself. And our argument had nothing to do with it. We made up this morning."

"Oh, I didn't know you made up," Vicki said, extracting a tissue from her bag, dabbing one cheek then the other, making a point of staring at Jenna's bagged hands before staggering over to her and Nate. Bending down, Vicki gave Jenna a small peck on the cheek, saying, "Oops, am I not supposed to touch you? I might be disturbing forensic evidence."

Jenna just looked at her incredulously.

It was Nate who came to Jenna's defense. "I think it would be a good idea if before speaking, Ms. Fortune, you put a filter on your comments."

"Well, I never," she said. "I understand you're sticking up for your cousin. But in this situation, I was just trying to console Roland's second wife.

Cousin! Nate and Jenna were cousins. That one hit me between the eyes. Served me right for assuming Jenna was cheating on her dead husband.

Vicki's gaze darted from Nate to Morgana. Morgana was watching the show and taking notes at the same time. It was all good theater, except for one thing. Roland didn't kill himself, because I'd been the one to throw the extension cord under the steps. By Vicki mentioning that Roland and Jenna had argued, it cast a very unfavorable light on Jenna. That, coupled with Jenna's bagged and bloody hands, didn't help either.

Kuri, who had gotten up from the sofa in the middle of Vicki's performance, was pulling leather volumes off the bookshelves, then thumbing through them. She looked over at Jenna. "Around four thirty, you told me Roland texted you to meet him at the pavilion. I think it's safe to say he was alive until then."

It was surprising that Kuri would throw Jenna under the bus like that. Just because Jenna had gotten a text from Roland it didn't mean Roland was alive when it was sent. Anyone could have sent it. Grabbed the phone after they killed him, then kept it until the time was right to frame Jenna. I'd been down to the beach around ten in the morning and there hadn't been a body, giving the time of death a window of seven hours, between ten and five. Anyone here could have killed him.

I was contemplating who had the most to gain by Roland's death when Morgana received a phone call. I got up and nonchalantly slithered over to a shelf of gold-spined antique books about the history of England. I cracked one open and peeked from the pages to read Morgana's lips as she whispered into the phone. Her eyes caught mine and she said, *Yes, sir . . . gun . . . I'll keep them here.*

Five minutes later, Chief Pell made his entrance by throwing open the double doors so hard that the door handles slammed against the paneling with a loud *bang!* He strode to the center of the room, then held up a clear plastic bag with a small silver gun inside. Fingerprint powder had sifted to the bottom of the bag like fine black sand. "Fess up. Whose gun is this?" For some reason he looked straight at me.

Had Roland been shot in the back of the head and strangled? "Not mine," I said, answering his piercing gaze. "Never owned one, never will."

From the back of the room, Jenna squeaked, "It's mine. Roland got it for me. It was for my safety when I had to stay here alone last weekend when he had to go out of town for business." She started to cry.

Everyone froze. We were as still as the pair of Chinese jade Foo dogs that flanked the fireplace.

Jenna looked up at Chief Pell with weepy eyes. "He wasn't shot, was he?"

Pell ignored her and pointed to Frank, and said instead, "I need you to come down to the station with me."

"And if I don't?" the ghosthunter asked, jumping up with his fists clenched, no longer intimidated by the oversized chief. "I have an alibi for being here. Ask her!" He pointed at me.

Pell didn't seem surprised as he jeered in my direction.

Frank protested. "I don't know one person in the room besides her." Again, he pointed at me. "And I don't even know the guy who was killed."

"Exactly," the chief said. "You don't belong here." He turned to Jenna. "Mrs. Cahill, I mean Eastman, I'm afraid you'll have to come along with me too. Perhaps one of your friends can get you a lawyer to meet you in East Hampton."

"I need a lawyer?" she croaked.

Chief Pell motioned for her to come forward. Then he looked over at Morgana. "Please send me the audio of both his" — he looked at Frank — "and Ms. Eastman's interviews."

I shot up from the sofa. "I have someone I can call for you, Jenna. He's the best lawyer in the area."

Chief Pell looked down his hooked nose at me. "Of course you do, Ms. Barrett."

"Am I being arrested?" Jenna squeaked.

"Not yet," Pell answered. Addressing Morgana, he added, "Get everyone's contact information and address," adding to the rest of us, "and don't leave the Hamptons." Then he corralled Jenna and Frank together and followed them out the open doorway.

I ran after them. "It'll be all right, Jenna. I'll call Mr. Marguilles; he's the best in the Hamptons."

Jenna's limp had returned, and she'd looked pathetic as she wobbled up the hallway. She stopped short and turned around. "Thank you, friend."

I was about to ask Chief Pell if I could come along to the station but decided against it. Instead I said, "Don't worry, Jenna. Call me when you're done. I'll pick you up."

Jenna looked at me with tear-filled eyes, then jutted out her chin, attempting to put on a brave face. I believed she was innocent of killing her husband, and if the police thought differently, I would do anything I could to help her. "Don't worry, Jenna. Everything will be okay."

But would it?

Chapter 15

After I called the Hamptons' number-one celebrity defense lawyer for Jenna—don't ask me how I knew who that was—I promised Morgana a tour of the main house. Other than the two CSI teams who were working the crime scene at the pavilion, Morgana and I were the only ones left in the main house. I'd brought her to the kitchen and was giving her an explanation about how Jenna had come in and made her announcement about her husband's death. Naturally, I left out the part where I'd snuck outside in my booties and did my own investigating. That was something I would only tell my diary. If I kept one.

Vicki had been escorted to Jenna and Roland's Amagansett rental, where she'd been staying while working on the showhouse, and was told to pack an overnight bag until forensics had a chance to collect evidence. I'd taken it upon myself to get Vicki a room at Montauk Manor. I figured at least I would know she'd be close by and available for questioning. I recalled her resentment and disgust when talking about her former stepfather, who also happened to be the chief operating officer of Veronica's Interiors. I also remembered the not so subtle way she made the comment about Roland and Jenna's argument. I ascribed to the saying *Make sure to keep your friends close and your enemies closer.*

Freya left the same time as Vicki. I'd heard her call someone to pick her up, explaining she'd been dropped off by one of her camera crew for some pre-shots of Enderly Hall for her show, *Hamptons Home and Garden.* When it came to Freya Rittenhouse's possible motive for killing Roland, I couldn't come up with a thing. I'd never heard her say a bad word about him, but of course he'd been so starstruck by Freya coming to him and asking to be on the decorating team that he'd been on his best behavior.

Maybe that was it! Why would Freya contact Roland about working on the showhouse? Wouldn't Jenna have been the logical contact for such a request? Freya did have an eye for décor, and she had promised to video my outdoor spaces for her show. When I gave it some thought, I realized she was one of those people who you immediately felt comfortable around. Even though she showcased wealthy estates in the Hamptons, interviewing their celebrity owners and top-notch interior designers, she never came off as pretentious or snobby. The same couldn't be said for most of her guests, the reason I chose to only decorate small Montauk cottages. I'd had enough social climbing in Manhattan, all the surface friendships only formed because of my ties to *American Home and Garden*. I didn't miss the invitations to social events that came as a perk for being the editor in chief of a national magazine, because even then I would have rather stayed at home and read a book, or gone shopping at the myriad flea markets in the city.

I also thought about the way she smiled and the caring in her eyes when she'd talked about her disabled sister. The only thing I couldn't wrap my head around was how friendly she'd seemed around Roland. Of all of us, including Jenna, she was the only one who didn't seem to despise the man.

When it came to Freya as a suspect, I needed to caution myself. It was early days, and with a little digging I might come up with a reason she might have killed Roland Cahill, recalling the time I'd trusted someone else's innocence, then almost paid the price with my life.

Frank, the paranormal investigator, was still on my radar, as was the entire ghosthunter crew. Mostly based on the fact someone had been in Shepherds Cottage yesterday and Jenna's claims of seeing lights inside the cottage and on the grounds. I'd locked the cottage's only door. Was someone looking for Captain Kidd's ghost? If so, they'd be better off traveling to Gardiners Island.

Nate and Kuri had apparently come to Enderly together in Nate's car and left together. Working in the same firm, Klein and Associates, I supposed it made sense. I'd learned from reading their lips as Morgana was writing down their addresses that they both lived in East Hampton. Nate and Kuri had harbored bad feelings toward the deceased. Kuri's hatred, more like disgust of Roland, had been apparent when Elle and I had seen them in Amagansett. However, Nate Klein's dissatisfaction with Roland I'd only learned about from word of mouth. Vicki's mouth. She'd mentioned that Roland must have been holding something over Nate's head to get the job at Nate's firm. Blackmail gone bad? One thing my father always taught me, unless you see it for yourself, or you have a credible witness, innocent until proven guilty must prevail.

Morgana gave me a light tap on my upper arm and I startled, realizing that she'd been talking to me and I hadn't heard a word.

"Sorry, you caught me. I was going over possible suspects and their motives. You know me. My mind's been swirling with all the possibilities. Even the one that Jenna might still be in danger, and whoever killed Roland also planned to murder Jenna."

"You understand things don't look good for your friend." I nodded my head. She said, "I'm lucky you're here. This is my first time on a homicide. I need to prove myself, and hopefully catch whoever killed Mr. Cahill. With your help, of course."

"I hope you're not trying to impress Chief Pell," I warned. "He's not easily impressed, and will be even less so if he learns we're friends. I also wouldn't follow the unprofessional way Pell is handling this case. I don't understand why he's showing us his hand by displaying all the forensic evidence—the gun, extension cord and Roland's phone. Arthur . . . Detective Shoner, would hold those things back, at least until preliminary reports came back on time of death."

"No, I don't care about what Chief Pell thinks,' Morgana said, reaching into the breast pocket of her black uniform shirt and retrieving a stick of gum that she opened then folded into her mouth. Morgana was a big gum chewer. As she'd once explained it, she had to make a choice between her three-pack-a-day cigarette habit or the morgue. She said gum seemed a healthier choice, confiding that another reason she'd stopped smoking was to get more men interested in her dating profile on her matchmadeinheaven.com dating site, saying, "You'd be surprised how many guys put nonsmoker as a nonnegotiable." Never married and in her mid-forties, I hadn't asked her more, not wanting to open the floodgates to one of her past matchmadein*hell*.com sagas.

"Pell's with Suffolk County," Morgana continued. "I'm more interested in not screwing up in my new position with the East Hampton Town PD. Just happy to be off traffic detail. Not much traffic here in Montauk. I'm lucky I was the only one around when the call came in from dispatch."

No, I thought, *I'm the lucky one because I no longer have Elle's fiancé to fill me in on case details anymore, but now I have you.*

I tested out our friendship connection by asking, "Can you share with me if Roland was not only strangled with the extension cord but also shot? Possibly with Jenna's gun? I know for a fact that Roland is the one who gave Jenna the gun for her protection. I bet it might even be registered to him."

Instead of answering my question, Morgana said solemnly, "I don't want anyone from East Hampton Town PD to know we have a connection because of my sister-in-law. Seeing you might have been on the grounds at the same time Mr. Cahill was murdered, I think after we leave here, we should keep things on the down low."

Her last sentence threw me off. Way off. I never considered myself a suspect. But there it was—like a slap in the face.

"I would never think you were involved," she added, "but you know the drill."

Unfortunately, I did. And, since my move to Montauk, I'd been drilled a few too many times. Even my father couldn't believe all my misfortunes. It hadn't stopped him from helping me and lending a hand in solving a few cases from afar. As I was contemplating on letting my father in on this latest development, weighing the pros and cons, my cell phone buzzed.

I tapped the Bluetooth feature on my right hearing aid and heard Jenna's breathless voice on the other end. "Meg, they're letting me go. Thanks for sending Mr. Marguilles. He was amazing."

"That's great."

She let out a long exhale that sounded like a rush of water in my hearing aid, then said, "I don't want to spend the night in Amagansett or at Enderly. Can you get me a room at Montauk Manor? I'll take a Pink Tuna Taxi, just text me the room number. And do you mind packing up a few things of mine from the attic? Toothbrush, toothpaste, change of clothes, my makeup bag, and, oh . . . the prescription bottle of sleeping pills next to the bed. And my laptop. I'm not a pill-popper but tonight I plan on taking one. Maybe two," she said with a laugh that ended in a sob.

"Sure. How about instead of Montauk Manor, you stay at the East End Yacht Club? I still have Cole's suite at my disposal. The press won't even know you're there. And in the meantime, we'll get everything straightened out." Having her stay at Montauk Manor, where I'd sent Vicki, would be a big mistake. Especially if it was Vicki who killed her former stepfather. I was starting to feel like the

Hamptons concierge for murder suspects. Who needed a room next? Frank the ghosthunter?

"That sounds perfect," Jenna said. "Thank you."

Don't thank me. Thank Cole. My stomach dropped as I boarded the Cole Spenser roller coaster—my first emotion was the thought of his safe recovery, then the downward plunge when I viewed the photo of the kiss. Letting us use his suite was the least he could do. Served him right for not asking for his keycard back. The jerk. Or was I being a jerk? We'd officially broken up. Cole had every right to move on. Too bad it had to be plastered all over social media. Hopefully, soon, I would find relief in the finality of it all. For now, I felt exposed. Gutted.

"You're welcome," I said into the phone, noticing Morgana pointing at her watch. "I'm sure Officer Moss will be able to escort me to the attic to get your essentials. Though I'm not sure about the laptop."

Morgana shook her head in the negative.

"Soon you'll have full access to everything," I added with false cheer. "It just depends on how fast the investigation proceeds."

"I didn't kill Roland," Jenna said in a raspy, drained voice. "Meg, you have to believe me."

"Jenna, I do believe you."

"Thank you for believing in me."

"Of course." I could have invited her to stay at my cottage, but I selfishly wanted my own space. A place to free my mind, and hopefully see things in a clearer light. The murder and Cole. Or was there another reason I'd hesitated? I'd told myself she was innocent. How could I know that for sure? I knew how. By finding out who had killed Roland Cahill. I said, "I'll call the yacht club and collect your things. Oh, by the way, I didn't know Mr. Klein was your cousin. It must be a relief to have him nearby."

"It is. Though he warned me about marrying Roland. I should have listened. Maybe Roland would still be alive? I know Nate's angry I made him hire Roland. I better go. Someone wants to use the phone. I feel a migraine coming on. With all this stress I'll probably have an aneurysm . . ."

"Sorry, Jenna, you're breaking up." Not really. "I better get up to the attic. I'll see you soon."

There was immediate relief in her voice. "Oh, Meg, what would I do without you and Elle? Please believe me. I didn't kill Roland."

"Of course I believe you," I replied.

But would Chief Pell?

Chapter 16

On the way up the narrow staircase to the attic, Morgana handed me a pair of disposable gloves. "The crime scene unit hasn't been inside yet, but I'm sure they'll be here soon. This way you won't leave any prints." She stopped on the second step from the top and looked down at me. "Unless you've been in the attic before? Even so, you might want to wear these so as not to disturb any other prints that don't belong."

"No. I've always meant to check out the attic but didn't want to run into Roland."

"It seems not too many people were fond of the dead guy," Morgana said, continuing up the steps. When she reached the top, she waited for me under the large arched opening.

I stopped next to her. "That's an understatement." I told her about Roland's subpoena but held back on Jenna's claim that Roland was trying to kill her with his car and the fact she'd asked him for a divorce. "He was a piece of work. The only person I saw him play nice with was Freya Rittenhouse. But most likely, that was so he could get Enderly on a *Hamptons Home and Garden* episode."

We stepped inside the attic and I moaned, "Nirvana! Attics are definitely my thing. Especially ones that take up the entire third floor of a mansion-sized cottage."

"To each his own," Morgana said, looking around. "I'm not a fan of old, dusty cobweb-crusted stuff."

"Cobweb-crusted? Oh, the dustier the better. Plus, it's what's found under the dust that's important." I wasn't an expert on antiques like Elle was, but I knew what surrounded us — the leftovers after Jenna had furnished the first two floors of Enderly — weren't shoddy second-class citizens. More like antique royalty.

Furniture from every century was scattered around the space, Elizabethan, Byzantine, Art Nouveau, Roman, just to name a few. "Amazing," I said, scanning the space.

On the southwest corner, hidden behind a tall gold Japanese folding screen, I saw the bamboo footboard to a queen-size bed. Jenna and Roland's makeshift bedroom. The folding screen butted up to a door that opened to a balcony with spiral steps leading up to the cupola. In my mind, another design feature cementing the fact that Sanford White, the Gilded Age tastemaker, had been Enderly's architect, owing to the fact another Stanford White *cottage* in Southampton had the same design. I hadn't had to decorate the third-floor balcony because no one was going to be allowed in the attic for the showhouse.

In the attic's northwest corner was a section filled with dead animal taxidermy. I supposed the word *dead* was a redundant adjective to use with the word *taxidermy*, but in this case, some of the animals looked ready to pounce and drag me away in their openmouthed saber-toothed jaws. Birds, lions, tigers and bears . . . oh my! Some had disintegrated into unrecognizable mats of hair, skin and sawdust. *Ick.*

Morgana had the opposite reaction. "Wow! Someone was a big game hunter," she said, moving toward the decaying zoo. "Did you know that Teddy Roosevelt was stationed at Camp Wycoff in Montauk during the Spanish-American War?"

"Yes. Him and his Rough Riders, recovering from yellow fever."

"Maybe Teddy was friends with Ms. Eastman's family? That would explain all these," Morgana said, patting a wildebeest on the nose, the ends of his tusks sharp enough to open a can of soup.

"Not beyond the realm of possibilities," I answered.

Morgana seemed quite intrigued by the zoological graveyard and went over to a brass tub filled with an assortment of antlers. Some of the antlers were mounted to pieces of wood, some loose. In season, Morgana and her brother Jack went bow-and-arrow deer hunting in the county park next to Montauk's Deep Hollow Ranch. A tough former Brooklynite, I'd never seen Morgana get squeamish about anything, including gory horror movies. Hunting the same way the Montaukett Native Americans had, with a bow and arrow, seemed a more humane way to thin out the overpopulation of tick-carrying deer compared to when a rich Hamptonite brought in a planeload of African lions and set them loose. A true story. Not well publicized for obvious reasons.

Personally, I couldn't kill any live creature, not even a spider. It might have had something to do with my favorite childhood book, *Charlotte's Web.* If I found one inside my cottage, I would capture it under a glass on a paper plate and free it outdoors.

"Oh, my, you've got to see this!" Morgana exclaimed. Her head was hidden behind the lid of an open steamer trunk.

"What is it?" I asked. "Something creepy? A clue to Roland's killer? You never answered me about the gun. Was Roland also shot?"

I cautiously stepped toward her. The attic's spooky vibes, the heads scattered here and there, along with what might be in the trunk had me on edge. Not my usual M.O. If it wasn't for the slight grin on Morgana's lips, I might have hesitated. When I came up behind her, I peered over her shoulder, expecting to see human remains or dozens of shrunken heads.

Instead, the crate was filled with old mid-century *Playboy* magazines. I burst into laughter. Nothing like a little comic relief to lighten the mood. "Those look like some oldies," I said. "Did you know if there's a December 1953 issue, the first one with Marilyn Monroe, it's probably worth ten thousand dollars or more?"

"I'm not going to even ask how you know that." She closed the trunk's lid and stood. "We better get going. I don't want to be up here when the team arrives. It's not like we're doing anything illegal because I'm your police escort. But like we agreed, it's better to keep things aboveboard."

Looking her straight in the eye, I asked, "Well, was Roland shot with Jenna's gun?"

"We are getting in some sticky-wicket territory here."

"Nod your head if he was."

Morgana kept still, until I broke the silence. "Okay, then. I agree. We should get moving. I have to bring Jenna's overnight bag to the yacht club."

I advanced toward the corner of the attic, where Jenna and Roland's makeshift bedroom was, remembering that I needed to collect Jenna's sleeping pills from the bedside table.

Once past the screen, I turned toward the bed. My mouth opened but nothing came out.

I felt Morgana behind me. "Holy dog ears!" she screeched into my left hearing aid.

In the center of the bed, covered by a white down comforter, was the outline of a body.

Who could it be? Everyone was accounted for. Apparently not.

We both stared, looking to see if the figure under the covers was breathing and ready to pop up like a jack-in-the-box.

There was only *dead* quiet.

Morgana hesitated for only a second, strode to the side of the bed and pulled back the covers.

Looking up at the ceiling with dead glassy eyes was the head of a huge white polar bear.

In its mouth was a wad of paper bills.

Could things get any stranger?

I had a feeling they could.

Chapter 17

I slipped out the back door and onto the Enderly's wide veranda and sat on a Victorian chaise that faced the invisible ocean, waiting for Morgana. She'd had to stay inside where there was wifi in order to send Chief Pell the audio interviews, as he'd requested.

After finding the polar bear rug in Jenna and Roland's bed, I'd filled Morgana in on how Grandpa Eastman died—on Enderly's beach with hundred-dollar bills stuffed in his mouth—adding the story of the trespasser Grandpa had shot and paralyzed. When we'd come down from the attic and entered the kitchen, we'd been met by three CSI teams. Morgana had filled them in on what we'd found in the attic and had pointed out the bloody sand on the kitchen floor. Afterward, they'd scattered into three groups, each team taking a floor.

Now, as I reviewed the past couple of hours, I couldn't help but feel spooked. Maybe there were such things as ghosts and curses. Ghosts of dead animals, grandfathers, trespassers and husbands. Curses by dead pirates. The night was calm, unlike the pounding of my heart while I waited for Morgana. The temperature had dropped ten degrees from when I'd gone out to see Roland's body and I couldn't stop my teeth from chattering. My jacket was in the car, but I was too exhausted, mentally and physically, to move. As my father liked to say, *Move a muscle, change a thought,* in other words, take action to get yourself out of a mental slump. I supposed instead of a polar bear rug we could have found a bloody severed horse head like in the movie *The Godfather.* Instead of the image of Ben Franklin on the hundred-dollar bills, the C-notes in the polar bear's mouth featured Mr. Moneybags from a vintage game of Monopoly.

Were Roland's death and the surprise in the bed related? If so, what was the message? Roland wasn't a relative of the Eastmans, only through marriage. Was someone trying to scare Jenna by mimicking her grandfather's death?

Too many questions. Not enough answers.

I was saved from my brain exploding when Morgana stepped out onto the veranda. "You ready to go?" she asked.

"Never more so," I said, jumping up from the chaise and moving toward the steps. Before stepping down, I glanced toward the ocean. The fog was as thick as ever, and I recalled Carl Sandberg's famous poem, noticing in this case it didn't look like our fog's little cat feet had any intention of moving on.

Morgana came up behind me. She said something I couldn't catch, then grabbed my elbow. Through the mist we saw a moving light in the direction of Shepherds Cottage.

"I'm going after them," she announced.

"Not without me you aren't."

We advanced as stealthily as we could in the fog, our feet making crunching noises on the stone and shell path. As we moved toward the ocean, a repetitious pounding splintered the still night. When we reached the entrance to a boxwood maze, I grabbed Morgana's elbow and led her inside, whispering, "I have a way we can sneak up on them." I took my phone from my pocket and turned on the flashlight function. Morgana took hers off her belt. We were invisible behind the dense hedges, the reason I'd chosen it as our way to sneak up on whoever was out there.

Last month, when Jenna gave me a tour of the grounds, she'd told me the story of how at age five she'd gotten lost inside the maze. Her parents found her asleep at the base of a fountain with a statue of Eros. Jenna said she'd thought Eros, with his raised bow and arrow, would protect her. After rescuing her, Jenna's parents demanded that Jenna's grandfather open up six exits — in case any other child wandered in and got lost.

I'd been a little disappointed at her story. I loved a good maze. One with a single entrance and exit. But now, I was thrilled. Because I knew exactly which way to go to get closest to Shepherds Cottage.

When we reached the opening, I turned off my light and whispered, "Follow me." Morgana clipped her flashlight onto her belt, then grabbed on to the fabric at the back of my dress and we stepped out from under a trellised arch into the murky night.

We listened and looked ahead. The pounding had stopped. The cottage was dark.

Now what were we supposed to do?

Morgana answered my question by drawing her gun. We slowly advanced forward, then stopped fifty feet from the front door of Shepherds Cottage. Our patience was rewarded. The cottage door burst open and a figure holding a flashlight, wearing a black hoodie and pants, bolted in the direction of the beach pavilion.

Still holding her gun, Morgana took her radio off her belt and shoved it in my hand. "Call dispatch for backup. I'm going after them."

After she charged off, I found myself staring down at the radio, wondering if I should pretend to be Morgana by adding a Brooklyn accent while chomping on a piece of gum. No time for that. I pushed the button on the side of the radio and said, "This is Meg Barrett, Officer Moss is in pursuit of a suspect, send backup to Enderly Hall. The pavilion near the steps to the beach. And hurry it up!"

There was static on the other end, and I couldn't make out what was being said because of my hearing loss. I pushed the button again and shouted, "Hurry! Officer Moss in danger. Go to Enderly Hall's beach pavilion." Then, instead of running for the front gate where patrol cars were still parked or to Enderly Hall in order to recruit the teams of unarmed CSIs, I went to the open door of Shepherds Cottage, reached inside and flipped on the light switch.

And felt like crying.

All the work. All the precious antiques and reproductions were scattered everywhere, most splintered in pieces. Even the large sideboard had been tipped over. Items weren't just lying on the floor, it looked like they'd seen both ends of a hammer. Pottery and glassware were shattered into thousands of pieces. Even a few of the floorboards had been pried up. I stepped inside cautiously, not wanting to disturb any evidence.

Then I moved to the bedroom and surveyed the carnage. It had also been tossed. It took everything I had not to rescue some of the priceless objects in the room. The feather mattress to the ornate four-poster bed had been pushed up against the wall, revealing the supporting bed ropes that were tied to the bed's frame. Deep slash marks in the mattress oozed feathers, some still floating in the air, signaling that this must have been the last room the perpetrator ransacked before running out.

All I could think about was how brazen an act it was to be searching for something while there was still a strong police presence on the grounds.

I checked the cottage's other room. It was also a mess. What had they been looking for?

"Meg, Meg!" Morgana called from the main room.

"In the bedroom."

She joined me, out of breath, spewing out two-word sentences: "Got away. Took stairs. Lost them. Foggy beach."

"Them? There was more than one?"

"No. Just don't know if it was a male or female." She glanced around. "What a mess! Any idea what they were looking for?"

"Not really. But this is where Jenna's grandfather lived at the end of his life."

"Well, you've done more than your share today. We can't go through anything tonight. I order you, as my deputy, to go home. I'll call you tomorrow."

I relaxed my shoulders. "Aw, I'm your deputy?"

"Not literally. How about my informant."

I joked, "Informants get paid under the table, don't they?"

She smiled. "Now you're pushing it."

Frankly, I'd had enough. Items that Jenna and I had spent months looking for were broken beyond repair. Even the blanket chest's top that came from Grimes House Antiques had been ripped off its hinges, its contents dumped out and the wood split from someone using the claw at the back of a hammer. Someone looking for a false bottom?

I yearned for my cozy chair by the fire and the company of my fat cat. Then I remembered I had to go to the yacht club and drop Jenna's bag that I'd packed, while a snarling, bodyless polar bear had looked on.

"Earth to Meg. You okay?" Morgana asked. "I'm sorry. I know this was one of your projects for the showhouse, right?"

Wordlessly, I handed her back her radio. She took it and gave me a quick hug. I'd never seen Morgana show emotion. But the hug said it all.

I squeezed her back and we walked out the cottage door and down the path toward Enderly. We parted company on the back veranda, where I grabbed Jenna's bag and headed for my car.

As I walked, I thought things could have been worse. It could have been Jenna at the bottom of those steps. And Cole could still be lost at sea.

But he wasn't. Just lost to me.

When I reached my car, I saw it was the only vehicle parked inside the gates. Beyond the entrance to the estate, I saw flashing lights atop two squad cars. It was surprising there weren't any news cameras, ghosthunters or lookie-loos. It seemed that even if the news had hit about Roland Cahill's death, it hadn't made a big splash on the media circuits. In the Hamptons scheme of things, Jenna's husband was a nobody. If it had been Jenna, an *Eastman*, that was another story.

There was also the possibility that nothing about the murder had been leaked to the press. Unlikely, especially when I thought of the brazen way Chief Pell had gone about brandishing evidence like guns, cell phones and extension-cord garrotes.

I opened my car door, tossed Jenna's bag in the backseat and got inside. Shivering, I grabbed my jacket from the passenger's seat. After I slipped it on, I felt a lump in the right pocket from the EVP ghost voice recorder. I laid it on the seat, retrieved my key from my handbag, which I'd hidden under the seat, then reached for the ignition. When I looked in the rearview mirror and caught my reflection, I knew what I had to do.

Find ghosthunter Frank Holden's cell phone. He'd been frantic about its whereabouts. Why? Maybe like me, he was too cheap to pay extra for cloud storage. The manic way he kept bringing up the loss of his phone made me suspicious. He hadn't cared about the EVP instrument in my pocket, only his phone.

For once, I appreciated the dense fog as I got out of the car and crept toward the area by the fence where I'd found the recorder. Turning on my phone's flashlight, I got down on my hands and knees and searched the damp grass, probably ruining the Doris Day dress Elle had loaned me. But if my sleuthing helped Jenna, I knew Elle would be all for it.

Ten minutes later, I gave up. Bedraggled and exhausted, I got back in the car and headed to the yacht club. There'd been no sign of his phone. It would have to wait for daylight.

Ten minutes later, Jenna met me in the yacht club's restaurant, and we went up to Cole's suite. I prayed my keycard would work. It did. After Cole's exciting rescue, I doubted he'd had time to call the yacht club and bar me from entering.

He had other things on his mind. Or should I say other people.

Once inside the sitting room to the suite, the first thing Jenna did was to grab the bag I'd packed. She withdrew the prescription bottle and took two sleeping pills. After everything she'd been through, I couldn't blame her for doubling up. I was just glad she didn't triple up.

Jenna told me of her time at the East Hampton station. It seemed everyone treated her well. Then she gave me a quick recap of her interview with Chief Pell and another officer from Suffolk County, confirming that Roland hadn't been shot with her gun. But he had been strangled and they'd determined it was a suspicious death. After changing into her nightgown, she shed a few tears for Roland, then begged me to stay with her until she fell asleep. I tucked her in, then sat next to her on the bed, holding her hand until she fell, more like plummeted, to sleep. Then I tiptoed into the other room.

Judging by her snoring, nothing would wake her. I was glad I hadn't told her about the surprise visitor Morgana and I found resting *its* gigantic head on her pillow in the attic.

Glancing around the sitting room, a great sense of unease descended, having nothing to do with the murder at Enderly Hall, more with the death of Cole's and my relationship. I wished him well, I truly did. But the jealousy monster on my right shoulder posed the question, *How long had Cole and his Billie been more than crewmates?* I backtracked to when he'd first hired her. Three months ago. We were still trying to make it work. At least I was.

I grabbed my jacket and the photo on the armoire taken last summer of Cole and me on one of his sailing yachts. Opening the sliding glass door to the balcony, I stepped out. Then I tossed the picture Frisbee-style into the cold dark water. The splash was an exclamation point to the end of our love affair.

Burial at sea.

How fitting.

Chapter 18

Sunday morning I woke with Jo's head on my feet. I propped myself up and glanced out the balcony window and saw clear blue sky and calm seas.

Hallelujah! The fog had lifted.

My first thought was what a beautiful day for the opening of the showhouse. Then I recalled my nightmare having to do with corpses and Cole. The two Cs. Maybe I should have swiped one of Jenna's sleeping pills. Luckily for me, Jo wouldn't let me wallow. I had to get food in her belly tout de suite.

Sundays were usually my lazy days, when I read the newspaper from front to back, either on my screened porch with a French press of dark roast by my side or in my comfy reading chair by the fire. There was no time for that today. I was too anxious about what had gone down at Enderly and needed to clear my tangled emotions by chatting with an old friend — the Atlantic Ocean.

After showering, dressing, adding minimal makeup and doing a quick check that Jenna was okay, I went down to the beach. Not only was the sky clear, but the temperature was near sixty. If only everything was as clear as the sky in front of me. Like who had killed Roland Cahill and why.

I hadn't called Morgana, wanting to stick to our pact of pretending we weren't anything but casual acquaintances, but she had texted me late last night from her sister-in-law's phone that Roland's time of death was sometime between ten and noon. That meant Roland had been killed soon after I'd been to the pavilion to make sure everything was status quo for the cocktail party. It also meant everyone involved with the showhouse had been there at the time. No one had an alibi. Including myself.

The confusing thing was, whoever sent the text to Jenna, pretending to be Roland, had to have gone back to the scene of their crime. Is that when they'd thrown the extension cord into the ocean? That meant there was another time everyone needed to be accounted for. Kuri is the one who said Jenna got the text around four thirty.

Last night when I got back from the yacht club, Elle had also sent me a text message with a link that led to a photo from *Dave's Papers* showing Freya Rittenhouse and Jenna's husband with their heads close together, all smiles, at Thursday evening's Guild Hall Gala. Thursday was the same day Jenna claimed Roland tried to run her over. That explained why Jenna wasn't by his side and Freya was. What kind of husband would leave his wife at home after what had happened to her? Even if Jenna overexaggerated her injuries, it seemed callous of Roland to go without her. I enlarged the photo and saw Freya's hand had been companionably on top of Roland's. He looked at her with admiration. Were Freya and Roland having an affair? Or was Freya just buttering up Roland because he'd allowed her to be one of the decorators for the showhouse? I'd suspected Jenna and Nate of the same thing, and they'd turned out to be cousins.

I needed to stay out of it. If Jenna was arrested, that would be a different story. Then, nothing would hold me back from getting involved.

Now, as I looked out over the water, I was determined to forget about the murder and instead concentrate on the clear, unfogged beauty that surrounded me. I strolled over to my usual flat-topped boulder and sat. A scruffy-looking seagull landed next to me, carrying what looked like a french fry in his mouth. "Fried foods aren't good for you, buddy, and I don't have anything with me as a healthy substitute. Can't eat a thing after what happened yesterday."

A male voice loud enough to drown out the sound of the crashing waves startled me.

"Do you always talk to seabirds?" Standing over my right shoulder was Patrick Seaton and his dog Charlie.

"As a matter of fact, all the time," I answered, laughing. "Don't you?"

Patrick tossed the piece of driftwood in his hand toward the narrow strip of sand at the ocean's edge. Charlie happily charged after it, then Patrick took a seat on a smooth boulder next to me and for a few minutes we silently watched Charlie play in the surf. Eventually he asked, "Everything okay? I heard you tell Jonathan Livingston Seagull over there that you had a bad day yesterday. Want to share?"

What came out of my mouth was almost like a vomitous explosion of words, Mt. Vesuvius spewing trapped molten lava, my voice rising and falling, depending on which tale I was telling. I told him everything, not just about Roland Cahill's murder, but also about Cole and the rescue photo with Cole's chief mate.

At first, he didn't respond. And I was glad because I was truly embarrassed by my outburst. At least I hadn't cried, and the strangest thing of all, the Barrett blotches hadn't reared their ugly red welts. Was it a sign that I felt comfortable with Patrick?

There wasn't time to ponder things because Charlie ran up to us with a crab carcass in her mouth, which for some reason reminded me of Enderly's attic. I realized I'd forgotten to tell Patrick about the polar bear head or how Jenna's grandfather had been found dead on the beach with bills in his mouth.

After I did, he said, "Sounds like quite a day. And quite a story. If this was one of my thrillers, or even a movie script, I would say it's too far-fetched to believe. Even the part about your ex's chief mate's name. But then Charlie is a guy's name and she's a girl."

"Stranger than fiction," I added, thinking, *Wow!* Patrick was right, Cole was an ex.

Charlie's ears had twitched when she'd heard her name. Glancing down at the decaying crab she'd dropped in front of him, Patrick praised her by saying, "Thanks for the present, gal," then petted the back of the dog's neck. She stood panting, waiting for him to throw another piece of driftwood, which he did. But Charlie didn't move; instead she kept her gaze on Patrick's right jean pocket. "My apologies," he said, "of course you deserve a reward for leaving me such a wonderful and odorous present." He reached into his pocket, withdrew a treat and held it in his open palm. Charlie lapped it up in a very ladylike manner. My fat cat could have used a few lessons from her.

Patrick tossed another piece of driftwood and Charlie took off in a gallop. He said, "I think the first thing you should do is nothing."

"But, I . . ."

"Aha!" he said, narrowing his gorgeous eyes. "I see how your mind works, rushing in where angels fear to tread."

"Not exactly. But seeing it's such a clear day and I didn't find Frank the paranormal investigator's phone, if I went back over to Enderly . . ."

"What's the rush?" he asked thoughtfully. "I know when I plot a thriller or a murder mystery, as in my *Mr. & Mrs. Winslow* screenplay, you don't want to tip off the murderer you're on to them until you have everything in place. Including backup. As Tolstoy said in *War and Peace*, 'The strongest of all warriors are these two — time and patience.'"

"Hmm, Tolstoy," I mused, "not one of our dead poets?"

"No. Just a dead author who thought and wrote like a poet."

"Okay. I have one: 'Rivers know this: there is no hurry. We shall get there someday.'"

He scratched at the stubble on his chin. "You've got me. A dead poet?"

"Nope. Winnie-the-Pooh."

Patrick grinned, the lines by his eyes crinkling in amusement. He was older than me, probably in his late thirties, but when smiling he looked like a little boy.

"Do you think your friend Jenna will be arrested?" he asked.

I thought for a moment before answering. "Well, I know for a fact that Roland wasn't shot, so Jenna's gun wouldn't come into play. And there's no proof that she strangled him with the extension cord. Before I threw it under the stairs, it was floating in the surf." Realizing what I'd just confessed, I put my hand to my mouth and said, "Oopsie."

Amused, Patrick laughed. "Oopsie? Seems you better be careful and keep all your tampering with evidence to yourself or I'll have to bail you out of jail."

He would? My heart hiccupped, and there they were — I felt the Barret blotches warm my neck.

The wind started howling, causing whitecaps on the ocean. Typical, changeable beachside weather in Montauk. Unless Patrick faced me, I had a hard time hearing him. And I wanted to hear every word.

Before asking him to turn his head when he spoke, I admired his profile. His nose was perfect and straight, almost noble, his strong jawline had just the right amount of stubble. His dark blond hair, which in the summer would be streaked with gold from his time surfing in the sun, fell at the back of his neck in short layers. Just to confirm it was as soft as it looked, I had an urge to run my fingers through it.

Get a of grip, Meg! Feeling tongue-tied and out of sorts at all the emotions filling my addled brain, I placed my hand on his arm. He turned to me. This morning the color of his blue-green eyes was more blue than green. "I'm sorry, but between the surf and the wind, I'm having a hard time hearing you. Do you mind repeating what you just said?" Then I pointed to my ears, reminding him about my hearing aids. Full disclosure: I had heard everything he'd said, I just wanted him to repeat the part about bailing me out of jail that had made my heart leap.

"My apologies," he said sincerely, then repeated himself, omitting the best part.

Had I been hallucinating? "No reason to apologize," I said, getting up from my boulder.

The tide was approaching. Soon the shoreline would be swallowed by the mighty Atlantic, along with the rocks we were sitting on. Patrick also stood, and we watched Charlie. The scars since her mistreatment as a racetrack dog were still visible on her flank, but she'd gained weight from the first time I'd met her, and her coat had a luxurious shine to it. Even Charlie's eyes looked healthy and alert as she came tail-wagging toward us, the stick making the corners of her mouth turn up like she was smiling. She stopped in front of Patrick and dropped the piece of driftwood in a puddle, then gazed up at her master with love.

"Wow!" I said. "She's a pro at fetching."

Patrick hesitated at putting his hand in the seaweedy pool to retrieve the stick, so I picked up a similar-sized stick and waved it in the air. "Here, Charlie. Look at this luscious specimen of a stick." I tossed it and she leapt after it.

Suddenly I thought of another dog, Cole's huge three-legged dog that we used to take with us on long beach walks toward the Montauk Point Lighthouse.

Tripod! If Cole's relationship with his Billie got serious, what would become of Tripod? Cole told me that his chief mate was allergic to dogs. At the time, I thought Billie was a man, not a female—and certainly not a love interest. As I watched Charlie frolic in the water, I worried about Tripod's future. His long shaggy coat was almost as hard to clean off my cushions as my mangy Maine coon Jo's. I could only imagine the dander.

"I think Charlie is part fish. She really loves the water," Patrick said, interrupting my thoughts about flying down to North Carolina and kidnapping Tripod.

Charlie came prancing back to us, lithely maneuvering over the stones and boulders. Patrick reached into his pocket and took out another treat. Charlie waited in a sitting position until Patrick placed the treat in his palm and held it toward her. Jo would have bitten off one of his fingertips, or scratched it away with her sharp claws, leaving a trail of blood. Patience was not one of Josephine Eater Barrett's virtues.

"She looks as happy as I am that the fog has finally lifted," I said. "'Keep your face always toward the sunshine and shadows will fall behind you . . .'"

"Whitman. How true. It's amazing how the weather can affect your mood." He looked pensive as he stared toward the lighthouse, reminding me of when we were neighbors and Patrick would pace the ocean at nightfall, looking forlorn and lonely. What was he thinking of? The people he'd lost? His wife and young daughter? A tragedy I couldn't even imagine.

He wasn't wearing a jacket. His black T-shirt fit his lean frame like a second skin, and so did his jeans. I couldn't help but compare him to Cole. Cole was also a fan of black T-shirts. Both men were about the same height. Both extremely attractive. But in different ways. Right now, I found myself being more attracted to Patrick than Cole. I realized why. I knew Patrick on a more intimate level than Cole. Not physically, mentally. I knew Patrick through the lines of poetry he left in the sand and the words he'd penned in his books. A portal into his soul, so to speak.

Like Patrick, Cole had had his own share of tragedy, but he never shared his feelings with me. His mother's murder was something that troubled him because of the unresolved issues they'd had before her death. I'd often wondered if the fact that I'd helped find her killer, and saw him at his most vulnerable, could have been the reason he had been so closed off emotionally. Why was I comparing the two men? Cole was out of my life. It was as clear as the brilliant sun in front of me.

Patrick tapped me on the shoulder. I turned toward him. He said, "Have you had breakfast? I make a mean eggs Benedict."

He had me at, *I make . . .*

Chapter 19

It seemed very irresponsible that I hadn't run up to my cottage to get my phone. I'd been too giddy from the fact that I would finally see the interior of Patrick's cottage. On my nightly beach strolls, I couldn't count all the times I'd looked up and pictured him sitting at a desk behind the lamp with the green-glass lampshade that glowed like a beacon in the twilight, while woodsmoke rose from his stone chimney, mixing with the salty evening air. Or other times, when there was only a faint glow in the front downstairs window, and I imagined him in front of a cozy fire, reading a worn book of classical poetry by Keats or Lord Byron—or some other dead or live poet.

I even knew how many wooden steps there were leading up to his cottage. Twenty-eight.

Did that make me a stalker?

Maybe.

"Grab my hand," Patrick shouted over the gale-force wind coming from the north. It whistled in and out of my hearing aids like the sound you got when holding a conch shell to your ear, only amplified by a hundred. I extended my arm, and when his hand grasped mine, it sent shock waves up my spine.

We walked west toward his cottage, and even when boulders turned to rocks, then small stones, and finally pure white sand, he still held tight to my hand.

I wasn't complaining.

Had I stepped onto the pages of a Nicholas Sparks book? All the components were there—two lonely people who meet by chance, one with a tragic past, one deceived by the person she loved, or thought she loved. Then throw in a romantic setting like the tremulous, whitecapped Atlantic to our left and there you had it—a possible recipe for disaster, especially if Patrick was already in a relationship with his publicist, Ashley.

When we passed the bluff where at one time my old four-room rental cottage stood, I paused.

"Sad, isn't it," Patrick said, following my gaze.

"Extremely," I answered. A huge modern beach house in the last stages of construction had replaced my former rental. After I'd fled

Manhattan and a cheating fiancé, the tiny cottage had been my refuge and safe port in the storm. There it was again. A cheating male. But in all fairness, Cole and I had already broken up before he'd left for Portugal. But as my father always told me, if there's even a wisp of smoke, you can be sure a flame will follow. My father had been referring to one of his murder cases, but I was sure his maxim could also be a reference to my love life. Cheated on once, shame on them. Cheated on twice, shame on me.

We continued on, passing in front of the nature preserve, where I'd first found Patrick's writing in the sand. Charlie waited for us at the bottom of Patrick's steps, yelping a few short barks to hurry us along.

When we reached Charlie, Patrick let go of my hand and patted the dog on top of her pale gray head. "You know the drill, young lady. First, shower, then breakfast."

"Hope that doesn't apply to me, I've already showered." There was an awkward pause after my ridiculous comment, and rightly so. As Charlie bounded up the stairs, I took a step to follow her, feeling like an imbecile, my mouth too full of my oversized foot to utter any more quips. Patrick said something from behind, but the raging wind made it impossible for me to hear. I looked back and saw that he wore a smile, no doubt from my creepy shower statement. He repeated what he'd said, and I read his lips, "I'll follow you up. I've been meaning to replace the rope handrails with wood but haven't been able to get a contractor to commit to a date."

His comment about a contractor reminded me of Roland Cahill's murder, and I felt guilt over not being with Jenna, holding *her* hand instead of Patrick's.

As we reached the wooden platform at the top of the steps, I paused and looked ahead. It was everything I'd pictured. And more. Larger than my cottage, but nowhere near as big as the beach houses surrounding it. It was built in a Cape Cod shingle-style, the shingles left in their natural woodgrain. Weathered with age and storms. I would guess it dated from the 1940s.

Patrick made sure I was looking at him before he spoke. "Believe it or not, this originally was what they called an Abercrombie and Fitch kit house, the original structure didn't use one nail."

"Like Lincoln Logs," I added.

"Exactly. Of course, over the years nails were added, either that or the cottage might have ended up in the ocean or on Block Island. I've tried to keep it in its original state.

Ahh, a purist. My kind of guy. "That's amazing. Need any help with Charlie's shower?" Not that I'd ever showered a dog before, but it would be fun to watch.

"I'll handle Charlie if you can go inside and pour us a couple cups of Joe? Fresh coffee's in the carafe on the kitchen counter. Mugs on the shelves to the right of the sink. I hope you like it strong."

"Only way I drink it." Could I get any luckier? Now I'd be able to mentally catalog every feature of Patrick's cottage without him glancing over my shoulder. I always said, you can learn a lot about a person by their home environment. Every item gave insight to the person that lived there.

Patrick and Charlie disappeared behind a row of rhododendrons bursting with clumps of lavender flowers. A reminder of spring. Though you'd never know it by the dismal weather we'd had over the past couple of weeks, but things were looking up.

I went up three wood steps and grabbed the handle of a worn screen door, opened it and stepped onto a screened-in porch with a view of the ocean on all three sides. The porch looked original to the cottage and even had a small potbellied stove in the corner. All the floorboards had been painted navy blue and were covered with a large sisal rug.

There were only a few pieces of furniture, making the view the star attraction. They included two wooden slat reclining chairs with navy cushions that looked like they belonged on the deck of the *Titanic*, and centered between the chairs was a round cottage-style bamboo table. Two seascape oil paintings hung from the white beadboard walls.

There was also a navy hammock hanging from the beamed ceiling. The hammock was only meant for one, reminding me of the pavilion at Enderly Hall and the impression of two bodies in the pillows. They hadn't been there when I'd done my late-morning walk-through for the party around ten. Did that mean Roland definitely knew his killer? *Stop*, I chided myself. I needed to savor my surroundings. There would be plenty of time to review yesterday's events. Unless . . . Jenna was still in danger.

His and hers (who was hers?) brass floor lamps with bamboo shades were stationed behind the deck chairs. Completing the porch décor was a large brass telescope for stargazing. I wanted to linger, happy that so far I hadn't been disappointed by Patrick's design choices. Actually, just the opposite: everything was classic, simple and welcoming. But in the few minutes I'd been on the porch the sky had clouded over. I shivered, needing that promised cup of coffee.

I opened one of the French doors and stepped inside, the anticipation killing me. The cottage's overall feeling was that of a manly fishing cottage. It could have used a woman's touch—a few soft pillows, a fluffy throw. Other than that, it was perfect. The great room housed a butterscotch tan leather sofa and easy chair, a wood coffee table with iron legs and a top made from a single slice of oak. If you counted the rings in the wood, you could probably guess the tree's age. The wood gleamed from layers of soft wax. Had Patrick made it himself? Was he a do-it-yourselfer like me?

On top of the amazing coffee table was a cribbage board. I hadn't played cribbage since I was a teen. Fond memories came rushing back of days in Northern Michigan on my grandfather's sleeping porch, where we would play marathon games of cribbage and backgammon, Grandpa smoking his pipe and me imitating him by smoking a strawberry licorice Twizzler.

Pipe! After Shepherds Cottage had been trashed, it smelled of pipe tobacco. It seemed even though I was trying to forget about last night, little things kept creeping in to remind me.

I stepped toward Patrick's flagstone hearth, noticing it was like mine, which I'd copied from my rental cottage. Only his flagstones covered the entire wall. The mantel was made from a wide cement slab that held a large mirror reflecting two wide bookcases on the opposite side of the room, separated by a window with an ocean view. As expected, especially knowing Patrick was an author, the bookcases were crammed with books, a mixture of antique and new. What was it about books that made every space feel cozy and insulated from the outside world?

Once again, I shivered and realized why. The only remnants of a fire were a few orange-and-scarlet embers that winked and spit up at me from inside the hearth. I grabbed some pieces of kindling from a leather tote and made a pile on top of the wrought iron grate. On top of the kindling I added three split logs. One thing I'd learned from living alone on the ocean was how to make the perfect fire. Matches. Where did Patrick keep the matches?

I spotted a box on the mantel and reached for it.

My hand froze in midair.

Next to the box of matches was a framed photo of a stunning dark-haired woman and a little girl who was around age five or six. The child had wheat-colored hair streaked with blonde. Just like Patrick's. She smiled big at the camera, like someone had said *Say che-e-e-se.* She also had Patrick's blue-green eyes. Her two front teeth were missing, and her face was covered in galaxies of golden freckles. It made my heart hurt to look at her. I switched my gaze to the woman in the photo. She was also smiling, but I could tell she wasn't smiling at the camera. She was smiling at the person holding the camera, her husband. Patrick. As clichéd as it seemed, I saw love in her dark brown eyes.

"You couldn't find the coffee?"

I hadn't heard him and Charlie come in. I jumped, not realizing I'd been holding the framed photo. It slipped through my fingers and went crashing onto the flagstones. "I, uh, was looking for some matches," I mumbled, scrambling to my knees to retrieve the photo. Lucky for me, the glass was intact.

As soon as I stood, Patrick wrenched the frame out of my hand and placed it back on the mantel, only this time facing backward— as if protecting his family's privacy from my prying eyes. If he would have slapped me, I would have felt better than I did. I gazed into his angry pain-ridden eyes. Eyes that refused to meet mine.

He stepped toward me and I flinched.

"I'm not going to hurt you," he said sharply, then reached over my head and snatched the box of matches from the mantel. In a gruff, emotionless voice, he said, "As I asked before, why don't you go into the kitchen and pour us a couple cups of coffee?"

I couldn't fault his reaction. I had no right taking down that photo, and I had no right invading his privacy.

Charlie came closer to her master and looked up at him, confusion in her dark eyes as to why the tension in the room could be cut with a machete. When only minutes ago we'd all been friends.

When would I learn not to be so nosy?
I left him staring at the fireplace, his back rigid, his face a mask of control, and went through the open doorway to the kitchen.

Chapter 20

I hadn't expected a full-blown epicurean's kitchen that was maybe a notch or two above my father's back in Detroit. It had every stainless-steel modern appliance possible, including a restaurant-grade Wolf gas range top and a double oven that even had a warming drawer. The wood center island looked custom-made, as did all the open raw-wood shelving stacked with white dinnerware. I took two white mugs off a shelf and filled them with coffee that smelled extra strong. The way I liked it. Jamaican roast would be my guess. Glancing to the right of the two double sinks, I spied a coffee/espresso maker that looked like it had been hijacked from the Starbucks in Bridgehampton. This guy made serious coffee, which was good because I was a serious coffee drinker. Although after what had just happened with the photo, I was already in hyper mode; caffeine might push me over the edge, and it probably wouldn't help soften Patrick's countenance, either.

I had no idea how he liked his coffee, so I took his cup and walked on tenterhooks to the open doorway and stuck out my head—afraid he might bite it off.

Speaking in a soft voice, I murmured, "I don't know what you like in your coffee?"

He'd been staring out the window at the ocean. At first I didn't think he'd heard me, but then he turned slowly and with a big grin said, "Black. I like it black. How about you?"

I handed him the mug, and when his hand touched mine, I felt relief that the awkward moment about the photo had passed. Or at least I hoped it had passed. "I like milk. No sugar."

"Almost a purest," he said, adding a wink. "How about I get going on those benedicts?"

I certainly wasn't going to stop him. As he passed me, I said, "Do you need me as your sous chef?"

He laughed, knowing all about my lack of culinary skills. "It's safer if you sit at the island and watch. But thanks for the offer."

My father had snitched about my gastronomic shortcomings during the last New Year's Eve party at my neighbor Claire's. "Hey, I resemble that remark," I said, feeling happy that his anger from earlier had passed.

He grabbed a white apron from a hook, tied it around himself, then asked, "Have you decided what meal you're making for your turn at the next Dead Poets Society Book Club's meeting?"

I took a seat at the natural wood countertop. "Don't worry, buster. I have things in hand." *Thanks to my father.*

Patrick went to the refrigerator, took out a glass bottle of milk, poured some into the cup I'd left on the counter, retrieved a spoon from the drawer, stirred and handed me the mug.

I drank my coffee and watched him prepare the meal. He was organized and efficient, cleaning up as he went, the opposite of whenever I tried to make even the simplest of meals.

We ate at the island, which he explained he'd made in his workshop in the shed out back. The eggs Benedict didn't disappoint. As I anticipated from the smells wafting toward me while he'd been cooking, it only took me five minutes to finish. And that was me trying to be ladylike. There wasn't even one tiny sautéed onion left on my plate from the crispy hash browns he'd whipped up. Crispy, just the way I liked them. The old adage *Food was the way to a man's heart* seemed reversed; food was the way to *this* woman's heart. Was he a mind reader? Or a stomach reader? The hash browns even trumped the Waffle House's. I thought no one did hash browns like the Waffle House, but I was wrong—Patrick Seaton did.

He'd even put sprigs of flat leaf parsley on top of the Benedicts' rich sunny hollandaise sauce. I gave him a five-star review, then we discussed different uses for herbs, with me telling him I would harvest a nice batch from my garden and leave them by his doorstep in the early evening.

"No need to leave them at the door," he said. "Knock. I'll answer. Unless I'm on a deadline and bunkered in my writing cave. Even so, I'll run down. We could share a drink on the beach."

Heat flamed my cheeks. Even though there wasn't a mirror around, I knew I was blushing at his invitation. Then, over bowls of fresh fruit and another cup of coffee, we talked poetry, even touching on politics and religion—a dangerous road to travel. I could tell we were both relieved that we shared similar views on both.

I wasn't sure which one of us brought it up, but the conversation switched to the murder at Enderly Hall. It felt freeing to talk to someone who didn't know all the players involved. It helped me see things more clearly.

After he asked me a few questions, he wrinkled his brow, then smiled. "Let's go up to my study."

"Said the spider to the fly."

Luckily, he smiled at my suggestive reply. "Yes, I have some etchings to show you."

"Welcome to my cave," he said a few minutes later, opening the door at the top of the second-floor landing. I passed through and stepped into a room that was exactly as I'd imagined. The window over his desk looked out to the ocean and the beach below. On the desk was the lamp with the green-glass lampshade. The space was more like a loft than a cave, though I could imagine a few bats hanging upside down from the wood rafters in the steepled ceiling. A worn Persian carpet covered the wide-planked wood floor. There was a vintage floor lamp standing behind a brown leather recliner and end table. An acoustic guitar, facing backward, leaned against the shiplap wall.

"Do you play?" I asked him. Duh, who else? I doubted it was a prop, like I occasionally used as décor in my clients' cottages.

"Used to."

By the way he said it, I let it drop. I had a feeling he hadn't played since the tragedy. Why keep it propped in full view? Maybe it was a hopeful sign he was thinking about picking it up again.

Patrick stepped toward the desk and pulled out the swivel desk chair, then pushed it in my direction, motioning for me to take a seat. Which I did. "So-o-o," he said, "the reason I've called you up to my lair is to do a little brainstorming."

He walked to a huge dry-erase board that was filled with writing. Before I could discern if he was working on a novel or another *Mr. & Mrs. Winslow* screenplay, he flipped the board over so that the blank side was facing us. "I use this board for plotting out my novels or screenplays. Writing a whodunit like *Mr. & Mrs. Winslow* is a little different from writing my suspense novels—more characters and a lot to keep track of. For *Mr. & Mrs. Winslow*, I added columns for each character and their motive to kill. I thought we could do the same for the murder at Enderly Hall."

"I like your thinking," I said, glancing at the bookcase next to his guitar. The top shelf was filled with glossy hardbacks of his *New York Times* bestselling corporate thrillers. I counted eight. The bookcase's second shelf held his stand-alone literary novel, *The Sting of the Sea*, a melancholy novel that was written in the dark days after his wife and child were killed. The opening scene had a woman jumping off the bow of a sailboat and into the sea, not to resurface again.

Next to *Sting of the Sea* was *Tales from a Dead Shore — A Biography of Tortured Poets*, an engrossing book that talked of classical poets like Keats and Lord Byron and the tragedies in their and other famous dead poets' lives. It was a good read but a tad on the depressing side, as evidenced in the title. I didn't want to slip down that rabbit hole, especially after what had just happened with Cole.

The final book on the second shelf was a glossy coffee table book titled *Montauk Moors*. It was filled with photographs Patrick had taken on Montauk's beaches. Below each photo he'd added a few lines of original prose. At the last book club meeting, he'd told everyone that *Montauk Moors* was the first time he'd penned his own poetry. The dead poets must have rubbed off on him because he'd done an amazing job. In a few short lines he'd managed to get to the soul of each photograph.

After *Montauk Moors* he'd written the screenplay for *Mr. & Mrs. Winslow*, a two-hour pilot episode for premium TV, still in production in nearby Bridgehampton.

Not on any shelf was *The Dark Light*, his most recent book. *The Dark Light* was a historical suspense novel based on the true World War Two story of German spies who came ashore in Amagansett, were caught and executed. The light in the book's title referred to the Montauk Point Lighthouse. I knew all this not from Patrick, or from reading the book, because it hadn't been released yet. Stalker that I was, I'd signed up at an online bookstore for news of Patrick Seaton's upcoming books. The book was due out in a week, and I'd already preordered it.

Patrick noticed me perusing his shelves. "I promise, I'm not an egomaniac by having all my books on display."

"Of course you're not. I'm impressed. I haven't read your suspense books yet, but I've read your last three books. I have a question."

"Shoot," he said as he put on a pair of black-framed glasses that made him look scholarly and sexy at the same time. "On page one of *Montauk Moors*, there's a photo of my old rental cottage. Why'd you choose it over all the others?" Under the photo he'd written, *Moonlight brightens the dull edges, where dark sand meets darker sea.*

He grinned. "I chose it because it was the quintessential shot of a lone cottage atop the moors. And I remember the color of the moon was the same shade as the light in your window."

"Are you the one who brought me kindling and cleaned up that mess someone left as a warning by my gate when I'd first moved in?"

"I've been meaning to ask you about that," he said, smiling. "You're no stranger to trouble, I can tell."

"I knew it!" Once again, I sounded like a stalker—Kathy Bates's character in Stephen King's movie *Misery*.

He seemed embarrassed by my outburst and picked up the dry-erase marker. He turned to the board and said, "Let's write down everyone's motive and opportunity. How many suspect columns do we need for our murder mystery?"

Our? I counted in my head, hesitating on including Jenna, but decided she had to be on the list. "Seven. I mean six. I don't count."

"Of course you don't," he said, grinning.

"Maybe add the victim's name, also."

"Yes, ma'am," he said, then turned his back to me and went to work. *Roland Cahill Victim* was written at the top of the board, then Patrick assigned columns for each suspect. His method of listing suspects was very similar to the way I analyzed past murders. Only I used my Cottages by the Sea corkboard, and instead of a column for each suspect, I used circles coming out from the spokes of a wheel, the hubcap being the person murdered, then I'd add index cards with the particulars of each person involved. When decorating my cottages, each circle would be a different room.

I decided not to share my personal detecting methods, afraid of scaring him away by drawing attention to the fact that Roland Cahill would be my fifth murder. I wondered if one day soon I'd be contacted by someone at *Guinness Book of World Records*. Or if word got out in *Dave's Papers*, I'd be persona non grata in the Hamptons. If I wasn't already.

For the next half hour, I called out as much information as I could for each person, starting with Jenna.

Jenna Eastman – Millionairess, owner of Enderly Hall, wife of victim. Claimed her husband Roland was trying to kill her by running her off the road in his silver Mercedes after she asked for a divorce. Wanted divorce because she overheard Roland tell his former stepdaughter, Vicki, he planned to sell Enderly Hall. Jenna got a text from victim's phone hours after he was dead to meet him in the pavilion. Owns gun, *she claims* (Patrick added, not I), Roland gave her for protection while he was out of town.

Vicki Fortune – Roland's former stepdaughter from when he was married to Vicki's mother, Veronica. Roland is chief operating officer of Vicki's inherited Manhattan interior design company, Veronica's Interiors. Poor interior decorator (Patrick turned and raised his eyebrows at that one). Company in financial trouble per Jenna. Not fond of Roland. Very interested in architect Nate Klein. Lives in Manhattan but has been staying in Roland and Jenna's Amagansett rental.

Nate Klein – Owner of Klein and Associates architectural firm in Amagansett. Architect who recently made Roland a partner in his firm. Jenna's cousin. Protective of Jenna. Possible friend of Chief Pell. Roland possibly had something on him in order to become partner.

Kuri Shui – Interior designer who worked with victim at Klein and Associates. Was physically manhandled by Roland. Threatened to tell Nate about his abuse. Roland mentioned if she did, he would tell her husband about something. Lives in East Hampton.

Freya Rittenhouse – Host and producer of local *Hamptons Home & Garden* television show. Was seen in photo with her hand on Roland's. She is the one who came to him about being on the design team for the showhouse. Not an interior decorator. Were Roland and Freya having an affair behind Jenna's back?

Frank Holden – Paranormal investigator who was found on the grounds the same time the body was found on the beach. Not a very good ghosthunter, he lost his EVP recorder (another smile after I explained what an EVP did). Frank was taken down to the station with Jenna. They were the only two. Claims to have lost his cell phone and was looking for it when the officer found him.

Under the column for our victim he'd written:

Roland Cahill – Jenna's husband of six months. Murdered with extension cord (another glance in my direction when he'd written what I dictated; I just shrugged my shoulders and batted my eyelashes). Wanted to sell Enderly Hall. Had a prenup with Jenna. Owned Queens construction company before marrying into Jenna's moneyed family. Manhandled Kuri's wrist. Was served court papers. Had Jenna on surveillance on his phone. Drove a silver Mercedes. Allowed paranormal investigators on the premises, which upset Jenna. Loved the limelight. Chief operating office of Vicki's company, Veronica's Interiors. Bought Jenna a gun for protection. Planned to forge papers saying that Stanford White was Enderly Hall's architect.

After everyone was listed, I got up and stood next to Patrick. We stayed silent and studied the board. "I think under Jenna's name we better add the way her grandfather died and that he shot someone who trespassed on Enderly's property right before his death. I think because of the polar bear head with the bills in its mouth, there's gotta be some kind of connection to the past. Also, the same day as the murder, Shepherds Cottage had been trashed. And I smelled pipe tobacco."

"Wow," he said, looking down at me, "good nose."

"Because of my hearing loss, I think I make up for it in other ways." He gently nodded his head like he understood, then I went on about the connection to Gardiners Island and Captain Kidd, along with Jenna having some kind of familial tie to the Gardiners, going way back to the seventeenth century. "What I don't get is how Roland's murder is tied to things only having to do with Jenna's family. It makes me wonder if perhaps Jenna might be next on the killer's list."

Patrick didn't answer, engrossed in the list before him. This was the first time we'd been alone together for any length of time—I could get used to it. Even though we were discussing a man's murder, I was feeling warm and fuzzy about being in such close quarters. But I'd been escaping reality for too long, and when I got back to my cottage, I'd have to face the facts—as sketchy as they were.

"I think I've taken up too much of your time. I really enjoyed breakfast. Can I ask a favor?"

"Of course," he said, taking off his glasses and rubbing the bridge of his nose.

"Do you mind taking a few photos of our board and texting or emailing them to me. I left my phone at home. Or maybe we could meet later to go over any new developments after I talk to Jenna and Officer Moss?"

A female voice called up from the bottom of the stairs, "Yoo-hoo, Patrick darling, you up there in your hidey-hole? Olly olly oxen free, come out, come out, wherever you are. What does that mean, anyway?" I heard Ashley say, the sound of her heels on the wood steps echoing up the stairwell.

Patrick hadn't answered my query about getting together.

Or maybe he had—by Ashley's arrival.

Chapter 21

After I'd hiked back from Patrick's, I found Elle sitting on the swing that hung under the eaves of my cottage.

"You have a key," I said, taking a seat next to her, "why didn't you go inside?"

"Uh, because this is the first day with no fog and I wanted to revel in it. Where have you been? And what's with that rosy glow to your cheeks? The Barrett blotches? What's up?"

Elle knew me too well. However, my flushed cheeks had nothing to do with Patrick Seaton, but more to do with his publicist and the fact that I'd agreed to meet her later at the cottage she planned on buying. Ashley had cornered me, saying, "When we were at your neighbor Claire's last New Year's Eve, I saw how spectacular her cottage turned out. She said it was all due to you, and I was really impressed. It's exactly the style I want, except for a few things my better half might want to add. But he trusts my taste." I hadn't even been able to glance in Patrick's direction after that statement, and when he offered to walk me home, I'd declined, mumbling something about enjoying the fresh air.

As I'd walked the shoreline home, I'd tried to come up with some way of getting out of meeting Ashley, let alone spending blocks of time with her as her interior decorator. Knowing she hadn't signed the closing papers, I could always call my friend Barb at Sand and Sun Realty and try to find some loophole that would keep Ashley from moving to Montauk. Selfishly, I didn't want her here, even if it was only for the summer season. Then I'd reasoned with the green-eyed monster. If Ashley wanted to move to Montauk to be with Patrick, there was nothing I could do about it. In fact, I needed to let the whole Patrick thing go. His reaction to me holding the photo of his wife and child told me volumes about the amount of baggage he'd bring with him into any relationship. Plus, I learned from watching tearjerker movies like *A Message in a Bottle*—it was hard to compete with a ghost.

"I just had breakfast at Patrick Seaton's," I reluctantly told Elle, knowing she would run with its possible significance.

"Well, that explains it."

"Not exactly." Then I told her the whole story, including the part about the photo and Ashley showing up.

"If you don't want to meet with her, why'd you say yes?"

I gave her "the look."

"We don't know for sure that she's in any kind of relationship with Patrick. It could be totally professional. Just a caring publicist and friend. Plus, it might be too soon because of Cole. I don't think you're totally over Cole. I heard how upset you were when you found out he was missing at sea, and I also heard how relieved you were when he'd been rescued."

"Rescued in more ways than one. And I'm over him. There's no doubt about that," I snapped.

"What's that supposed to mean?"

"Hold that thought." I got up and went inside to get my phone. Jo was nowhere to be found, a good sign she was up to something naughty. She liked to find small pieces of clothing, things like a sock or a scarf, then bury them in her litter box. It was her way of telling me she wasn't happy that I'd cut her down from three meals a day to two. The brat.

When I came back out to the deck with my phone, I scrolled through my photos for the screenshot I'd taken of Cole in a lip-lock with his chief mate. After finding it, tapping it, then enlarging it so that all you saw were Cole's and Billie's faces, specifically where their two mouths fused into one, I flashed it in front of Elle's face.

"Oh, jeez! What a rat," was all she could come up with.

I sat back down. "I said yes to see the cottage because Ashley is so darn nice . . ."

"But you don't want to see Ashley and Patrick together, in case they're in a relationship. I get it," Elle said. "Especially after the quaint little morning you two shared."

"I'm swearing off men," I said, gazing out at the open expanse of sea and sky. "Don't say it."

"Say what?" Elle asked innocently.

"What you always say when it comes to my love life . . . 'There's plenty of fish in the ocean.'"

"I wasn't going to say that. But if I did, I usually say fish in the sea, not ocean. What I planned on saying is we have bigger fish to fry than your love life." She laughed at her own joke. "Like, what we're going to do about Jenna. I just spent the last couple of hours with her. I made her call the psychiatrist that her husband had mentioned when we ran into him Friday in Amagansett. Was that only a couple of days ago? Tragic. Roland Cahill was a buffoon, but he didn't deserve to be murdered. Anyway, Dr. Sorenson couldn't come into his office because it's a Sunday, but he did prescribe some medication for her, which we picked up."

"Wow. You just reminded me of something. The afternoon that Roland mentioned the psychiatrist, I had a feeling he saw the guy too. Maybe Morgana can take a look at his files?"

"That might backfire if she has to look through Jenna's also. What if Jenna told the doctor she thought Roland was trying to kill her. It wouldn't help eliminate her as a suspect. That's for sure."

"Where is Jenna, right now?"

"She's back at the yacht club. Hey, isn't she staying in Cole's . . ."

"Suite. Yes. The least he could do!"

Elle high-fived me. "Atta girl. You always preach, anger's better on the emotional scale than depression. I should know after spending time with Jenna. She's definitely depressed, and rightly so."

"Thanks for being with her. When I ran into Patrick on the beach, I didn't have my phone. Speaking of which, I better read my messages." I opened my phone again, and sure enough there was a message from Morgana that I needed to go to the East Hampton Town Police Department substation in Montauk and give a formal statement. I handed my phone to Elle so she could read it.

"It sounds like you're lucky Officer Morgana Moss showed up yesterday. Arthur wanted me to let you know he would keep in contact with her about the case. He tried to go through the proper channels, but Chief Pell must have put him on the Do Not Share list."

"I can't understand what's going on with the chief. He's never been this bad. Is there something you know that I don't?"

"If there were, Arthur wouldn't share it with me. Something is going on with him. I plan on having a chat with him the next time he's in town. We decided to make this long-distance thing work contingent on the fact that he'd come to the Hamptons every weekend. Well, guess what? I haven't seen him in two weeks. He better show up for the engagement party or you'll need to change the venue to a broken engagement party," she said wistfully, handing me back my phone.

I stowed it in my pocket and pressed my hand against the left side of her jaw until she faced me. "Look me in the eye, Elle Mabel Warner. You don't mean that. Do you?"

She shrugged her shoulders, looked away and said, "I guess not. We'll get through it, I suppose."

"There's no supposing. I know Arthur Shoner. He loves you with all his heart. Buck up, things could be worse."

"How?"

"You could be like me, an old maid living alone with a one-eyed cat."

"Meg Barrett, since you've moved to Montauk your love life has been epic. I'm not shedding any crocodile tears for you. Let's say we go inside and make a plan—"

She couldn't finish her statement because the light blinked on my phone, telling me I had an incoming text.

It was from Patrick. Elle must have seen my hand tremble when I held the phone screen closer to my face. It was a photo of our suspect list. Nothing else. No cute quip like *Let's do breakfast again* or *Drinks on the beach?* What did I expect? And if I did expect more than this so soon after breaking up with Cole, I was out of my mind.

Elle glanced over my shoulder and I said, "It's from Patrick. I'll forward it to you."

She took out her phone from her vintage Chanel tweed blazer. I knew it was Chanel because of the interlocking gold CC logo on the buttons. I was sure it was vintage because Elle was wearing it. Plus, on the lapel were six colorful rhinestone broches that glittered when the sun hit them. The brooches, along with a ton of vintage clothing and accessories, had been willed to Elle from her Great Aunt Mabel. Aunt Mabel had been an assistant to the famous mid-century movie costume designer Edith Head, who did the clothing for *To Catch a Thief, Sabrina, White Christmas,* and many others. Elle had been toying with the idea of opening an Edith Head museum, until she realized she wouldn't be able to wear any of her designs and accessories.

After a few taps on her phone screen, Elle grinned and said, "Boy, you and Patrick have been busy. I'm glad you value my input for a change. It'll keep me busy, instead of worrying about what my fiancé is up to twenty-four-seven."

"Well, we're partners in crime when it comes to our vintage treasures and refurbishing antics. So why not bring you along on this one. But don't share the suspect list with Jenna. Or anyone else for that matter."

"You don't usually involve me in your detecting shenanigans. Why now?"

"Two heads are better than one. And you know Jenna just as well as I do. Plus . . ."

"You want me to send this on to Arthur."

"It couldn't hurt," I added coyly. "Even if he's having a hard time getting info from the Suffolk County Police Department, maybe he has a few ins with his alma mater, the East Hampton Town Police, or even knows someone from the New York State Police."

"I will, but I'm up for the challenge. You might be surprised how much Arthur and you have rubbed off on me. Not to mention that this is the fifth time I've gotten drawn into a murder investigation because of you."

"Hey, I seem to remember you had ties with our second and fourth murders."

"Semantics. Not that I don't appreciate what you did at Sandringham."

We discussed the suspect list for a while. Elle was sharper than I thought when she asked how I knew Roland hadn't offed himself. And there was no surprise in her gaze when I told her about my part in throwing the murder weapon under the steps.

When it was close to noon, I walked Elle to her car, giving her an assignment as my sworn deputy to find out how Vicki was doing at Montauk Manor. We didn't want her leaving town, but we also didn't want her blabbing about Jenna and Roland's fight the night before his murder.

"But I don't even know her. How will I manage that?"

"Pretend you're part of the set design crew for *Mr. & Mrs. Winslow*, which technically you are. Tell her you need her expert advice on something. Explain that I sent you because of her stellar reputation. She'll believe that, or anything else that pumps her magnificent ego."

"And what is my covert mission? Wait, let me record you." She took out her phone and tapped the screen. "Okay. Shoot."

"Your mission is to find out her home address in Manhattan. Maybe your fiancé can check things out there and see how solvent her business is. If Roland oversaw the financial end of the business, it would be good to see if by killing him it would somehow be to her advantage. Also check into Roland and Veronica's divorce, maybe there's a story there. I know from experience Vicki hated Roland, yet she had no problem being one of the designers for the showhouse or staying in their Amagansett beachfront rental."

"Should I record her without her knowing? I think that would be too nerve-racking."

"I don't think that's necessary. Plus, it wouldn't be admissible in court."

"Maybe you should go into law enforcement."

"I think I'll stick to my serene life, decorating small cottages with the stuff we fix up in your carriage house. Now you've done it. You made me remember that I'm meeting Ashley. Hope she comes alone."

"You'll be fine. I have a good feeling about you and Patrick. It's funny, now that you've shown me that photo with Cole's chief mate Billie, I think it's meant to be a godsend. No more hanging on. And if your reclusive author is in a relationship with his publicist, that would make it a rebound affair. After her, you'll be next in the circuit."

"Screwy logic, Ms. Warner. Because that would mean I need a rebound relationship from Cole, and I don't think that would be happening with anyone but . . ."

"You're right. I'm going. Leave things to me. I'll report back after I get more information. I told Jenna I'd have lunch with her at the yacht club. Anything I should pass on?"

"Oh, that's great 'cause there's something I want to do after I meet Ashley."

"Should I ask what? Or leave it?"

I smiled but didn't answer, and instead said, "If you can, when you're with Jenna, find out everything there is on her cousin Nate. I can't believe I thought they were lovers."

"The architect, right?"

"Yes, Klein and Associates in Amagansett. It would be interesting to find out if he's related to Jenna's mother's side of the family or her father's. If it's her father's side, he could be the one who stuffed those monopoly bills in the polar bear's mouth. I'm having a hard time figuring out what that little scene in the attic has to do with Roland Cahill's murder."

"So, you saw his body before the police came. Did he have anything in his mouth?"

"Not that I could see."

"Okay, I'll try to bring up Nate to Jenna, but you have no idea how distraught she is. And drugged."

"I can imagine. Also, tell her to be strong and don't let anyone intimidate her, especially Chief Pell. And not to talk to anyone but her attorney, Justin Marguilles."

"That's easy enough. But it's not like you to pawn off things on me. What exactly are you doing after you see Ashley? I bet it's more dangerous than my two assignments."

"Never you mind. I'll be fine. Now, be on your way, my little sleuth. Report back at twenty-hundred."

I watched her try to figure out what time I was talking about.

"Eight tonight."

She gave me a salute, opened the pickup's door and got inside. After manually rolling down the window, she said, "Thanks, friend, this will keep my mind off Arthur. And I'm only sharing my findings with you. Serves him right."

She started the truck, and as I watched her pull away I thought, *What have I just done?*

Chapter 22

I turned off Embassy Street and pulled into the tiny parking lot of the East Hampton Town Police Department substation. I was happy Chief Pell had decided to keep it local. If he'd wanted, he could have directed everyone to trek out fifty-six miles to Suffolk County Police Headquarters in Yaphank.

Before leaving my cottage, I'd checked the internet for anything about the murder. So far, nothing. Why was Chief Pell keeping things under wraps? Maybe he wanted to charge onto Main Street atop his white stallion and make an arrest before the news got out. I couldn't blame him for not wanting to face the press and explain that there'd been another murder in the exclusive Hamptons. Until we found out who killed Roland Cahill, I had to make sure Pell kept Jenna out of his crosshairs.

When I walked into the station, Morgana greeted me in a professional manner—almost as if we'd never met. I followed along, even though the only other person in listening distance was a young officer behind the counter who looked barely of drinking age and was playing with his Apple Watch. He hadn't even looked my way when I'd passed by and walked over to Morgana's desk.

The substation was so small there was only one main room with a counter separating the officers from the public. I assumed there was a bathroom, but there was no holding cell or metal detectors to pass through. Everything about Montauk was cozy, even their police station.

Morgana had my statement already written up on her laptop, the only thing she needed to add was where I'd been between the hours of ten and noon. I couldn't remember my steps exactly, but I knew before ten I'd been busy adding the florist delivery plants to the verandas, porches, and gazebo. I'd checked the pavilion, and no one had been there, certainly not Roland. And the fairy lights had been lit when I'd left. I didn't tell Morgana that I'd made another trip to the beach to look at Roland's corpse, or about the extension cord rearranging, and I certainly wasn't going to mention it now. I trusted Officer Morgana Moss but didn't want her to have to compromise her new position at the department, or for that matter feel pressure to arrest me for disturbing a crime scene.

During the two-hour window of his time of death, I hadn't seen any of the other decorators, not even Jenna. I assumed everyone had been inside, working on their allocated spaces. We'd all met in the kitchen at one for gourmet lunches that Nate brought in from Montauk Melissa's food truck. The truck was parked a couple of miles down the shore from Enderly Hall, at nearby Ditch Plains Beach. Even my foodie-snob father made it a must-do stop when he came to visit. I told Morgana it would be easy for her to find out exactly when Nate picked up the food because the food truck had a surveillance camera. Sometimes, if the mood hit, Melissa would leave the truck unattended to go out surfing. If that happened, then everyone was on an honor system, leaving cash for whatever food or drink items they took. A couple of years ago, some rich summer kid from East Hampton stole all the money from Melissa's till. He'd been caught by Elle's fiancé, Detective Shoner, who talked Melissa into getting surveillance cameras. She had them installed, albeit reluctantly, seeing as Montauk was the kind of beach hamlet where everyone trusted their neighbor.

After Morgana printed my statement and I signed it, she slid a piece of paper across her desk, glancing over at the counter to make sure the young officer wasn't watching us. He wasn't. I picked it up to read it, but she gave me a stern look and shook her head no. I quickly stuffed it in my pocket, then stood up to go.

"One more thing. I need your prints."

"They're already on file with IAFIS."

Morgana gave me a surprised look.

"Don't ask," I said under my breath as I headed for the exit.

As I opened the door and stepped out, I heard Morgana say in a motherly tone, "Hand it over, James. I guess I'll have to put the watch in my drawer, next to your cell phone."

I hopped in my car and looked around, waiting until a woman pushing a baby carriage passed before taking out Morgana's note from my pocket. Written in what looked like doctor's script was a short but to-the-point missive: *Meet me outside the gates to Enderly Hall after sunset.*

Of course I'd be there. After all, it was a police directive. What could go wrong? Only a million things. Especially if the past was any gauge.

I hesitated about how to destroy the note. Morgana's paranoia was rubbing off on me. Should I swallow it? Burn it? But I didn't have matches. Instead, I ripped the note into tiny pieces then dropped them inside my Yeti cup that still had a half inch of coffee in it. Then I closed the lid and shook the contents for good measure.

I had time to kill before meeting Ashley at the cottage she planned to purchase. It was early afternoon, but I was still full from my breakfast. I knew I was overthinking things, but why would Ashley want my opinion about how to decorate the interior once she bought it? And why wasn't I running over to comfort Jenna, as Elle had done? Could it be that in the back of my mind I still considered her a suspect in her husband's death?

In order to kill an hour, I decided to go to The Old Man and the Sea Books. I needed to pick up the book we were reading about Walt Whitman. My heart did a small leap when I realized I was holding the next Dead Poets Society Book Club and Patrick would be attending. It's not that we'd left things on a bad note, in fact it had been quite nice until Ashley showed up. All awkwardness from when I'd been caught holding the family photo had vanished and we were like a team of investigators from a prime-time cop show going over our board of suspects.

Not the type to wallow, I brushed off my fears and drove the quarter mile to Montauk's only bookstore. The septuagenarian proprietor, Georgia, knew more about Montauk and the Hamptons than anyone. Maybe she could shed some light on Jenna's grandfather and how his death could be tied to Roland Cahill's murder. But when I parked in front of the white picket fence, covered in Georgia's climbing peach-tipped roses, I saw there was a *Closed* sign in the window.

I got out of the car, my nose sniffing the air like a dog on scent. The Montauk Bakery's door was open, yeasty smells escaping and mixing with the salt air. I was tempted to step inside for my weekly boule of dense sourdough bread. I always had them slice the loaf super thin so I wouldn't feel guilty when I slathered layers of butter on top. Even though I was tempted to go inside, I was still stuffed from my meal with Patrick.

Opening the white picket gate in front of the bookshop, I stepped onto the red brick walkway that led to what had once been a fishing cottage. When I reached the door, I saw a handwritten note in Georgia's neat printing taped to the brass mail slot: *Gone to the opening ceremonies at the lighthouse, will open Monday at ten. Come see me and say hi, I'll be at the Save the Seals table.*

Disheartened and wishing I could go to the lighthouse instead of meeting Ashley, I went over to the bookshop's large plate-glass window and peered in. Butting up to the front window was a wide rectory table stacked with recent bestsellers, along with books by local authors. On the far wall, two wing chairs flanked a small fireplace, embers still burning in the hearth. I must have just missed Georgia. Covering the walls where there weren't bookshelves was art by local Montauk artists. Naturally, most were of seascapes.

My favorite spot in The Old Man and the Sea Books was the back room, where Georgia sold used books, some rare, but most well-loved and well-read. The bookshop was my favorite place to kick off my shoes, or boots, depending on the season, sip a cup of Earl Grey with a new (or old) book in hand, while ignoring whatever Mother Nature was doing outside its cozy walls.

As I pressed my nose to the window, I saw the tip of Mr. Whiskers's silky, thick tail flick back and forth from one of the armchairs by the fire. He must have sensed I was there. I'd been the one to find him in a Dumpster behind the bookshop. Georgia claimed custody and Mr. Whiskers was now the bookshop's official mascot. I'd babysat him once. Long story short, Jo was *not* the hostess with the mostest. I tapped the glass. Mr. Whiskers popped his head out from the chair, and I was able to read his lips when he meowed — *Keep your fat beast of a feline away from me, forevermore!*

I waved and blew him a kiss, then followed the bricks back to the sidewalk and headed south.

I knew exactly what I needed.

The bell jingled when I stepped into Fudge 'n Stuff. I ordered a double scoop of Barrett's PBB ice cream, my own signature flavor that the owner made in one batch because she couldn't stand me ordering three separate scoops of peanut butter, banana and brownie, then asking for one of her large mixing bowls to mix them all together.

As I walked out the shop's door, I took my first spoonful and felt better already. So much for not being hungry.

I still had an hour and a half to kill before meeting Ashley, so I walked both sides of Montauk's small downtown, window shopping while eating my ice cream. As I passed the plate-glass window of Catch of the Day, with its sign *Wanted: Piano Player who can Shuck Clams*, I saw them. Nate Klein and Kuri were sitting in a booth, snuggled together in deep conversation. I know Kuri saw me, but Nate hadn't. Kuri quickly looked away, then whispered something in Nate's ear.

Pretending I hadn't noticed them, I rushed past the window. Just because they were together didn't mean they were an item. Maybe they had met up when signing their statements at the Montauk substation. Roland had threatened Kuri with telling Kuri's husband about something she'd done. Was that something a someone? And even if she was stepping out with Nate, what did that have to do with Roland's murder?

After finishing my cup of ice cream, I threw it in the bin outside Rockin' Retro, smiling at the sign in the window that said they would be opening next Friday. Rockin' Retro was one of my favorite shops in Montauk. They sold fun reproduction memorabilia gift items from the thirties to the eighties, including old-school candy like Dots, Milk Duds, licorice whips and my favorite mints, Coward's Violets. At the thought of the mints, I recalled Cole loved the way they made my breath . . . Enough.

I walked slowly back to my car thinking about Kuri, and how she told Morgana that she got along fine with Roland Cahill. A lie, witnessed by yours truly.

With still a half hour to kill before meeting Ashley, I got inside my car and put the address she'd given me into GPS. I would get there early and do a little background research while I waited for her.

There was one person in particular I wanted to learn more about — ghosthunter Frank Holden.

Chapter 23

I sat in my car, looking toward the exterior of the cottage Barb had found for Ashley. It was stunning. The views alone were worth a cool million. Patrick's publisher was one of the big five, possibly number one, but I didn't think publicists got paid enough to have a summer cottage like the one before me. Ashley probably had family money. One more feather, more like diamond, in her gold tiara.

The cottage Ashley planned on buying was made from new construction but was meant to look like it had been there for decades. It was set on top of a hill surrounded by pines. Each side of the house had a second-floor balcony. The balcony facing the north looked toward the Block Island Sound and Lake Montauk; to the south was the Atlantic; to the west, Fort Pond, and to the East a glimpse of the Montauk Point Lighthouse.

I'd learned all this because I'd found Sand and Sun's listing on my phone, displaying dozens of interior and exterior photos. Most of the exterior shots were taken at sunrise and sunset. I'd been right about the million-dollar view. The cottage was listed for more than that.

With twenty minutes until Ashley and my appointed time, I typed "Frank Holden, Montauk" into the search bar of my phone's browser. Nothing came up. Next, I went to my *Long Island Newsday* app and typed in his name again. The only thing that came up was a death notice listing Frank Holden as the only surviving relative of Norman Holden, longtime Montauk resident. I entered both Frank and Norman Holden into the search bar and bingo! "Holy moly!" Norman Holden was the man Jenna's grandfather had shot, mistaking him for a trespasser. "Wow!" I said to the steering wheel. A coincidence? Or more? More was my guess. At the exact moment I clicked on an article about the trial, Ashley pulled up in a navy Range Rover.

Ashley got out of the car and came toward me. As she approached, a gentle breeze blew back wispy sections of hair that had escaped her French braid.

I put my phone away and got out of the car, then met her on the slate walkway.

"Hope I'm not late?" she asked, all sunny and smiling. She wore a cashmere aqua sweater that made you want to touch it, black leggings and black to-the-knee boots with gold buckles. The sweater looked store-bought. Probably from Sophia's, the exclusive cashmere shop in East Hampton. Ashley's sweater was quite different than the last knitting project I'd attempted after a few lessons at Karen's Kreative Knitting in Montauk. My alpaca wool pullover ended up having one sleeve that covered my hand, while the other went to above my wrist. It was partially my churlish cat's fault. We'd had a tug-of-war over one of the sleeves moments before Jo planned on burying it in her litter box. *Bad cat!* never worked, so I'd pretended she'd done nothing wrong. Big mistake. It took me a week to find where she'd dragged the other sleeve.

"I was early," I said.

I could tell she was excited about showing me the cottage. No matter what I thought of it, I wouldn't burst her bubble. I'd learned long ago that home décor was a personal thing, and not to decorate the way I thought the cottage's interior should be by ignoring my client's wishes. That being said, I always managed to stick a few vintage or antique items inside even the most modern homes. It was my calling card, so to speak. If they wanted to toss them in the trash after I left, so be it.

Ashley linked her arm through mine and we strolled up the flagstone walkway like two childhood pals. Stopping at the bottom of the steps to the porch, Ashley said, "Thank you for coming. Patrick told me about what happened at Enderly Hall yesterday. Such a tragedy. If you want, we can reschedule. Was the guy who died a close friend?"

"More of an acquaintance. But his wife is a good friend." I was happy that Patrick hadn't told her Roland was murdered because it still hadn't hit the news.

"Well, let's make it quick then." She used her left hand and pointed to the cottage. Her unusual ring with its amber stone caught a ray of sunlight like a beacon. "First impressions?" she asked, looking as if she was holding her breath. I had to wonder why my opinion seemed so important. She didn't lack confidence and she didn't seem the wallflower type—the complete opposite, more like an exotic hothouse orchid.

"I think it's magnificent. And so is your ring." I had to know.

"I'm so glad you like the cottage, you can thank your friend Barb for that. As for my engagement ring, it was purchased from a little fine jewelry shack after a day of deep-sea diving off the Great Barrier Reef in Australia. What a magnificent day we had. One I'll always remember. Hurry. Let's go inside. I can't wait for your suggestions."

There it was—the *e* word—*engagement*. I felt myself deflate, like I'd been stuck with the thickest and pointiest of needles, all hope evaporating in a single word.

We went up the stone steps, Ashley's arm still holding mine tight, two sorority sisters on a fun romp. Not that I'd ever been in a sorority, but I was sure Ashley had.

If I could feel her excitement, did that mean Ashley could feel my disappointment? To cover for my blotched face (I felt the prickles of heat, I didn't need to see them), I asked, "What does your fiancé think about the cottage?"

"Oh, he'll go along with anything I want." She put her hand around my shoulders. "Who needs men with it comes to interior design. Us girls can carry on, can't we? I have a vision, hope you and I are on the same page. It has to be a melding of masculine and feminine styles; I was thinking modern cozy. If there's such a thing," she said with a quick smile. "We plan on living here together in the summers until we make wedding plans."

I couldn't believe Patrick would live in such a modern home. How could he be willing to give up the ocean for hilltop views— even if they were magnificent? I could tell how. I was looking at the reason. The complete package. I fast-forwarded to the future. No more poetry quotes in the sand. No more chance meetings. No eggs Benedict at his handmade wood island. Who was I fooling? It didn't matter; after they were married, I couldn't have expectations on anything having to do with Patrick Seaton. And rightly so.

"Come," Ashley said excitedly as she nudged me toward the front door. "You go first. I can't wait for you to see." She handed me the key with a tag on it from Sand and Sun Realty.

I took it, inserted it in the doorknob, and walked in.

• • •

Thirty minutes later we'd completed the tour and were standing in the marble foyer. The cottage had been staged using lots of glass, chrome, and dark fabrics. The masculine style wouldn't be my first choice if it was my cottage. Thankfully, the photos I'd viewed online showed the space empty and I could see its potential. During the walk-through, I'd kept my comments neutral. If there was one thing I prided myself on, it was following my clients' directives, not mine. Holding my breath, I asked, "If this is the look you're going for after the staging company removes everything, I'll try to copy the style and feel of the furnishings and accessories."

"Oh, no," she said, shaking her head. "Way too stark and uncomfortable. That's why Barb recommended you. She knew I would hate the way the owners had staged it. I think she used the word *cozy* when talking about your design aesthetic. I want a cozy little love nest. What would you do if this was your cottage?"

Ugh. The more I spent time with her, the more I liked her. I gave her my vision, even showing her photos from some of the cottages in the area I'd done.

"Oh, Meg, they're wonder—" Before she could finish her sentence, the front door burst open and Justin Marguilles walked in toting a bottle of champagne in one hand, paper cups in the other. For a moment I was reminded of how Nate Klein had come into the kitchen last evening with the hopes of toasting the showhouse's opening. That surely hadn't happened. I was surprised Ashley would bring the Hamptons' ace lawyer in on the deal. The same attorney that I'd called to represent Jenna. It truly was a small world, especially in the Hamptons.

"My apologies, ladies. Sorry I'm late. Business called." The first time I'd heard about Justin Marguilles, I'd been intimidated by his reputation alone. Adjectives such as shark, brutal, smooth talker caused anxiety before I'd even set eyes on him. But after the court case, I realized he was just a darn good lawyer. He dressed impeccably. He wasn't thin, more muscular, over six feet tall, handsome in a rugged, pirate kind of way, his eyes the color of cognac when you held your glass in front of a fire. He had a sardonic smile, keeping you on guard, and rightly so. As far as I knew, he'd never lost a case. As I'd found out, he wasn't someone you'd want as opposing counsel. That was the main reason I'd suggested him to Jenna.

He also had a way with women, a lifetime bachelor, never condescending, always polite.

"Business always calls," Ashley said in a pout that turned into a grin.

"Well, darling, did Ms. Barrett here give you her green light?"

Green light? Darling?

"Is it time to toast our future summer retreat?" he asked, popping the cork on the champagne. It almost hit the skylight, then bounced onto the marble floor like a child's rubber ball. The same way my heart felt at the news.

Justin Marguilles and Ashley Drake were engaged.

Not Ashley and Patrick.

"Oh, I love it!" Ashley said, clapping her hands. "And Meg knows exactly how to transform it. It checks all our boxes."

Justin raised an eyebrow. "She does, does she?" He handed each of us a cup, filled it to the brim, then wove his arm through Ashley's. They locked gazes and he said, "I approve, my darling. It's perfect." Then he glanced over at me. "Ms. Barrett, how would you like to decorate our modest honeymoon cottage?"

Modest? "Please call me Meg."

"And call me Justin. No more formalities between us. Hopefully we will never be on opposite sides of a courtroom again. By the way, thanks for the reference."

"You're welcome. It would be my pleasure to have Cottages by the Sea at your disposal," I said, adding a huge grin. If there'd been a ladder propped outside the cottage, I would have climbed it and shouted from the rooftop, "Hell, yes!"

"In that case," he said, "let's have a toast." We raised our glasses. "One my Irish grandmother would approve of—May joy and peace surround us, contentment latch our door, and happiness be with us now and bless us evermore."

"Hear, hear," Ashley said, tapping her fiancé's cup, then mine. "Bottoms up."

The champagne went to my head. Caught up in their excitement, or more honestly, in my own excitement at what their news selfishly meant to me, I said, "I also have an Irish toast that I usually say to my clients after the completion of their cottage. In this case, I think it's apropos to use it now." Justin refilled our cups, and I said, "To Ashley and Mr. . . . . Justin, bless the corners of this house and be the lintel blessed. And bless the hearth and bless the board and bless each place of rest. Bless each door that opens wide to strangers and to kin. And bless each crystal windowpane that lets the sunshine in. And bless the rooftree overhead and every sturdy wall. The peace of man, the peace of God, the peace of love to all."

We tapped our cups together and drank.

All was right with the world.

For the moment . . .

Chapter 24

After leaving the lovebirds inside their new summer nest, I walked to my car on cloud nine, only to plummet to earth when I remembered what I'd found on Frank Holden moments before Ashley had shown up. It was obvious Frank had been a novice at tracking down spirits who'd traveled to the other side. Had his ghost hunting been a ploy for him to seek revenge on the Eastman family for what had happened when Jenna's grandfather shot his father? Now that Frank had a motive, I hoped it would take the spotlight off Jenna. Frank was obviously a phony paranormal investigator, but was he a murderer?

Instead of heading home to feed my bratty cat and change my outfit into something spy-worthy, like black sneakers, pants and a hoodie, I made a kneejerk decision and passed the turnoff to my cottage. Continuing east toward Montauk Point Lighthouse State Park.

Morgana's note had me meeting her at sunset, which gave me plenty of time to take a detour to see if Frank, or his boss, Mac, were hanging around the lighthouse looking for Montauk's favorite ghost, Abigail.

As expected, there was traffic leading into the park because of the Montauk Point Lighthouse Week festivities. As with every trip I'd taken to the lighthouse, I always stopped at the park's scenic overlook. Not that the view from my cottage deck wasn't as magnificent, just different. What I loved about the small hamlet of Montauk was all its different parts. Each section, from the Block Island Sound to the Atlantic, offered up its own majestic views, wide assortment of wildlife and even different smells—pine trees, salt breezes, and just plain clean air. It was amazing that New York City was only eighty-five miles away. Thankfully, years ago someone had been smart enough to set aside more public park land than residential. I was happy that Carl Fisher, the man who thought he could make Montauk into the next Miami Beach, had failed. The Great Depression had something to do with it. Montauk was the *un*Hampton; unpretentious and unspoiled. I hoped it would stay that way.

The overlook's parking lot was packed. Dogs, children, young couples (yay, Patrick and Ashley would never be sitting in a tree, K-I-S-S-I-N-G). There wasn't one parking spot, so I moved on.

I traveled up the one-way entrance to the park, my windows down. When I pulled up to the parking attendant's kiosk, I talked my way out of paying, telling her I was picking up someone who was ill. Not a lie. If Frank Holden turned out to be Roland's killer, you couldn't get sicker in the head than that. I drove slowly, looking ahead to the vine-entwined low fence sprouting pale violet clematis that fronted the walkway leading up to the lighthouse. Its stature always took my breath away.

The air was nippy but the sun was out. Seagulls dove and coasted on the stiff breeze, sometimes dive-bombing the area at the back of the snack bar for scraps. I pulled into the yellow-lined *No standing or parking* spot and saw Mac the ghosthunter's tall form, his distinctive gelled-up spiky dark hair and oversized black-framed eyeglasses. He was holding court to a bevy of male and female followers who were dressed in identical black T-shirts that read *Keep Calm and Ghost Hunt*.

Getting as close as possible, I pulled the Wagoneer a hundred feet from the fence and laid on the horn. The line of people waiting outside the gate for the tour that would take them up the lighthouse's one hundred and thirty-seven steps gave me dirty looks, as did a park ranger who looked torn between coming over to sanction me or staying to collect the tickets.

Paranormal Investigator Mac finally glanced my way. I waved. He waved back, but then turned back to one of his ghosthunter groupies. He had a sharpie in his hand and was autographing the girl's T-shirt in a very strategic place. I tapped the horn, gently this time, giving off a weak beep. Mac didn't look my way. Darn! Best laid plans and all that. Then I had an idea. I dug in my handbag for the business card he'd given me on Friday when I'd come to Frank's rescue, then shot him a text from my phone. *Need to talk to you about Frank Holden. You could be liable for what he's been doing at Enderly Hall.*

I watched him pull out his phone, glance at the screen and start typing. The light on my phone flashed, and I read, *You mean Frank Mullens? I don't know a Frank Holden. A little busy now. Who are you?*

*Meg Barrett. I saved Frank's arm from the fence at Enderly Hall and
talked the cops out of pressing trespassing charges. I'll make it worth your
while. I'll pick you up in front of the snack bar.*
Ok. But I only have fifteen minutes till I go on camera.
White Woody Wagoneer.
I see you.
It seemed Mac wasn't the only one who saw me. The ranger in
front of the gates to the lighthouse must have called for backup,
because he was pointing out my car to another ranger. Ranger
number two took a step in my direction and I gunned it, parking in
front of a Hamptons Jitney bus parked just north of the snack bar.

Mac showed up just as I was in the middle of reading a text from
Elle saying that when she went to Montauk Manor to interrogate
Vicki, she'd been told Vicki had checked out. The desk manager said
she'd left without paying her bill. That wasn't a surprise. What was
a surprise was that Vicki left town while being a suspect in a murder
case.

I unlocked the car door and Mac hopped in, bringing with him
the scent of the briny ocean and too-strong spicy aftershave. I
shoved my phone in my handbag.

He said, "You gotta make it quick. I go live in fifteen. They're
clearing out the lighthouse museum for our crew to do a short
segment."

"I'll be quick," I answered, taking my pointer finger and swiping
it across his long nose where an eyelash had fallen. "Make a wish," I
said, holding it in front of his lips.

"I *wish* we could hurry this along," he said ungratefully, but
superstitiously blew on the eyelash anyway.

"I just need to know if Frank Holden was with you or any of
your ghost . . . paranormal investigators on Saturday between ten
and noon?"

"First of all, Frank's last name is Mullens. At least that's what he
told me. Second of all, he was let go a couple of minutes ago. I'm
surprised you didn't see him. He stayed overnight with us in the
lighthouse. Showed up last night around seven—two hours later
than scheduled. Didn't contribute a thing. Funny thing was, he
didn't seem too upset about being fired. After his incident with the
fence and the loss of my EVP recorder, not to mention his complete

lack of interest in what's going on here at the lighthouse . . ."

"How about yesterday between ten and noon? Was he with you and your crew?" I repeated.

"I have no idea where he was during those hours. Just last night and today."

"Do you have an address for him?"

"No. He's not part of our usual band of brothers."

"How come there's no band of sisters in your ghost hunting enterprise?" I asked.

He shrugged his shoulders. Apparently he'd never thought about it. "We travel the country and pick up extras if one of my PI's is ill or is needed at home. And before you ask, I paid Frank by cash. That's the way he wanted it. He didn't even squabble like they usually do about the eight dollars an hour. Ghost hunting isn't as lucrative as some might think. Do you mind telling me what's going on? Does it have anything to do with the dead guy? We picked up a lot of strange (pause) disturbing (pause) anomalies on our geomagnetometer when we were at Enderly Hall the other day." He projected his voice like he was talking in an auditorium without a mike, occasionally waving his hands spastically for extra emphasis.

"What ghost did you pick up on? Captain Kidd's?"

"Why would Captain Kidd be there?" he asked, his interest piqued. "I thought Kidd buried his loot on the banks of Gardiners Island. We tried to check out the island, rented a skiff, but had to turn around at the point of an assault rifle. That family takes their privacy seriously."

And rightly so, I thought.

I quickly explained about Shepherds Cottage and its link to Gardiners Island. He seemed surprised at the story.

"Surely you know about the money ponds near the lighthouse?"

"That treasure is supposedly buried there. Yes. But I didn't know anything about Captain Kidd having a connection with Enderly Hall. That might explain a few readings we had."

"So, if you weren't looking for Captain Kidd's ghost, why were you at Enderly Hall? Or more succinctly, what ghost were you hoping to run into? Or should I say run through. Ha, ha. Get it? They're transparent."

"Good one." He was getting fidgety, a step from annoyed. He

answered, "It was your guy Frank Mullens or whatever you said his name was . . ."

"Holden."

"Frank told us that there were numerous ghost sightings at Enderly Hall. His family had been witnessing them for ages. When I told him we were only interested in the lighthouse ghost, he said that the original owner had been a keeper."

"As far as I know, that's not true."

"He told us he had some documented proof that there was recent paranormal activity going on. Some story about a suspicious death and rumors of a demonic presence. He also said he got permission from the owner so we could go on the grounds to check it out."

That confirmed what Jenna had told me about her husband allowing the ghosthunters on the property to help with publicity.

"Hey, why are you asking about this unless the dude's death was suspicious? With everything going on this week at the lighthouse, I don't know if I can get back to the estate. Maybe I could send one of my guys over to see if he can get a reading?"

"That's not necessary. But I will talk to the man's widow and ask her permission." I couldn't imagine Jenna wanting them on Enderly's grounds, and he must have read something in my remark, because he said, "Ms. Barrett, I think if you came with us when we go back inside the lighthouse, you would see how paranormal investigators roll and be quite impressed. Everything is scientific. On top of that, we use groundbreaking equipment. I can show you documented proof that there are at least two entities inside the Montauk lighthouse. One evil. One pure."

I coughed. "Gee, I wish I could tag along, but I have somewhere I need to be. Thanks for the info on Frank, though. Just one more question . . ."

He rubbed his chin, then leaned in closer, using his eyes instead of a piece of equipment to read my face. "A nonbeliever. Anytime you're up for the challenge, send me a text. I'll show you a few things that will not only make your hair stand on end but also make you see that what we do is a good thing. Ridding the world of evil . . ."

"One demon at a time."

"Exactly. What's your last question?" He looked down at his

gold Rolex, then back at me. Frank might have been getting eight dollars an hour for ghostbusting, but Mac with his syndicated television show was doing much better.

"What kind of car does Frank have?"

"A late-model silver Lexus. Probably the reason he didn't squabble over eight dollars an hour. The guy must have money."

The fact that Frank drove a silver Lexus, similar in body and color to the car Jenna said ran her off the road, put Frank at the top of my suspect list. I couldn't wait to tell Patrick . . . oops, Morgana.

"Now, I have a favor to ask of you," he said. "I go on camera for our next segment in a few minutes. Let's see if I can convince you with my intro that something truly evil is living inside the lighthouse."

"Can ghosts really live inside anything? Aren't they free to go anywhere they wish—willy-nilly, uncontained."

Once again he ignored me, most likely because he was used to nonbelievers and ghost-related puns.

"Okay," I said after an awkward silence, "what can I do for you?" I couldn't turn him down. I needed to keep him on my good side in case we needed him to throw Frank Holden under the ghosthunter bus, if only for using an alias last name.

"I need to rehearse my monologue as to our findings last night when we were in the attic of the lighthouse museum gift shop. Where we encountered two restless entities . . ."

"One of them Abigail?"

"Precisely. It's the other I'm worried about. We'll be recording live for my show. They're closing down the lighthouse just for me and the team. So, if you're game, I need to get the opinion of a nonbeliever on my opening monologue. I think I've got most of the history of the lighthouse ghost Abigail down."

"You should have filmed yesterday when we had all that fog and mist. Would've been the perfect setting for a ghostly hoedown."

"This isn't a game, Ms. Barrett. And we did film yesterday, all night until the park opened for the public."

"Please, call me Meg."

"It's a five-minute intro, Meg. Let me know what you think?"

"Okay. But first answer one more question. Do you think Frank really wanted to be a paranormal investigator, or is it possible he was up to something illegal?"

"He certainly didn't have the experience he said he had. Didn't know a spirit box from an SLS camera."

"SLS?"

"Structured Light Sensitive camera. You ready?"

I could tell Mac was at his tipping point. "Yes."

"Here we stand"—Mac gestured behind him, the ring on his right hand whacking the passenger-side window—"in front of the Montauk Point Lighthouse, commissioned by George Washington himself in 1790."

"I think it was 1792."

He sent me a threatening glance, the dark intensity of his eyes magnified by his thick lenses. He took his job seriously.

"Shall I continue?" he asked, continuing anyway. "You are about to see footage of a harrowing, (pause) disturbing (pause) twelve hours of credible (pause) proof that there is a murderous entity living inside the historic Montauk Point Lighthouse. Numerous ships and lives have been lost off the shoals of Turtle Hill (pause) never to resurface again. What I am about to show you will set to rest the until-now unproven legend of Montauk's ghost, Abigail. First let me tell you the backstory. We travel back in time to the year 1860, when young Abigail, the daughter of one of the construction workers renovating the battered lighthouse, fell in love with one of the masons working to fortify the lighthouse's outer walls. I will tell the murderous (pause) tale of an innocent (pause) young couple who paid the price of falling in love with their lives. (pause) Stay tuned for a segment we call 'Trapped. Abigail, the Montauk Point Lighthouse Ghost.'" He looked at me instead of a fake camera. "Pretend we are stopping for a commercial break."

"Okeydokey. Don't you think this might be more exciting for me if I watch it when it airs?" I really wanted to get going. So far his spiel was a snooze-fest.

"It will still be exciting to watch later. Mark my words, you'll be riveted by the scientific proof we've uncovered. I promise you."

"Okay, okay."

"Does this help?" he asked, turning to me after switching on the flashlight function on his phone, placing it on his lap so it made his face drain of color. The area under his cheekbones sunk in, and he resembled a good-looking vampire, like Tom Cruise from the movie *Interview with a Vampire.*

"Ready?"

"As I ever will be."

He gave me a dirty look.

Unsmiling, and in a serious voice, he began, "Even though I am alive to tell the tale of what transpired last evening when my crew and I spent the night inside the lighthouse with the goal of protecting Montauk's famed ghost, Abigail, I don't want you to think we are out of the woods yet. (pause) In four hours we will go back inside, prepared for a battle with a supernatural entity so evil (pause) that we seriously reconsidered the challenge. Rumor has it that in 1890, when soon-to-be president Theodore Roosevelt visited the lighthouse, he told the lighthouse keeper that on his way up to the light in the tower, he felt an unearthly presence and blast of cold air. I, myself, have seen his signature in the Montauk Point Lighthouse guestbook, which can be viewed at the East Hampton Library.

"Now, back to our innocent lighthouse ghost. It seems Abigail fell in love with an unsuitable man. Unsuitable to Abigail's father. We are fairly certain from our communication with Abigail that it was her father who killed her lover by stuffing him between the walls of the lighthouse during one of its renovations. Our goal tonight is to locate the bones (pause) of Abigail's true love and rid the lighthouse of Abigail's father, who's been keeping guard over the young man's remains. Our only problem (pause) is we are dealing with an entity so dastardly, so foul, that its made our high-tech geomagnetometer malfunction, giving us a reading we haven't witnessed in our ten years of ghost adventures. You will hear the entity called Abigail literally (pause) crying for our help. Using other high-tech equipment, one piece of which is a thermal UV camera, you will see for yourself that Abigail exists. Our top priority will be to find Abigail's lover's bones so the pair can free themselves from being tethered to the lighthouse and travel to the light. And if we can, (pause) we will lead her father's demonic spirit into our RGR, revolutionary (pause) ghost (pause) receptacle, (pause) then toss the RGR to the bottom of the Atlantic Ocean."

He stopped, took a deep breath, and with his huge round brown eyes opened wide, he asked, "Well?"

"It all sounds very exciting. You sure have a way with words." *And pauses.* "However, I think people might be disappointed if you rid Montauk of its lighthouse ghost. Stick to throwing the father in the sea, but keep Abigail and her boyfriend around to live happily ever after inside the lighthouse."

He looked like he was considering it, then said, "Naw. This is good."

"You know there is another version about Abigail. It's even painted on canvas inside the museum. Did you see it?"

"Yes." He waved his hand in a dismissive motion. "We found no proof that Abigail was the only survivor of an early-nineteenth-century shipwreck, then climbed the tower steps and died when she reached the top. All our readings point to my version."

"Okay. Well, good luck. Thanks for your input on Frank."

He got out of the car, but before closing the door he leaned in and said, "Be sure not to disturb us when we spend our second night in the lighthouse. I have to keep my phone on. My wife's pregnant with our first child. Due any minute."

"Congrats. I promise not to contact you. Boy or girl?"

"My wife wants to be surprised. I want to know."

"Can't you use some of your equipment on her while she's sleeping for a look-see?"

"Ms. Barrett, you're too much."

I swore I saw him thinking about it as he closed the car door.

As I was about to pull away, I thought of something. I lowered the passenger-side window and called out, "Mr. Zagan!!"

He turned, looking annoyed, but came back to the car.

"I forgot. I have something for you." I reached behind me to the backseat and grabbed the bag with the EVP recorder, and handed it to him.

He took the bag and looked inside, a smile spreading across his wide mouth. "Frank's?"

"Frank's," I answered.

He saluted, then walked away.

Chapter 25

I took my time leaving the lighthouse, enjoying the long drive to the center of town while thinking of my to-do list for Elle and Arthur's celebration in my walled garden. It was only three weeks away.

Lucky for me, my father was coming, and he'd been instrumental in choosing the menu that would be brought in by our favorite restaurant, Pondfare, prepared by TV's Top Chef Pierre Patou. Elle's shop assistant, right-hand man and my fashionista, Maurice, was also on team Elle and Arthur. He'd been in charge of invitations, beverages and hiring the waitstaff. Soon, many of the perennials in my walled garden would be in full bloom, one of the reasons I'd chosen the end of May. In case of inclement weather, I'd reserved a couple of white party tents and stocked up on two cases of fairy lights. At that thought, my mind wandered back to the fairy lights at Enderly Hall's pavilion and the missing-then-found extension cord, aka the murder weapon.

All in all, I really didn't have that much to do for the party. Elle's fiancé had only to show up and make sure to bring with him a surprise guest that would blow Elle's mind—hopefully in a good way.

When I reached tiny downtown Montauk, I slowed to let a young couple cross the road. They took their time. As they walked, the man pushed aside the woman's long dark hair, then kissed the base of her neck. She pushed him away, laughing, then they walked hand in hand to the curb. A couple of hours ago, the scene would've rubbed salt in an oozing wound. But now, knowing that Patrick wasn't involved with Ashley, the romantic spectacle I'd just witnessed had my heart thumping deliriously.

Putting my foot on the gas pedal, I continued west with a huge smile on my face and a song in my heart, until the photo of Patrick's wife and daughter came to mind. How could someone compete with that?

At Montauk's town green I saw a familiar figure sitting on a park bench. Nate Klein. Minus Kuri. He held a phone to his ear and didn't look happy. I coasted to a stop, put the car in Park, got out and fed the parking meter a quarter. Trying to make it appear as if I was aimlessly strolling by, I stopped short in front of him and feigned surprise.

Still talking into the phone, Nate motioned for me to have a seat. Which I gladly did. "Okay, I'll be there around four to pick you up," he said in a soothing voice. "Don't talk to anyone but your lawyer about anything. Things will work out, I promise." He tapped his phone screen and pocketed his phone.

"Was that Jenna?" I asked, knowing it was. "Is she okay? Nothing's happened, has it?"

"She's fine. But she's been ordered to show up in South Hampton to identify Roland's body. A ridiculous formality in my opinion. She's with her friend Ellen, says she's okay. Sounds a little out of it."

I didn't correct him that Jenna was with Elle, not someone named Ellen. And I didn't think it was any of his business that per Elle, Jenna had been given a prescription from her psychiatrist, which would explain the "out of it" part. Jenna being the hypochondriac that she was, in this case the pills seemed warranted. I said, "I brought her to the yacht club last night. Made sure she was sleeping before I left her."

"Thanks for that," he said. "I just hope they don't charge her."

"Do you really think they will?"

"I can't see how. I've talked to Chief Pell. So far, there's no concrete evidence. But just being *his* wife makes Jenna look guilty." When Nate was being interviewed by Morgana, unlike Jenna and Vicki, he hadn't disguised his contempt for Roland Cahill. What surprised me was his mention of Chief Pell. I'd forgotten that in the library, Pell had called Nate by his first name. What was their connection? In this case, Nate's relationship to the chief might be to Jenna's advantage. Unless Nate murdered Roland. Then it would be to Nate's advantage.

"Did Jenna tell you that she thought Roland tried to run her over the other day?" I asked.

"Yes. And I brushed it off. Wish I hadn't. You know Jenna," he said, turning to me. "I thought she was exaggerating."

"Did she also tell you that she overheard Roland say that he planned to sell Enderly Hall?"

"Yes. And he also planned on faking Stanford White papers

proving White was the architect. The jerk even asked Kuri to make copies at the Montauk Library of the architectural renderings on file for one of Stanford White's sister cottages. Thankfully Kuri told me about it before she did it. Knowing what he was up to, I blew a gasket." He balled his fists. "It wasn't a pretty confrontation, but well deserved."

"Is that why you gave him a black eye?"

"Jenna told you?"

It had been a guess. Obviously, a good one. I evaded answering, not wanting to lie. Instead I said, "Not to talk ill of the dead, but he seemed to have it coming. Not the murder part. The black eye part."

Nate put his head in his hands and mumbled something my hearing aids couldn't pick up. I waited until he sat back up. I'd never been this close to him before. He was quite a looker; no wonder Vicki was enamored with him. He also smelled good, citrus and some other earthy scent. He moaned, "I wouldn't have hired him if I'd known the truth behind his Queens construction firm. Kuri did a little digging into his past and found more than a few skeletons, but it was too late. I couldn't get rid of him after promising my cousin."

I would have loved to ask him what those skeletons were, but I could tell I had to tread gently. Nate looked like he was ready for a breakdown. "My friend Elle and I were sure tricked when we met Roland at the wedding. He was so charming. Jenna seemed truly smitten. Is that why you agreed to have him join your firm? Because he made Jenna so happy? Did your relationship start out better in the beginning?"

"Relationship? With him?" he snarled. "It was never smooth. Yes, I was doing Jenna a favor. Just as she and her father had done for me many years ago, paying for my tuition to become an architect, then introducing me to all her high-society friends in Manhattan. When she moved to the East End and I opened Klein and Associates, I told her I didn't want anyone knowing we were cousins. I wanted to make it on my own credentials, not cling to her shirttails. She agreed wholeheartedly. Now it's my turn to be there for her."

"From what I've heard, you sure have made a success out of it. She's lucky to have you in her corner. The few times I interacted with Roland at the showhouse, he could be pretty rough around the edges."

"And controlling. He had Jenna on a short leash. When it came to the firm, Kuri and I had to constantly smooth things over with our clients, putting out one fire after another." He stopped for a moment, looking pensive as he gazed in the direction of the ocean, only a few short blocks away. "Roland paid no attention to detail," he said, continuing. "Tried to use substandard materials, then invoiced me for more than he paid. Kuri found him out and snitched, even though he threatened her with . . ."

He didn't finish his sentence and didn't need to because I had heard the same threat when Elle and I saw him in Amagansett. He was threatening to tell Kuri's husband something. I wanted to ask if she was stepping out on her husband. Weighing my options, and Kuri's possible relationship with Nate, I decided to zip it. Plus, I didn't want to stop the flow of information he was so freely spewing. So I asked something that had nothing to do with his relationship with Kuri. "When I bumped into Roland on Friday in Amagansett, he was served with court papers. Seemed quite taken aback. Any idea what they were for?"

"No. I wonder why Kuri didn't tell me? Well, whatever it was for, it has died with him, unless . . ." He said more to himself, than me. Probably realizing that Roland, being a partner in the firm, might make Klein and Associates liable for whatever the subpoena was for.

I stood, knowing we'd talked long enough, not wanting to push it. "Please pass on to Jenna that she's more than welcome to stay at the yacht club as long as she wants."

"You're a good friend," he said, also getting up from the bench. "You must think she's innocent. That's good."

And he didn't?

"But after I take Jenna to East Hampton to identify the body, I am determined to have her come stay with me. I don't want her anywhere near that Vicki creature who's been freeloading off of Jenna and using the Amagansett rental. I saw Vicki and Roland going at it Friday. There must have been some reason he asked Jenna to include her as one of Enderly's interior decorators. Per Kuri, she didn't inherit one ounce of her mother's design genes. And Roland never did anything unless it helped Roland. I think his former stepdaughter felt the same way."

"Vicki's not in Amagansett. She supposedly left for Manhattan this morning."

"I thought we were told to stick around. Well, that's a relief. Jenna doesn't need Vicki piling on any more stress. Plus, Vicki told everyone yesterday that Roland and Jenna had gotten in a fight Friday night. If I was Jenna, I'd never let her set foot at Enderly Hall again."

We walked together to the sidewalk. Nate turned to the left, I to the right. "Take care," I said to his back. "Oh, Mr. Klein, one more thing."

He turned around.

"Tell Jenna to call anytime. I'm only a text away."

"Thanks for being so kind to my cousin. I'll pass it on."

If Nate and Jenna were cousins and both were blood relatives of Jenna's grandfather, then Nate might have a motive to get Roland out of the way. And then possibly Jenna. She'd told Elle and I how her father and uncle had fought for Enderly Hall. It was only after both men died that she inherited the estate. Jenna had no siblings. Far-fetched as it seemed, if Nate was an Eastman, he might have a motive for murder. I left caution to the now brisk wind and asked, "I'm so happy Jenna has family to lean on. Are you related on her mother's or father's side of the family?"

He ratcheted his head toward me. Scowling, he snapped, "Why? What does that have to do with anything? What does it matter which side I'm related to?"

Oops.

I guess that answered my question.

Chapter 26

"You know, I shouldn't be doing this. We were going to try to keep our relationship on the down low. This can't be an official visit," Morgana whispered as we used my keycard to walk through the gates of Enderly Hall. I raised the volume on my hearing aids and asked why there weren't any police vehicles parked inside or outside the property.

"There's an officer who swings by every half hour. That's why we need to be quick. In and out," she repeated for the tenth time.

"Did you get the photo I sent you." I'd forwarded Patrick's text of our suspect list.

"Yes. I like that it gives me your take on everyone. My sister tells me this isn't your first rodeo, however, I don't know this Patrick guy, so I wouldn't share too much. Pell doesn't want the fact that Mr. Cahill was murdered in the press yet. They're still calling it a suspicious death."

I explained who Patrick was.

"Oh, the author. I'm impressed you two are friends."

"Not exactly friends, but we're getting there."

"What happened to that handsome rich Spenser guy you were dating?"

"We're over."

"By the look of those pink, rosy cheeks under the lamplight, you've moved on with a certain author? Am I right?"

I didn't answer and she continued, "I'm a big fan of his writing. Love his thrillers. But I've never seen him hanging around town. I do know he's good-looking from his dust jacket photos. Heard he was a recluse because of some tragedy."

"He seems to be coming out in public a little more. Seems happier. Which might have something to do with *Mr. & Mrs. Winslow*. He wrote the screenplay for an upcoming television series, similar to the Thin Man movies based on Dashiell Hammett's books."

"Nick and Nora. I loved those movies. I especially loved their dog Asta, a wire fox terrier. That breed can be a little high-strung. My aunt had one, and it used to nip at our ankles when we came for Sunday supper. Talk about a coincidence, I just got a request for filming at the lighthouse by *Mr. & Mrs. Winslow's* production company. It's for next September, after the summer season ends. Hope my boss approves it. Anytime Hollywood comes to Montauk, it calls for extra recruits and costs the taxpayers lots of money."

"On the other hand, it's great for publicity. It should be a closed set. People on the East End are used to camera crews and A-list stars." We stopped at a fork in the path. "So, enough chitchat, Officer Moss. Why am I here?"

"Frank Holden's phone," she said. "We need to find it. When I had Frank in the office to sign his statement, he brought it up again. There must be something on that phone that incriminates him. I need you to tell me where you saw him when he lost his paranormal investigating thingie."

"EVP. Sure thing. And I bet I know why he wants the phone."

"If you're going to tell me his father was the one that Ms. Eastman's grandfather shot, then I already know."

"Did Frank tell you that?"

She laughed. "Contrary to all the cozy mystery books that we both like to read, the police are capable of handling murder investigations. It didn't take DNA testing to find out Frank Holden's ties to Enderly Hall."

"Okay, okay. Speaking of DNA, anything?"

"Another misconception. DNA results don't come back from the lab in TV time, only real time. Like a week or two. They have to be sent to Riverhead."

"You've made your point. But would you tell me if you did get results pointing to anyone?"

"Now you're pushing it, Ms. Barrett."

"Why is finding his phone important? He lost it the day before Roland Cahill was murdered."

"I have a feeling whatever is on it will shed an unfavorable light on our Mr. Holden." She took a piece of gum out of her mouth and tossed it in the shrubbery. "Barb tells me that I smack my gum too loud, what do you think?"

"I never noticed." Not true. But my mother always taught me that sometimes a white lie isn't really a lie, especially if an unimportant truth would hurt someone's feelings. "You're right, though, the guy's no Bill Murray."

Morgana stopped on the gravel drive, looked at me and raised an eyebrow. "Is that a reference to the movie *Ghostbusters*?"

"Yes. I'm just sayin', he's no paranormal investigator. He doesn't even know any of the lingo or equipment names." I told her about my meeting with Mac Zagan. "And get this, Frank drives a silver Lexus, probably the car that Jenna saw in the fog when she thought her husband was trying to run her off the road."

"She what! I know nothing about this. Are you withholding key information to protect your friend?"

"Morgana, you have to trust me. I know Jenna didn't kill Roland."

But did I?

I braced myself for a good talking-to; instead, Morgana grabbed my wrist and pulled me to her. "Stop!" she whispered.

"What the heck?"

"Shush. Look." She pointed in the direction of Shepherds Cottage.

Sure enough, a light glowed in the cottage's northern window. It wasn't coming from a moving flashlight like last time. It was from the electrified oil lamp I'd placed on the bedside table for the showhouse tour.

"Let's go," I said, moving toward the path.

"No. I'll check out the cottage, you go search the area where you saw Mr. Holden on Friday."

"I already did that."

"There's a lot of bushes and underbrush. Here, wear my headlamp."

She handed me a high-powered flashlight attached to a headband. "So, basically, I should be crawling on my hands and knees back here, while you check out the cottage without backup?"

"Exactly."

"Don't you want me to lead you through the maze? I did good last time."

"I'm not going through any maze. I'm walking straight toward the cottage with my gun drawn. Now scoot!" she said in a low growl.

"But what if while you're over there Roland's killer gets me. Safety in numbers, remember?"

"With your track record, I'm not worried about you. More about them!"

"Well said." I wasn't really being a ninny or a whiner, I just wanted to be around when she caught whoever it was. What was in Shepherds Cottage that was so important? Again, Frank was the only one who had ties to Jenna's grandfather, who had lived in the cottage before his death. Maybe Jenna's not-quite-right-in-the-head grandpa had told Frank's father about the link to Captain Kidd and the cottage. Maybe Frank's father had been shot by Thomas Eastman not as a trespasser but as a possible thief? All these thoughts funneled through my brain as I turned to go back toward the gate.

"Should I call for backup?" I said over my shoulder.

"No. You aren't supposed to be here. Remember?"

"Got it. Be safe."

"I've got this. Stay where I told you."

"Text me."

"Meg, let it go." She did look pretty formidable holding her Glock in front of her as she advanced toward the cottage. I waited until she disappeared into the dusk.

Instead of checking inside the property for Frank's phone, this time I went back out the gate and checked the area outside the fencing.

The night was warmer than it had been in days. Stars twinkled and a crescent moon looked like one from a child's fairy-tale book. To the west, there was still a thin strip of pink sky, giving hope that our gloomy weather pattern had moved away for good and tomorrow would be fog-free.

I didn't turn on the headlamp until I was on my knees about five hundred feet from where I'd helped Frank get his arm unstuck. Luckily, no gardeners had come since Friday. The rhododendrons and hydrangeas were spaced evenly in front of the wrought iron fencing. Most of the big estates in the Hamptons had tall privet bushes blocking views from the road. Jenna felt differently, she'd wanted whoever was passing by to get a glimpse of Stanford White's renovated masterpiece.

Five minutes later I hadn't found anything but a 1957 copper penny and was about to give up. I was also worried about Morgana. She hadn't texted me as promised. Nor had she returned to her car. I stood up and glanced toward Shepherds Cottage. *What was that?* A figure passed in front of the bedroom window, and it wasn't someone dressed in an East Hampton Town Police uniform.

Something akin to a premonition told me to abandon my search and instead go seek out Officer Moss. Not that I believed in premonitions. I just knew what living, breathing humans were capable of. I took a step toward the gate, then changed my mind. It would only take a second to check one other place. Instead of searching for the phone where I'd freed Frank's arm, I got back down on my hands and knees and crawled toward where I'd seen the ghosthunter van parked. *Voilà!* The headlamp's beam caught the shine of a cell phone's glass screen. I scooped it up, stood, then bolted toward the gate. I aimed my remote and watched the gates slowly open. When there was just enough room for me to pass through, I sprinted toward the cottage.

Now that my mission was complete, I needed to help Officer Moss with hers.

I wasn't worried about the crunching of my sneakers on the stone and shell path because as I got closer to the cottage, I saw that the door was flung wide open. Weak light spilled onto the small porch. I tiptoed inside, whispering, "Officer Moss? Are you here?" then more fervently, "Morgana! Where the heck are you!"

The cottage was empty, still a mess from the carnage on the night of the cocktail-party-that-wasn't.

Defeated, I looked around for a weapon. I grabbed a weighty copper bed warmer attached to a long wooden stick and went back outside.

I checked the gazebo. No Morgana. I scurried to the pavilion, my breath raspy and labored as I ran. When I reached the steps, I noticed that the yellow crime scene tape had been broken, its ends flapping on the ocean breeze, more terrifying than if it was intact. I shined the headlamp around the interior before bolting to the railing. Holding my breath and saying a prayer, I directed my light onto the rocks below.

Thankfully, nothing.

The only place left to check was Enderly Hall. I walked toward the house, turning my head left and right, scanning the terrain for any clue to Morgana's whereabouts. When I reached one of the entrances (or exits) to the boxwood maze, I stepped inside, holding the bed warmer in front of me like a sword. For all I knew, Morgana could be lost inside — like Jenna had been when she was a child — or worse.

Morgana wasn't in the maze. I made my way out the exit closest to Enderly Hall.

There, on Enderly's back veranda, I saw a dark figure dressed the same as me, in a black hoodie, pants and sneakers. The person was crouched over Morgana's unmoving body. She was laying on her side with her back to me. I punched in 9-1-1 on my phone and whispered our location.

Adrenaline and anger took over. I turned off the headlamp and crept toward them, holding tight to long handle of the bed warmer. The hooded figure held something in his right hand. As I got closer, I saw it was a pair of eighteenth-century iron sheep shears that I'd left as a prop on top of a basket of shorn wool inside Shepherds Cottage.

I stepped cautiously. When I was fifty feet away, I heard a male voice saying something to Morgana. He had no clue I was behind him.

Morgana wasn't moving. I charged forward, brandishing the bed warmer. I brought it down full force on top of the man's head. *Whack!* He fell facefirst to the veranda floor, flopping like a fish out of water, jerking his arms and legs like he was having a seizure — which hopefully he was. Even in his flailing, he held tight to the shears. I waited a few seconds in case I had to deliver another blow. Finally, he lay still.

Putting the bed warmer out of reach, I pried the shears from his hand. They weighed at least fifteen pounds. Then I bent next to Morgana and took her pulse. Thank God, she had one. Crowning from the back of her head was a large bump the size of an egg, a goose egg. Her hair was matted with blood. "You son of a bitch!" I cursed as I took off my hoodie and made a pillow for under the left side of her head. Her eyelids fluttered.

"Help's on the way, Morgana. Hold tight. I won't leave you."

Holding back tears, I turned back to her assailant, worried that Roland Cahill's murderer might rise like a phoenix for one last assault like in every horror movie I'd ever watched.

He lay still. The sound of sirens came closer. I knew I should wait for them. Instead, I went back to Morgana and took her gun from her holster. It felt strange in my hand. I'd never used a gun before. It wasn't one of those things on my bucket list. But I'd be sure to use it if I had to. I released the safety and moved next to the man. Just by the shape of his body, I thought I knew who it was.

With the gun in one hand, I used the other to push him over.

It was no surprise that I was looking down at Frank Holden.

He smelled of pipe tobacco and sweat.

"I'll take that gun, Ms. Barrett," a deep voice said from behind. Chief Pell stepped onto the porch, his grim features illuminated under the porchlight.

"Gladly," I answered, handing him the gun. "Where's EMS?"

"They're right behind me."

A pair of attendants carrying a gurney scurried up the porch steps, lowered it, then rolled Morgana's limp body onto it. They each took an end and went down the steps. When they reached the shell and gravel walkway, they extended the gurney's wheels.

As they pulled away, I shouted, "I'm going with her!"

"You're not going anywhere, Ms. Barrett," Chief Pell commanded. "You've got some explaining to do."

I went up to him, nose to chest. My knees were shaking, but not from Pell. More from worry about Morgana. "Don't you want to handcuff Mr. Holden? Look, I think he's moving." I pointed to him.

When the chief looked over at Frank's still body, I took off after the stretcher.

Chapter 27

"Well, I guess it's no big deal that Vicki took off, seeing we have Frank Holden in custody."

"We?" Morgana said from her hospital bed. "I suppose I can give you that one, owing to the fact you saved my life. But you're still in a lot of hot water with Chief Pell for leaving the scene. You didn't have to ride with me in the ambulance. But I'm glad you were here when I opened my eyes."

"Does that mean you're so grateful that you can share what Frank Holden said when he was interrogated? What his motive might have been for killing Roland, trashing Shepherds Cottage and stuffing monopoly money in the polar bear's mouth?"

"I can only tell you that he did confess to the last two things. But he claims he didn't murder Mr. Cahill."

"Are you pressing charges for what he did to you?"

"You betcha! Attempted manslaughter. If it wasn't for you, he'd probably be up on murder charges." She winced and moved her hand to the back of her bandaged head. "The lump seems to be going down, but they want to keep me for another night," she said. "I'm ready to go now. I want to be there for the press conference."

"Doctors know best. Listen to them. Thank God Frank only used the handles of the shears to wallop you, he could have used the blades. If that had been the case, I wouldn't be talking to you right now. Do you have any idea what he was looking for in Shepherds Cottage?"

"Kind of. Please hand me my tablet," she said, pointing to it on top of the nightstand.

I passed it to her and asked, "Can I get you anything else? Water?"

"I'd kill for a Diet Coke and a cigarette, but I suppose a piece of gum inside that drawer over there would do."

After I gave her the stick of gum, she said, "Shut the door. Make sure you're out of view of the window. I'll let you read the transcript from Mr. Holden's interview. He had a public defender with him, but I'm sure the guy will get a top lawyer soon. We've looked into his bank accounts, he has almost a million in savings and CDs."

"Jenna told me that after her grandfather shot Frank's father as a trespasser, he paid a million in settlement money."

Morgana typed in her password, then handed me her tablet.

"Thanks for sharing," I said with a smile. "Wow, I've never been handed police files *legally* before. I usually find other means. This is so much easier."

"I think you've earned it. I just don't know if anyone else will feel the same way if they find out. Especially Chief Pell. I think we're both in the doghouse. He wasn't even listening when I sang your praises last night. Quick thinking with that bed pan. He was slightly appeased when you turned over Mr. Holden's phone."

"Bed *warmer*," I corrected.

"I think the chief's threatened by you. However, when this does go to press in a couple of hours, we need to give him full credit for capturing Frank Holden. It will make both our lives easier."

"You're okay with that? I wouldn't be. This is your first big case."

"I am. I shouldn't have brought you along. It could have been you at the end of those prehistoric sheep shears."

"I don't think Pell's got it out for me. It has more to do with Elle's fiancé and the fact the chief hasn't solved one Hamptons homicide in the last couple of years, while Detective Shoner has been front and center for the last five."

"Along with you right next to him," Morgana said, chomping her gum. "Owie, chewing hurts my head."

"So, stop chewing."

"Are you going to read the transcript or not?"

I got up, locked the door and pulled my chair against the wall. After making sure I was out of sight of anyone looking through the window in the door, I sat back down and started reading. In Frank Holden's quasi-confession, he admitted to breaking into Shepherds Cottage looking for a yellow diamond that his father had told him about, which Jenna's grandfather had claimed came from Captain Kidd's treasure on Gardiners Island. Frank's father befriended Jenna's grandfather, who at the time was out of his mind. Then slowly, over the course of a year, Frank's father pilfered small items from the main house: sterling, small statues, and even a few pieces of Jenna's grandmother's jewelry. But when Grandpa Eastman claimed that somewhere he'd misplaced an uncut yellow diamond, Frank's father made it his life's mission, or in this case, his death's mission, to find it.

In the interrogation, Frank said he had no idea why Jenna's grandfather shot his father. Maybe he wasn't so crazy after all and found out that Frank's father had been stealing. Frank went on to say that when he heard about the showhouse, he planned revenge against Jenna for the sins of her grandfather. He wanted to scare her away so he could continue the search for Kidd's yellow diamond. That's why he'd signed up as a paranormal investigator, so he'd have access to the estate. He was the one that scared Jenna with his car, claiming he never came close to hitting her. He also confessed to stuffing Monopoly money in the bear's mouth as another scare tactic. But he was adamant about not killing Roland.

"You're right he claims not to have killed Roland," I said.

"Well, what else is he going to say?" Morgana said. "We don't have forensic evidence tying him to the murder, but I'll make sure to be there when the judge sets bail."

"I don't blame you. I just don't understand why he would kill Roland. If this was a revenge plot, wouldn't he go after Jenna, not Roland?"

"Maybe Mr. Cahill caught Mr. Holden snooping around. It doesn't matter, we have enough to keep him for a while. You should be relieved. Your friend Jenna is off the hook. Especially after you let it slip that she thought her husband was trying to kill her, giving her a motive to kill him." Morgana yawned.

"I think you need your rest. I'll come back later. Need anything before I go?"

"I would like a sip of that ice water from that pitcher over there. All these painkillers give me cottonmouth, and maybe you can fluff a few pillows behind my back."

"Of course."

I served her the water, adjusted the pillows, then dragged my chair closer to her bed. I handed back her tablet in the nick of time because the door opened. Thankfully, it was a nurse who walked in, not the chief. "You need anything, Officer Moss?" the nurse asked.

"No. We're good. Thanks, Nurse Marie."

Nurse Marie winked at me. "We like to keep our officers well taken care of. Just like they take care of us. Lunch should be here in a half hour, I noticed you didn't fill out your preference card."

"Surprise me," Morgana said.

"Will do," Nurse Marie answered.

When the nurse turned her back, Morgana grabbed her throat and mimicked she was having the gag reflex. I stifled a laugh. The nurse took Morgana's temperature, checked her fluids in the IV bags, and said, "Don't overdo it. You have a nasty bump on the back of your head, and you look quite pale. It might be from your low iron and vitamin D levels. You have to eat your spinach, take vitamin D, or even better, get twenty minutes of sun every day."

We all looked out the window that overlooked a forest of pines. All we saw was a milky opaqueness. Yes, this morning the fog and chilly temps had returned. Thankfully, last evening had been clear or I might not have found Morgana in time.

Nurse Marie added, "And every morning, have a bowl of Total cereal. It's rich in iron." She refluffed the pillows behind Morgana's back. Doing a better job than I did, she tucked her blankets tightly under the mattress and said, "I'll be back with lunch in a half hour."

After Nurse Marie squeaked out of the room on her white rubber-soled nurse shoes, I said, "I'll smuggle you in some shrimp fritters from Mickey's Chowder Shack. How does that sound?"

"Heavenly. Any last takes on Mr. Holden's interview?"

"I don't know. Something seems off. Vicki Fortune left Montauk Manor yesterday morning. I stopped by before coming here, and the hotel manager said she didn't leave a forwarding address." I didn't tell her that I'd talked the manager into giving me Vicki's pink iPad, which she'd left under a stack of towels by the bathtub. His mother was one of my Cottages by the Sea clients. Any time I came across a piece of white antique ironstone, I sent it her way.

"Do you think Vicki and Frank Holden were in it together? I'll look into where she went. But I think you're overthinking things."

"I've called her number—no answer."

"Now that you mention it, she never showed up to sign her statement yesterday. Not that it matters, seeing we have our guy."

"Innocent till proven guilty, Officer Moss."

"Not innocent of almost killing me."

"True." I got up. "I'm going to let you rest. Text if you need me."

"I will. And Meg?"

"Yes?"

"Stay out of trouble."

"Yes, ma'am," I said, saluting. "But only if you get better so we can celebrate."

She didn't answer because she'd nodded off to sleep with her mouth open. I grabbed a tissue from her bed tray and removed the wad of gum dangling from her lips, then blew her a kiss and exited the hospital room.

I was happy to leave. Hospitals weren't my thing. The smell of disinfectant and moans from open doorways, not to mention the waiting rooms filled with anxious family members praying for good news about their loved ones, brought back memories of a sad time in my life.

My mother had wanted to go home. The arrangements had been made with hospice care. But she didn't make it through the night. Fortunately, my father had been lying next to her when she'd passed.

I wondered if Patrick Seaton had been able to say goodbye to his wife and daughter one last time.

With dark thoughts swirling, I stepped out into another dismal, fog-drenched day.

Chapter 28

Jenna was waiting for me, suitcase in hand, outside the lobby of the East End Yacht Club. I swung my Wagoneer around the circular drive, parked and got out. Before putting Jenna's suitcase in the back of the car, I gave her a bone-crushing hug. "I'm so happy things are settled and you can go home."

She hugged me back and said with tears in her eyes, "I'm so grateful for all you did in capturing that monster."

"Anything for you, dear friend."

I expected Jenna to look wan and washed out, but there was a blush to her cheeks and a sparkle in her eyes. She wore a tan sweater set and dark jeans with boots. Her long hair extensions were gone, and her shiny auburn hair was pulled back in a high ponytail. She appeared just as I remembered her when we'd worked together at the magazine. Now that the weight of who killed her husband had lifted, she looked ready to face the world. And as she walked to the car, there was no sign of a limp.

My assessment was confirmed when she said, "I had an epiphany while holed up in my room for two nights. I plan to embrace each day as if it were my last, and not complain about anything."

I liked the new-and-improved Jenna. I just hoped it would last. "Sounds like a plan." I grabbed her bag, put it in the back and we both got in the car.

"How's Officer Moss doing?" she asked.

"She's doing amazingly well. If she could, I know she'd escape from Southampton Hospital and hitchhike back to Montauk."

"That's a relief. I hear you're her savoir. I'm not surprised," she said.

"I wouldn't go that far." I started the engine, put it in gear, and took the lane that led us off Star Island to the main road. At the stop sign, we had a choice of going left toward downtown Montauk or right, toward the harbor. I asked, "Did you have lunch?"

"No. Breakfast in the suite. I had to charge it on your account, they wouldn't take my debit card. By the way, thank you for that."

"No problem." *Thank cheating Cole,* I thought, smiling inside. "Hey, let's do Morgana a favor. Save her from the awful hospital food. You'd think in the ritzy Hamptons the hospitals would serve gourmet food. Let's go to Mickey's and drop her off some real food. We'll still have time to meet everyone at Enderly at three. Are you sure you're up for going back to the house?"

"Yes, I'm up to it. Mickey's sounds good. I need some normal in my life. I made cremation arrangements this morning after the coroner called to say he's releasing the body. I know Roland would want to be interred in the Eastman columbarium."

"Elle and I are here to help with any arrangements. You only have to ask."

Jenna remained silent.

I glanced over and saw tears spilling from her beautiful emerald eyes, making tributaries through the peach blush on her cheeks. "Oh, Jenna. You don't have to be strong for me. Why didn't you go to Nate's last night? When I saw him yesterday, he said he invited you."

"He offered, but I told him I would stay another night at the yacht club until I could get in contact with Vicki to tell her I would be staying in the Amagansett rental until they caught Roland's killer. But now that the maniac is behind bars, I plan to move into Enderly Hall. I'm going to kick Vicki out. I'm not happy about the way she acted in front of Officer Moss and Chief Pell. So, I'm sending her packing, anyway. She never said a kind word about Roland. I'll sublet the Amagansett beach house before I let her stay there."

"Good for you."

She looked out the passenger window, where stunning water views would be if not for the fog. Her voice had a slight edge to it when she said, "Vicki left a voice mail at six a.m. yesterday morning saying she needed to see me about something. When I called back, her mailbox was full."

"Maybe she was calling to say goodbye. She left town yesterday morning."

"Well, if I decide to move forward with the showhouse, she *definitely* won't be invited back. I was thinking Labor Day weekend for our new date. What do you think? That's why I called everyone together for this afternoon. I'm also going to pay for anything you, Freya and Kuri spent on your spaces. I love everything the three of you have done, and I look forward to living at Enderly Hall among all your choices.

"What to do about Vicki's rooms is simple. If she doesn't answer my calls, I'm going to pack everything up that didn't come from Enderly's attic and put them in storage. Good riddance!" With that, she broke into heaving sobs.

I pulled the car over at a scenic overlook, took out a package of tissues from the storage compartment under the center armrest and handed it to her. Jenna removed half of the pack, then alternated between drying her tears and blowing her nose.

"Darn! I thought I was doing so good," she said between sniffles.

"You are doing good. You're doing amazing. And don't worry about putting Shepherds Cottage back together. Elle and I will take care of it."

She blew me a kiss. "Thanks, friend. Please don't worry about me. I held off taking the benzodiazepines that Dr. Sorenson prescribed. But maybe that was a mistake?"

Uh-oh, was the old Jenna back?

"On second thought, no," she said. "They make me sleepy and my head gets as foggy as what we're seeing out the car window. Plus, I need a new doctor. I only had one session with Dr. Sorenson and Roland was there. I don't think that was appropriate, do you?"

"Not really. Was he Roland's doctor too?"

"Yes. Roland went through a traumatic event about twenty years ago. He would never tell me what. Just that Dr. Sorenson helped him make peace with it. Of course, I'm heartbroken and sad about Roland's death. How could I think he wanted to kill me? The police told me that Frank Holden owns a silver car and admitted to trying to scare me when I was jogging. I was also told that Frank's father is the man my grandfather shot. What kind of twisted mind would kill my husband to get back at me?"

"Things will get better. You have a lot of people pulling for you. Elle, me, and your cousin Nate. Have you and Nate been close since you were children?" I asked. "What does he think of your grandfather's story?" Even though Frank Holden was in custody, I still had a niggling doubt that it hadn't been him who killed Roland.

"Oh, Grandpa Eastman wasn't Nate's grandfather. Grandpa was Nate's great-great-uncle. His great-grandmother and my great-grandfather were siblings. And sadly, no, we just reconnected about six years ago. Being an only child, it would have been nice to have him in my life. At least he was there for me when my father died. And he's here for me now."

Did that mean if something happened to Jenna, Nate would inherit Enderly Hall? I didn't have time to contemplate all the Machiavellian scenarios, because we'd reached Mickey's Chowder Shack's parking lot.

I turned in, found a spot close by the door. Through the wipers I saw a trio of commercial fishing boats rocking wildly in choppy waves. We waited until there was a break in the rain, and I said, "Ready for some chowder and shrimp fritters?"

"You bet," she said.

I waited for her to complain about the blustery cold wind that lashed our faces on the way to the restaurant's front door, but she didn't complain then, or through the whole meal. The conversation was light, with Jenna deciding that Elle would take over Vicki's spot for the showhouse. I thought it was a happy solution to the Vicki problem.

It was only when a local news station broke through regular programing on the TV over the bar that we were reminded of the past few days. The camera zoomed in on a familiar hulking figure. The caption at the bottom of the screen read *Chief Pell, Suffolk County Homicide.* I motioned for the check and asked Jenna, "Do you want to leave? I don't think he'll say anything we don't already know."

"No, I'm good. I want the world to know what happened to Roland. Then everyone can feel safe and sleep better tonight, knowing his killer was caught."

I didn't want to tell her that the chief hadn't told the press that Roland's death was a homicide until now. Knowing Pell, he wanted to keep it under wraps until he could charge in, shove Morgana off her white stallion, hop on, take the reins, and get all the glory. But what if Frank Holden only did the things he confessed to? *Not* the murder of Roland Cahill?

That was a question that would keep me from sleeping tonight.

Chapter 29

Jenna and I dropped off Morgana's takeout from Mickey's Chowder Shack at Southampton hospital. You would have thought we'd served her a meal from a three-star Michelin restaurant. Jenna tearfully thanked Morgana for capturing Frank Holden, then Morgana deferred to me as the true heroine in his capture—the opposite of how Chief Pell had just painted things at his news conference.

After Nurse Marie shooed us away, Jenna insisted I call Elle to invite her to Enderly Hall for the three o'clock meeting to discuss the showhouse.

I put the call through as we walked to my car in the hospital parking lot. It was fortunate that I'd connected the small wireless microphone to the lapel of my jacket and used the Bluetooth feature on my hearing aids, because when I told her that Jenna planned to move into Enderly Hall, Elle shouted loud enough to puncture an eardrum. "She what! Alone in that rambling mansion! The press is gonna go crazy after that news conference, not to mention those paranormal investigators will be circling to talk to Roland's ghost."

Watching how I answered, because Jenna was looking over at me expectantly, I said, "Yes. We're going to discuss the new date for the showhouse. Jenna wants you to take Vicki's place. Apparently she's gone back to Manhattan."

"What about Roland's funeral? The whole grieving process?"

Ignoring Elle's questions, I said, "She's thinking Labor Day Weekend for the showhouse and she wants you to take Vicki's place. Oh, you'd love to. I will tell her." I gave Jenna a thumbs-up, opened the passenger door of my Woody and closed it after she got inside. Then I whispered into the microphone, "Elle, this will be good for her. Get her mind off things. Just be at Enderly Hall at three."

"Okay. But I think this is a recipe for disaster. She should go away to an island or something and recuperate. I'll be there. Don't forget tomorrow we have to meet on the set of *Mr. & Mrs. Winslow*. I have the perfect 1940s dress for Zoe Stockton to wear, the same one Rita Hayworth wore in *Gilda*. And you promised to bring that silver samovar you found at Fort Pond Thrift that the set designer was looking for."

"I haven't forgotten. Can you do me a favor?" I didn't wait for her to agree. "Please ask Arthur to check Vicki Fortune's apartment in Manhattan. Jenna told me she lives above Veronica's Interiors on Bleecker Street in the Village. Something's up with her leaving town yesterday morning before Frank Holden was even arrested."

"All right. I had the worst nightmare about Jenna last night . . ."

"Oops. Jenna's waiting for me. Gotta go." I pressed the button on the microphone, disconnected the call and got into the car. Once Elle started analyzing her dreams, I would be in for the long haul. Plus, I had my own bad feelings about Jenna staying alone at Enderly Hall.

On the outskirts of Amagansett, Jenna spoke for the first time. "I know I should stop at the rental and get a few more things to bring with me to Enderly Hall. I just can't bear going in and seeing all of Roland's things." She'd been putting up a brave front about her husband's death, which was confirmed when she said, "Meg, I feel such guilt and remorse that I accused Roland of trying to kill me. I wouldn't blame him if he haunted me to the end of my days. And how did I let my obsession with Enderly Hall get so out of control. I'm no better than my father and uncle. I have the resources to build a hundred Enderly Halls. They are just things. I think I got caught up in all the fanfare of having a Stanford White house. It's just a house. No more, no less."

I kept quiet because I knew Jenna had to deal with her feelings. But I wanted to say that even though Roland hadn't been the one behind the wheel of the car that ran her off the road, he still planned on selling Enderly Hall out from under her and also intended to forge architectural drawings that may or may not have been by Stanford White.

"I hope Frank Holden gets the electric chair," she said, anger clouding her green eyes.

I didn't want to tell her that New York didn't have the death penalty, but as Elle had recently reminded me, anger was a step up from depression. I said, "We still have an hour and a half until three. I'll drop you at Enderly and go to Amagansett. Just text me what you need."

"You're a lifesaver. What would I do without you?"

"You'd be fine, Jenna. You're tougher than you think."

And I truly believed it.

About a mile from Enderly Hall, we got caught in a hailstorm. As we pulled through the gates, lightning flashed, with thunder soon following. It wasn't the best welcome home for Jenna, so when she left me to go to the kitchen to make a pot of tea, I ran up to the attic to make sure there weren't any more surprises in Jenna and Roland's bed. There weren't. Just fingerprint dust on top of the nightstand.

I turned to leave, when a large hardcover book under the nightstand caught my eye. It wasn't the book *Stanford White: The Man, Murder, and his Legacy* that caught my eye. It was the gap near the end of the book, where a white envelope peaked out.

I reached down and picked up the book. It had to weigh five pounds. The cover photo showed Stanford White with his handlebar mustache and piercing eyes, standing next to the Triumphal Arch in Washington Square Park.

The story of how he was murdered in 1906 by the jealous husband of his mistress, actress Evelyn Nesbit, had been one of the biggest scandals of the new century. But I wasn't interested in learning about Stanford White's murder, more about Roland Cahill's. Flipping to the center of the book, I took out the envelope. I wasn't surprised when I saw it was the subpoena Roland had been served with on Friday. I quickly glanced at the plaintiff's name, Marjorie Salerno. The name didn't set off any warning bells, but at least I had the court document number, which could be looked up legally. I got out my cell and took photos of all five pages. Then I sent them to Morgana with a note to please look into the case. I returned the envelope to the book and went downstairs.

When Jenna came into the great room a few minutes later, holding a silver tray laden with a full tea service and a plate of shortbread cookies, I had a fire burning in the hearth.

She set the tray down on a small brass serving table. I grabbed a shortbread cookie and said, "I better run to Amagansett. We only have an hour until everyone arrives."

"Thanks, Meg. There's a key hidden under the green urn on the porch."

"Be right back. Text me if you've forgotten anything."

I went into the hallway, grabbed my jacket, then stuck my head through the great room's open doorway to check on Jenna. She was safely ensconced in a cushy armchair by the fire, a cup of chai tea in her hand and a copy of *Architectural Digest* on her lap.

Good. Maybe she would be okay staying alone at Enderly Hall.

I left quietly, going out the front entrance, where I grabbed an umbrella, then hurried to my car. I needed to make this trip a quick one, which would be hard in all this fog and rain. I got into the car, started the engine and headed west toward Amagansett. On the way, I tried Vicki's phone number. A recording said her mailbox was still full. I had ulterior motives for wanting to go to the beach house rental. I wanted to see if there was anything in Vicki's things that might help rid me of this nagging feeling that Vicki had something to do with her former stepfather's murder.

Frank hadn't been formally charged, and until he was, I didn't want to take any chances that Vicki was holed up somewhere, waiting to pounce on Jenna.

It was only a ten-minute drive to the rental Jenna and Roland had called home while they were renovating Enderly Hall. The exterior of the beach house was on the modern side with lots of floor-to-ceiling windows on the second level. I'd been to the house once before and knew that the bedrooms were on the first floor and the great room and kitchen/dining area on the second level. I hadn't needed to use Jenna's key because the door was unlocked. I went inside and made a beeline for the master bedroom, knowing if Vicki was staying here, that would be the one she would choose.

When I stepped through the open doorway, my mouth flew open. What a mess. All the drawers were open and the bed unmade. Vicki had been in a hurry. I did a quick scan for anything left behind. I didn't find a thing except for a pink hairclip. I searched the other three bedrooms, but they looked untouched.

I went up the curving wood staircase to the second floor. The space, with its pitched open-beamed ceiling, reminded me of a loft apartment you mind find in Soho. The only difference was that a Soho loft didn't look out to a white sandy beach and the Atlantic Ocean. I could only imagine the view on a clear day. Literally. Because now all I saw was torrential rain streaming down the windows and sudden flashes of lightning.

The upstairs looked untouched. Not even a dirty dish in the sink. Like me, Vicki must not be a cook. The fridge only had an unopened bottle of *pink* champagne (what a surprise) and something furry in a plastic bag that might, at one time, have been a piece of cheese. There was nothing to be found tying Vicki to Roland's death.

Defeated, I went downstairs and grabbed the things Jenna needed from one of the bedrooms that had been turned into a designer closet. I took one more look around the master bedroom and remembered I'd almost forgotten to check the small trash can in the bathroom, something my father had taught me when discussing some of his cases—not to mention, also shown on every cop/detective show on TV when detectives were looking for clues to someone's whereabouts.

Instead of digging through the trash, I took out the bag lining the wastebasket and tied it off. I'd take it with me and look at it later. I ran out the door, locked it and put the key back under the urn. It was two forty, soon everyone would be arriving at Enderly Hall.

Everyone but Vicki Fortune, that is.

Chapter 30

Nate and Kuri were seated next to each other on the great room's sofa. When I'd pulled through Enderly's gates, they'd followed behind me in Nate's black Infiniti. Elle had texted me that something big had come up, but she would try to make it by three thirty.

Jenna was in the armchair by the fire, and I'd chosen to sit on the window seat with its mullioned windows that looked out toward the gazebo. It had stopped raining, but the fog and mist remained, the sky still dark and threatening.

When the doorbell chimed, I shot up and said I'd get it, thinking Elle was arriving earlier than expected. I wanted to make sure Elle didn't say anything to upset Jenna; she always meant well, but like Jenna, Elle could be an alarmist.

It wasn't Elle. It was Freya, who had brought her sister Emma, who was in a wheelchair. "Hurry, come in, it's nasty out there," I said as Freya pushed the wheelchair through the open doorway. "How did you get up the steps?" I asked. "You should have called on the intercom, someone would have come out to help you."

Freya looked down at her sister and said, "Emma can walk with assistance, but only for short distances. Meg, I'd like you to meet my sister, Emma."

Emma looked up at me, her pale blue eyes almost ghostly, matching her pale skin. She reminded me of an elfin fairy, or a similar ethereal creature. Her left hand was bent at the wrist, her fingers cupped inward, close to the waist of her floral cotton dress. I would guess she was in her mid-twenties, at least fifteen years younger than Freya. Emma extended her right hand and said with much effort, "I Em-ma Po-ost."

"Nice to meet you, Emma Post." Then I said to Freya, "Everyone's in the great room."

I followed behind them. Freya went over to Jenna, apologizing for bringing Emma and explaining that her sister's caregiver had been called in for jury duty, adding that all she needed was a quiet place where she could leave her with a stack of adult coloring books and markers. "You love your coloring books, don't you, Emma?" she said, glancing down at her sister with love.

Emma glanced up at Freya but didn't smile. However, her

cornflower blue eye lit up when Freya took out a book from a pocket behind the wheelchair and showed it to the room like she was an elementary school teacher introducing a new book at circle time. The coloring book was titled *Exotic Birds*.

"This is your new book we got from East Hampton Bookworks, isn't it, Emma? What's this on the cover of your new book?" Freya asked her sister.

"Bird," Emma replied, the word *bird* coming out in four syllables instead of one. Emma resembled a bird, a canary with her yellow print dress, petite form, and fair hair.

"What a wonderful subject," Jenna said. "Of course Emma is welcome. Anytime. How about you take her into the study? Does she need to be sitting at a table?"

"No," Freya answered, "I brought Emma's lap desk. The study will be perfect, I'll be able to see her through the glass doors.

Freya wheeled Emma into the study and we waited until she returned before discussing the future of the showhouse. Everyone agreed that Labor Day would be the best time. Freya, Kuri, and I agreed that we would present Jenna with our receipts for the things we'd brought in and she would reimburse us. Jenna told us she wouldn't change a thing and looked forward to living among our choices.

The subject of the trashed Shepherds Cottage was brought up. Jenna had contacted her homeowner's insurance and they would be by first thing in the morning. Then with teary eyes, she told us that Roland's ashes, per his will, would be sent to his family crypt in Queens, and his wake, sometime in the near future, here at Enderly Hall. "I just need some time to get things together. I don't want the press to interfere with our celebration of his life and I'd also like to see justice for that fiend who murdered him. I hope you all understand."

"Of course we understand," Nate said.

Jenna got up from the armchair and faced us. "Do you think I'm making a big mistake, rescheduling the showhouse?" She wrung her hands together and pink flushed her cheeks. I couldn't bear for the old Jenna to surface, second-guessing herself and playing the victim. "Who would want to come see a house where someone had been murdered?" she asked.

A lot of people, I thought, but instead I said, "One day at a time, Jenna. We're all here for you. I'm your neighbor, remember? Roland wanted the showhouse. Opening Enderly Hall to the public would be part of his legacy."

"You're right, Meg," she said, collapsing back into the armchair. "One thing that is going to change is I am removing anything Vicki put in her rooms for the showcase. Elle Warner is going to take over. Vicki never had a kind word for Roland or was appreciative of anything we've done for her. If it wasn't for Roland funneling money into Veronica's Interiors, the company would have folded years ago. Now that he's gone, she won't get a red cent from me."

I thought it was the perfect time to exit the room and find out what was keeping Elle. It had been a long day, and I'd been neglecting my chubby kitten, plus I had an ulterior motive of walking the beach toward Patrick's cottage on the off chance he would see me and we could discuss all the new developments.

"Can I get anyone something to drink? I'm parched," I said, standing and heading toward the door leading to the kitchen.

Everyone declined.

"Freya, how about Emma. Can I bring her anything?"

"Oh, that would be great. Just some water, no ice and a straw. Plastic or paper cup if you have."

Looking toward Jenna, who was now staring into the fire, I realized I'd have to find the cups on my own. "Okay, I'll be right back."

I found a stack of plastic cups next to a box of paper straws in a pantry the size of my kitchen. Everything was neat and organized, with enough staple ingredients to rival those shown on cooking competition shows. Jenna was a good cook, but I think half of the items were meant to be on display for the showhouse. The vintage aqua glass Ball jars that were filled with dried beans had come from Mabel and Elle's. Open shelving held dinnerware in the Spode pattern that Jenna had been collecting over the years, enough to service a royal banquet at Kensington Palace. I took a cup and a straw, then walked into the kitchen, where I grabbed a bottle of water from one of the refrigerated drawers to the right of the double farm sink.

Before pouring the water into the Emma's cup, I sent a quick text to Elle: *Where are you? We're all leaving soon.*

She answered like her fingers had already been poised over her phone's keyboard. *Don't go anywhere. I'm waiting for a call from Arthur. He said he has some important news to tell me. I'm scared. Need my friend. Be there in fifteen.*

I'm here. I'm sure it's nothing.

Boy, was I wrong.

Chapter 31

Before going back to the great room, I brought Emma her water, holding it to her lips while she drank. She didn't say thank you, but nodded her head and smiled instead.

"What a beautiful picture. You have a real talent." I wasn't just serving platitudes, her choice of colored markers for the peacock she was working on was spot-on. "When you're finished, I think that could hang in a museum." She gave me a puzzled look. "When you're finished, I bet Freya will hang it on your refrigerator." That brought a big grin.

She carefully took four markers in her right hand and held them up to me. Her left hand remained stationary. "Do you want me to choose your next color? She nodded her head yes. I chose an iridescent royal blue. Emma put the other markers on the tray, and I handed her the marker. In a few deft strokes, she filled in the area around one of the peacock's eyes in its tail. I had to wonder if she'd ever seen a peacock before. She must have because she'd gotten the color and shading exactly right. And there wasn't one area where she'd gone outside the lines.

"Do you need anything else, Emma?" She shook her head no. "I'll leave your water then." I placed the plastic cup in the cupholder on her lap desk and noticed the tube coming from her right ear. Freya had told me on Friday that her sister had cochlear implants. I tapped her on the shoulder, and when she looked up at me, I tucked my hair behind my ears and pointed one at a time to my hearing aids, then to her cochlear implant. I gave her a thumbs-up.

At first, I didn't think the fact that we were kindred spirits in the hearing department had registered. Then she put down her marker and reached for my hand and squeezed it. I squeezed back, fighting the scratchy feeling at the back of my throat.

After she released my hand, I said goodbye and went toward the glass doors leading into the great room. I pulled the brass handle and opened the door. Just as I was about to walk through, Elle burst into the room. She was drenched from the rain, mascara trailing down her cheeks like she was an Alice Cooper groupie. She stood on the Persian rug, water dripping from her black raincoat.

What could be so important that she wasn't cognizant of the value of the rug?

With her next words I found out.

"Arthur called. They just found Vicki Fortune's body at the bottom of a ravine nicknamed Massacre Valley."

Massacre Valley was a nickname for a Montaukett Native American site that butted up to Montauk Manor.

"Is she dead?" Freya asked.

"Yes."

Tough Kuri, who'd stood up for herself with Roland, looked panicked. She asked, "What does this mean? Is the killer coming after everyone who has something to do with the showhouse? Picking them off one by one, like in an Agatha Christie book? I thought the guy was in jail?" Kuri grabbed Nate's hand. I saw him squeeze hers back, then she pulled her hand away and placed it on her lap. No one noticed but me.

"He is in custody," Nate said, locking his eyes on Kuri's face. "He probably killed her before Chief Pell caught him last night."

I opened my mouth to correct him that it was Officer Moss who should get the credit, then thought better of it. If Nate and the chief were pals, nothing I said would change that. Morgana was right, we didn't want to rock the already sinking boat when it came to communication with the Suffolk County Police.

Jenna jumped up. Addressing Elle, she said, "Could it have been an accident?"

Elle said, "No. It wasn't an accident."

"How was she killed?" Freya asked.

"Choked."

Jenna let out a little cry. "The same as Roland." Then she promptly fainted into the armchair.

Nate got up and ran to her, gently slapping her cheeks until she opened her eyes. "Jenna, you need to be strong. Vicki was killed by that same maniac they have in custody. He can't hurt anyone."

Not necessarily true. I believed we had a different maniac we should be looking for.

Vicki went missing sometime early Sunday morning. Mac Zagan said that Frank Holden had spent Saturday night in the lighthouse with the paranormal crew, only leaving when I showed up Sunday afternoon after meeting with Ashley and Justin at their future cottage. I didn't speak up, knowing we would have to wait for the medical examiner to give us the exact time of Vicki's death.

If she was killed during the hours Mac said Frank was at the lighthouse, that meant he hadn't killed Vicki. And if he hadn't killed Vicki, what were the chances he hadn't killed Roland.

Pretty darn good, I thought.

It appeared Vicki and Roland's killer might be in this room. The Barrett blotches started their ascent, and I had the urge to run out of the front door, pulling Elle and Jenna with me.

Wait. If it hadn't been Frank,. could I be wrong? Could Jenna have killed both her husband and Vicki?

I hoped not. But just in case, I wouldn't be inviting Jenna to stay with me. And until the real killer was caught, I planned to stay away from Enderly Hall. Let Nate, Jenna's cousin, take care of her. Oops. Unless he was the murderer with the help of his adulterous girlfriend Kuri. Then there was Freya: if she was having an affair with Roland and something went south, she could be our killer. But why would she kill Vicki?

Longing to leave, I stood up and said, "Nate, I'm sure you're right."

Even though I knew — he was *dead* wrong.

Chapter 32

I almost collapsed liked Jenna had done earlier when I walked into my cozy, welcoming, serene—extra emphasis on *serene*—cottage. The first thing I did after taking off my raincoat was to light a fire. As if on cue, Jo got up from her favorite chair, which also happened to by *my* favorite chair, and rubbed her Maine coon body against my legs, sending up plumes of cat hair. I wasn't fooled that she'd missed me. She just wanted to be fed.

The next thing I did was go to the landline phone and check my messages. There were six from Cole, and zero from Patrick. Cole had also left messages on my cell phone that had been translated to text. They all basically said the same thing: We need to talk. I need to explain something. *Blah, blah, blah.*

I deleted them all.

Earlier, after the police arrived at Enderly Hall to officially talk to Jenna, and asking her permission to get entry to the beach rental that Vicki had been staying at, I'd pulled Elle aside and told her about Frank spending Saturday at the lighthouse and that he didn't leave the park until around one in the afternoon on Sunday. She'd promised to pass it on to her fiancé. I was happy he would know about it because Morgana was out of commission until she was well enough to leave Southampton Hospital, and there was no chance I would tell Chief Pell.

Then I'd had a thought. Morgana could let her fingers do the walking from her hospital bed. I called Morgana and told her about Frank's possible alibi for Vicki's murder. "Holy moly!' she'd yelled into my ear. "I need to get out of this prison. There still might be a killer on the prowl!" I'd also asked her what Vicki had been choked with. Instead of an extension cord, she'd told me the killer had used one of Vicki's pink scarves. I could tell by the hesitation in Morgana's voice that she was starting to believe that Frank Holden hadn't killed Roland or Vicki, but she also warned me that before doing anything, we would have to wait for the coroner's report. Then she promised she would personally have a talk with Mac Zagan and also get ahold of footage from Montauk Point Lighthouse Park's security cameras.

There was nothing else I could do.

Well, maybe something.

After feeding Jo a dozen cat treats, because it was too soon for dinner, I grabbed my raincoat, ran out the French doors to my deck, then down the steps to the beach. I had one destination in mind—to see someone with the initials P.S. and talk over the latest developments.

There was some good news as I followed the shore west: the rain, thunder and lightning had stopped, but a hazy mist remained. That was the best I could come up with as I looked toward the turbulent sea. The whitecaps and pounding surf were a mirror to my churning thoughts. I broke into a fast walk, worried Roland's and Vicki's killer might take advantage of the mist and my hearing loss to sneak up behind me before I could reach safe harbor. Safe harbor in the form of Patrick Seaton.

I didn't have to walk the mile to his cottage because up ahead I saw the outline of his tall body. He and Charlie were standing in front of the nature preserve where we left each other dead poets' verses in the sand. I hurried toward them and was thrilled when Patrick smiled as soon as his eyes met mine. Charlie bounded up to me and licked my hand. I wasn't sure if it was in greeting or because my hand still had the scent of Jo's cat treats.

"Fancy meeting you on a day like this," Patrick said. In his right hand he was holding a thin piece of driftwood resembling a cane; its tip had a carved point. Next to him, written in the sand, was a single word—*Who*.

I laughed. "That's one fancy stick you've got there, Mr. Seaton. No wonder your words come out so much clearer than mine."

"Yes. Now you know my secret. I whittled it myself. I have a heck of a time keeping it out of Charlie's mouth."

"Whittled," I said, grinning. "Haven't heard that old-fashioned term used in, well . . . ever."

"Okay, carved. Better?"

It felt good to laugh. I wished I could just forget about death and murder for a while. But here I was, once again in the thick of things. Maybe Elle was right. I should run for hills, or at least hide out in my cottage at the first inkling something sinister was about to happen. Death in the Hamptons was taking its toll. Murder was a cute game of whodunit in my cozy mystery books. But when life imitates art, there seemed to be something not so pleasing about flesh-and-bone corpses.

"So, what were you about to pen in the sand?" I asked, petting the velvety dark gray fur on Charlie's back. "Finish what you were writing. Then I'll guess which dead poet's quote you've chosen."

"I doubt you'll guess this author."

"A challenge! Something I can't resist." That answered the question I'd just asked myself about getting involved in mysteries.

He looked over at me and gave me a knowing look. Then he took his stick and wrote *naught suspects is easily deceived.*"

"Who naught suspects is easily deceived," I said, reading the apropos verse out loud. "That's it? Only one line?" I racked my brain for who it could be. It could have been a hundred dead poets. "I'm stumped. How about just giving me one initial for the poet's last name?"

He quickly added a *P.*

"Pope?"

"Nope. I'm telling you—you'll never get it."

"Poe? Pitt? Proust? Plato? Procter?"

"Nope. Nope. Nope. Nope. Nope."

I put both hands in the air. "I give. Who is it?"

"Petrarch."

"You certainly got me on that one. Never heard of them. Male or female?"

"Male. Like Shakespeare, he was known for his sonnets."

"Of course. Most classical poets were men. Only a handful were of the fairer sex. But think of all the female unpublished poets who stuffed their poems in drawers, or hid them under their beds."

"Like Dickinson," he said.

I gazed into his eyes. Today they were dark green. "Exactly. Only about twelve of her eighteen thousand poems were published when she was alive."

"It's a writer's curse," he said. "Even though you might not get published, you keep on writing."

Charlie barked, interrupting us. She had wandered away and returned with an old tennis ball someone had left on the beach. Patrick reached down and held out his hand, palm up. Charlie dropped it into his hand. He tossed it and she went bounding away, getting lost in the tall seagrass in front of the nature preserve's cyclone fence. Patrick said, "I'm trying to keep her away from the water today. It's too cold for an outdoor shower." He took a hand towel from his back pocket and wiped his hands.

What a guy, I thought. Patrick had to have some flaws. So far, I hadn't seen any red flags. Even his anger over me invading his privacy seemed warranted.

"How's your murder mystery progressing?" he asked.

There it was. A chink in his armor. I realized he hadn't contacted me once since the morning we spent going over the suspect board. Not one peep.

"I've tried to call you on your cell, but your mailbox is full," he said, as if reading my mind.

Because of all of Cole's voice mails filling up my mailbox.

Sweet relief. *Patrick likes me. He really likes me,* I thought, referring to actress Sally Field's famous Academy Award speech when she won an Oscar for *Norma Rae.*

I put Patrick back in the to-good-to-be-true column, then filled him in on the latest about Frank Holden's arrest, Morgana being in the hospital, and now, Vicki's death. Or murder.

After he gave my words some thought, he said, "I told you not to take out the wife as a possible suspect."

"I still don't believe Jenna's involved. But she's the only one with ties to both Vicki and Roland."

"Does she have an alibi for when you think Vicki Fortune was killed?"

I shivered, and he noticed. "Let's go to your place or mine to go over our suspects. It's getting cold."

Before I could answer, he took the decision out of my hands. "Let's make it mine. I don't think you want Charlie tracking sand all over your cottage."

I didn't protest. Thinking about Jo and Charlie meeting for the first time, it might not go too well on Jo's part. Although she had gotten along with Cole's dog, Tripod. Charlie tracking sand into my cottage wouldn't bother me in the least. It was something every beachfront property owner lived with—sandy toes and salty kisses . . .

The first thing I noticed when I walked into Patrick's cottage was that the photo of his wife and child was no longer on the mantel. Where had it gone? Its absence tugged at my heart.

He led me into the kitchen and offered me a glass of wine, which I accepted. "You're not drinking?" I asked. Maybe he didn't drink because of what happened to his family. But then I thought back to last New Year's Eve, when I saw him drinking a glass of champagne.

"I'm on a deadline for the next *Mr. & Mrs. Winslow* script. I think coffee, lots of coffee, is a better choice."

"Does that mean they'll be keeping you on as the screenwriter for all eight episodes?"

"Looks that way," he said modestly, shrugging his broad shoulders. "I would keep it under wraps for the time being, though. You know showbiz. It took four years after one of my thrillers was optioned before it finally went into production." He grabbed a stemless wineglass from the open shelving by the sink and placed it on the counter. Next, he reached for a bottle of wine from the wine cooler under the center island. Again, I thought of how well Patrick and my father would get along in the kitchen, and how well I would get along consuming whatever gourmet goodies they presented to me on their silver platters.

"Rosé good?" he asked, holding up the bottle sporting a Wolffer Estate label. My mind fast-forwarded to the local winery's Candlelight Fridays: wine tasting, small tapas plates, and romantic candlelit tables butting up to acres of grapevines . . . I realized he was waiting for my answer.

"Yes. Rosé's perfect. I loved your pilot script when I read it."

"You read it?"

"Yes. I never guessed whodunit." I didn't elaborate that I'd read it while on Shelter Island last December, not wanting to bring up the last murder case I'd been involved in. Instead, I said as he uncorked the bottle and poured it into my glass, "The color pink reminds me of Vicki Fortune. She always wore pink." Then I remembered that her pink iPad was in the seat pocket of my Wagoneer. I didn't mention it because he might be one of those by-the-book types, wanting me to turn it in to the cops. The same reason I didn't tell Morgana about it, not thinking at the time that Vicki was dead. I would give it to her.

After I looked at it.

"Unless you have a dinner date, would you like to go upstairs and rework our suspect board?"

"No dinner date," I stuttered. "Good idea."

A few minutes later, we were both staring at our suspect board, like there was something obvious we'd missed.

"See anything useful?" he asked.

"No. You?"

"No. Why don't you have a seat at my desk and tell me what I've missed since the last time you were here. Then I'll update the board."

Before sitting down, I'd had to remove a spiral notebook from the chair. It was open to a page with Patrick's writing on it. At first, I thought he was in the middle of writing a poem, but then I saw that above the words he'd jotted musical notes. Patrick was a songwriter. Wow. What didn't he do? I glanced across the room and saw his guitar leaning against a wood stool—no longer facing the wall, like it had last time I'd been up here. For a moment, I wished instead of going over a list of murder suspects—a dwindling list—that we were sitting on the beach, him with his guitar, me with my glass of wine, Charlie frolicking in the surf.

Breaking into my Fantasy Island scenario—after all, Montauk was on an island, Long Island—Patrick said, "You do know that Mr. Holden could have killed Mr. Cahill, and someone else could have killed Ms. Fortune."

"If you want to go down that path," I said, "then perhaps Vicki killed her former stepfather, and someone else found out and killed her."

"Then there's scenario three. The obvious, but most confounding. Kuri, Nate, Freya, or Jenna killed them both."

"Well, there's also the possibility, like in one of Dame Christie's books, that they all did it together."

He threw his hands in the air. "Okay, I give. Let's just concentrate on Vicki Fortune and what you know. Nothing else has changed with any of the others, has it?"

"Well, I'm pretty sure Nate and Kuri are in a relationship, and she's married. Also, Nate is related to Jenna through a great-great-aunt on her father's side. There's the possibility that if Jenna dies, he might inherit. But why kill Roland and Vicki? Jenna had a prenup.

Nothing new with Freya, except those photos I told you about, where she and Roland were holding hands, along with the fact she wasn't invited to be a decorator and had approached Roland to be on the team. I know Jenna was mad at Vicki for telling the police that she and Roland had gotten in a fight the night before he died." Patrick raised an eyebrow, but I kept talking, "As for alibis for Vicki's murder, we will have to wait until we hear from Morgana about the time of death." I realized he didn't know that Morgana and I were friends, so I gave him a brief outline of what happened Saturday night with Frank Holden.

"I saw it on the local news that he'd been caught and had wounded an officer, but there was no mention of you being involved."

"Just a little," I said, avoiding his gaze.

"Why do I doubt that."

He took an eraser and removed Vicki as a suspect, then added her name under Roland's. With his back to me he said something that I didn't catch. Then he must have remembered about my hearing loss. He turned to face me. "The only ties between Vicki and Roland Cahill are the interior design business . . ."

"Veronica's Interiors. Yes. He was the company's chief operating officer, controlled the purse strings."

"Well, I don't know what it all means. Except one thing. "You need to stay away from Enderly Hall."

"But . . ."

"We should just give up for now. Finish your wine, I'll heat up some leftover osco bucco from Pondfare, their portions are ridiculous, then I'll walk you home."

Before I could give him a resounding *Yes!* he added, "Unless you already have plans?"

"Nope," I answered quickly. Maybe too quickly. Then I decided, what did it matter?

I wasn't the type to play games or hard to get.

Chapter 33

I took off my fleece jacket and draped it across Jo's chubby body, only her furry raccoon head was sticking out. The temperature in the cottage was bordering on freezing, and I didn't blame Jo for not thanking me. I prayed that come Memorial Day things would warm up, or I'd have to invest in portable heaters for Elle and Arthur's extravaganza, only three weeks away.

Patrick had left me at the bottom of the steps leading up to my cottage. Before coming inside, I'd grabbed Vicki's pink iPad from the backseat of my car. Did I feel a stab of guilt for not mentioning its existence to Morgana or Patrick? You betcha. But in my defense, I never suspected that Vicki would be dead. Let alone murdered.

After feeding Jo, I listened to a voice mail from Elle. She told me that her fiancé had called to tell her they found Vicki's pink van parked in front of Veronica's Interiors. If Vicki never left Montauk, then that meant her killer went to the beach house and packed up Vicki's things to make it look like she'd left for Manhattan. Someone didn't expect Vicki's body to be found and was trying to make it look like she'd left town.

I made a fire, stared into it for a few seconds, then sat on my white down-cushioned sofa and toggled Vicki's iPad to the On position, bringing up a screen showing Vicki's face. Sadness enveloped me. I realized she wasn't a cardboard cutout (pink cutout) figure. She was flesh and bone. Or had been. Who would claim her body after the M.E. was done with it? Jenna?

Feeling like a voyeur, I searched the iPad like a forensic CSI— well, more like a novice forensic CSI. I was about to give up when I saw an unedited video where Vicki was in the bathroom giving makeup tips for her cyber fans. There was a knock at the door; the screen was covered but the audio was still recording. I played it once. Then twice. Then three times. But because of my hearing loss, I couldn't get a fix on who had come into Vicki's Montauk Manor hotel room. The voice was female. That was all I knew. It wasn't Frank Holden, and it wasn't Nate Klein. That left Jenna, Kuri and Freya. I searched the video for some kind of time stamp but didn't see one. However, in the beginning of the video, you could see sunlight coming in from a window behind Vicki's head. The only day there had been sunlight in the past few weeks was yesterday.

Jo had waddled over to where I was sitting, jumped onto the sofa and sat on top of the iPad. "Bad girl! This is evidence in a murder case." She didn't budge and I was worried her weight would cause the screen to implode. I changed tactics. *Praise your children, never scold* was a new mantra I was trying out on Miss Chubs. "What a good kitty. What have you been up to today? How about some stinky, I mean delicious, sardines for a reward."

That did the trick. She got up, stretched, then hopped off the sofa and headed to the kitchen. After turning off the iPad, I went to the bathroom for some rubbing alcohol and cotton balls and erased all of my prints. If Chief Pell wasn't in the equation, I would have just handed it over to Morgana as is.

Then I went into the kitchen to feed Jo. "Oh, you bad cat!" I screeched when I saw all the garbage covering the kitchen floor. I must have left the cupboard door open that held the small covered bin of food that would go in my organic compost pile. Odorous items. The garbage can was one of those step-on ones. Jo had obviously stepped on it, and had tipped it over.

I removed a clean garbage bag, broom and dustpan from under the sink, put on rubber gloves, then got down on my hands and knees. I swept the garbage into the dustpan while Jo sniffed around. Nothing was to her liking. Too many vegetables. She'd already scavenged the good stuff. She looked at me expectantly. When she saw my expression, she knew that her snack of sardines was off the table. And would be forevermore.

A few minutes later, as I was tying off the garbage bag, it hit me.

The trash bag that I'd taken from the Amagansett rental master bathroom was still in the back of my car.

After scrubbing the floor with wood floor cleaner, I ran out to the car to retrieve the bag. It was a garbage kind of night.

What I found inside was a revelation. So was what I'd found online, after a little digging.

I grabbed my jacket off the chair, and sneezed a few times from the cat hair. Jo looked over at me expectantly. I said sternly, "Don't you even! Momma has to go talk to someone."

Someone who might turn out to be our murderer.

Chapter 34

"Meg, what are you doing out on a night like this?"

A good question, I thought, glancing around at Freya's mammoth home in East Hampton.

"Come into the kitchen. I have the kettle plugged in. I was just going to make a cup of tea."

I didn't answer her, just followed her into the huge kitchen. I took a seat at a long wood farm table that smelled of beeswax and lemon. She'd told me she was a big fan of Grimes House Antiques, and it showed in all the pieces she used sparingly in her décor.

"Is everything okay? There hasn't been another murder, has there? Jenna's okay, I hope. That poor thing," she said, wringing her hands.

I opened my mouth to speak, then shut it. Looking back at me on the refrigerator, behind a magnet that said *Star Student,* was the completed page of the jewel-toned peacock that Freya's sister, Emma, had been working on earlier today at Enderly Hall.

Something must have shown on my face because Freya turned to me and asked, "So why are you really here? You've found out about my connection to Roland Cahill, haven't you? Even so, I didn't kill him." She held the unplugged electric kettle in her hand—a shaky hand that just might take it upon itself to toss scalding water all over me. I looked toward the wood block holding carving knives. Freya followed my gaze, blinking rapidly. She grabbed the papa bear of the group from one of the slots with her free hand. She put the kettle down, but still held the knife, pointing it downward in front of her.

"I just have a couple questions. But they can wait," I answered, my voice betraying me with its mouselike squeak.

"You must also know about Emma. I can tell by the way you looked at her artwork." She and the knife stepped closer to me.

"Oh, you mean about the lawsuit your sister won against Roland Cahill. That's why I'm here. I came to tell you that your secret is safe with me, because it has no bearing on the murders. You see, Frank Holden was caught on camera in the parking lot of the hotel where Vicki was staying, which coordinated with the coroner's estimation of her time of death. For Emma's sake, I thought you'd be relieved that you wouldn't be a suspect when they found out about Roland's negligence that caused your family so much pain. She's such a special girl." The *special girl* part was true.

Freya looked down at her hands. Still holding the knife, she went to the refrigerator, opened it and took out a covered pie plate. Turning to me, she said, "How about a slice of raspberry pie? My mother's recipe and Emma's favorite."

"Sure."

She got out two plates from behind a glass cupboard door, placed them on the counter, and then cut two slices of pie. After putting the knife in the sink, she used a sterling pie server to remove the slices, then put one on each plate. She put the pie server in the sink, grabbed a couple of forks from a drawer, then brought the plates and forks to the table.

"Well, it's a blessing that Montauk Manor had surveillance cameras," she said, taking a seat across from me. "And, as to the other thing, yes, Roland Cahill was the cause of all of Emma's developmental problems. I had already moved out of the house and was at Stony Brook University when my mother, stepfather, and Emma, only a toddler at the time, moved into Roland's condo of horrors."

"So, Emma is your half sister?"

"Yes," she said, glancing at my uneaten pie.

I quickly took a bite. She got up and returned with two napkins, not paper but pressed white linen napkins. She handed me one, and I wiped my mouth. Raspberry filling stained the napkin, looking like blood. Hopefully not a foreshadowing of the rest of my visit. "Oops, sorry."

"Don't worry, Emma's live-in caretaker, Rosie, loves to do laundry and iron. I don't know what I'd do without her. She also loves Emma like she's her own. After what that monster did, concealing all that poisonous lead and paying off the building inspector, it wasn't surprising when I heard that Frank Holden had been arrested for killing Roland. People are still suing Roland for other things he's done: not removing asbestos, faulty wiring, gas leaks. The only blessing in the whole mess was that Emma wasn't part of any class action lawsuit. Her case was the first. And so far, she's received the most money. Every penny going to her care. But money can't change what's happened to her."

I glanced again at Emma's art on the refrigerator. The page had come from the adult coloring book titled *Exotic Birds* — the same title listed on a receipt from East Hampton Bookworks. The same receipt I'd found in the garbage bag I'd taken from Vicki's room at the Amagansett beach house. I'd gone online and put the names Emma Post and Roland Cahill into the search bar and found that Roland had been sued for covering up the existence of lead paint and lead pipes in a prewar building he'd renovated into high-priced condos. The name of his company back then was Five Star Construction. I'd also found a news article explaining that Emma had been exposed to lead paint after peeling the wallpaper next to her crib and eating it. The toxicity of the lead paint that had been clinging to the backside of the wallpaper caused her severe mental and physical damage. I also found a photo of Emma in her wheelchair, along with a couple who must have been Freya's mother and stepfather, standing next to the lawyer who'd won the lawsuit.

Now I was in a quandary. I'd just lied to Freya about Frank Holden being on Montauk Manor's surveillance camera. And Freya had just proved that she was guilty of killing Vicki by naming Montauk Manor as Vicki's hotel. I hadn't told anyone but Morgana and Elle where Vicki had been staying Saturday night; I'd even booked it under my name. It must have been Freya's voice on Vicki's iPad Sunday morning. I'm sure a forensics team would be able to match it.

On the way to Freya's house, I'd told everything I'd learned about Freya to Morgana. Morgana had warned me not to confront Freya, saying she was sending a patrol car to Freya's address. Of course, I hadn't listened. Before the police arrived to arrest her, I had to make sure Freya was guilty.

And if she had killed Vicki, then I wanted to know why. Not, however, at the price of becoming her next victim. I had to tread carefully. One thing I'd learned from the past, never back a killer into the corner.

"Thanks for the pie," I said, standing up, wanting to leave before the police arrived. Freya was guilty, and I needed to vamoose.

Unfortunately, that didn't happen, because as I was putting my plate in the sink, I heard sirens. Darn! I glanced into the sink at the knife covered with red gel, half thinking of grabbing it and running for the door.

Too late.

Freya tapped me on the shoulder. I turned to see she had a clean knife from the knife holder. Not as big as the one in the sink, but big enough.

She said, "I'm not letting them arrest me for killing someone who should have been sent to prison for life. Roland Cahill didn't deserve to live. He laughed when I told him who I was and what I wanted. Which was for him to apologize to Emma and to use his new wife's money to pay out all the other victims' families he'd destroyed. He'd filed chapter eleven after Emma's case, and since then, not one person has received a penny in any of the cases that followed Emma's settlement." Beads of sweat bloomed above her upper lip. "When we were at the pavilion, I took advantage when Roland turned around to answer a call about *another* lawsuit he was involved in. I pulled the extension cord from the socket and slipped it around his neck. And pulled.

"At first, he thought the choking was some kind of amorous *Fifty Shades of Grey* move. I'd been leading him on since I joined the decorators for the showhouse. Just to watch him fall. I planned on tricking him onto my show as an up-and-coming Hampton contractor, then instead, doing an exposé on all his heinous past acts. Destroying him where he lived—inside his inflated ego. I heard him arguing with Jenna the night before, so I knew she wouldn't miss him. She'd be better off."

"But you set Jenna up by sending that text." I inched my way toward the open doorway.

"I had to. You don't understand how important I am to Emma. With a strength I didn't know I had, I dragged Roland's body down the steps to the beach. He was still alive, so I took off my jacket and used it to pick up his head, not wanting to leave prints or DNA. Then I banged the back of his head against a sharp rock to finish him off. Then I unwrapped the extension cord from his neck and threw it into the ocean. I hadn't counted on it washing onto shore. Later in the afternoon, I sent Jenna the text from Roland's phone, climbed down to the beach and put the phone in his cold, dead hand."

I tried to bite my tongue, but it still wagged, "Why did you kill Vicki?"

"Saturday morning, Vicki saw me with Roland in the pavilion.

And then when I left Enderly Hall Saturday night, she was waiting for me. She told me she was happy that I'd killed him. But that didn't mean she'd keep quiet about things. She wanted money. That wasn't initially what set me off. It was when Vicki saw Emma. Rosie came to pick me up from Enderly Hall because I'd come in the morning with the camera crew so they could do some test shots. Vicki saw Emma in the backseat and said she looked familiar. I knew then, I couldn't spend the rest of my life waiting for her to blackmail me. Emma needed me."

"But wasn't the trial fifteen years ago? What were the chances Vicki would recognize her?" I asked, trying to keep her talking until the police arrived.

"I realize that now. I wasn't thinking straight. I just knew I couldn't go to jail and leave Emma. Vicki called me from her hotel room later that night and said she changed her mind, she couldn't keep quiet about me and Roland. She said after she checked out of her room at Montauk Manor, she planned to go to the police. I pretended to understand, saying it was better if it was all out in the open, all the while maintaining my innocence.

Early Sunday morning, I went to her room with ten thousand in cash and a promise to feature Veronica's Interiors on my show. I even offered to make her my cohost. She fell for it. I talked her into getting in my car to go to the studio and do some headshots, telling her I had a team waiting."

Freya stepped closer, knife in hand. I pivoted to the right and said, "When she got in your car, you grabbed the scarf around her neck and choked her with it. Then dumped her body."

"The narcissistic thing. She was primping in the car's vanity mirror. Didn't see it coming. Why couldn't it have been her that ate the lead paint in one of her former stepfather's buildings, not Emma? Her mother, Veronica, was married to Roland during the time of the trial. After getting rid of her, I drove her pink van to Manhattan. I parked it in front of Veronica's Interiors, then took the Hamptons Jitney back to East Hampton."

"How come Roland didn't recognize you as Emma's sister?"

"I was in Europe, finding myself, when the case finally went to trial. It took five years after my mother and stepfather filed for the case to be settled. Roland's lawyers kept postponing and postponing. I wasn't here for her or my mother, but after my mother and stepfather passed, I made up for it by taking care of Emma."

Another thing I'd learned. Well, maybe not. When a killer started confessing and you were the only one in earshot, you better make a move. Dead men, or women, tell no tales.

I pushed her back against the table and headed for the door. But she grabbed me by the back of my sweater. The sirens sounded close. Just not close enough.

She held the tip of the blade against my jugular. "I'm sorry, Ms. Barrett, but Emma needs me."

"The police are minutes away. How will you explain things?"

"Hand me your phone!"

I did. She turned it off. "Now your car keys. Move slowly."

I reached in my pocket and handed them to her.

"Now move it. Hurry."

"Which is it? Slowly or hurry?" I was trying to buy time, but she wasn't going for it. She pressed the tip of the knife into the middle of my back.

"You were never here. They have no evidence I killed Roland or Vicki."

I tested her by staying put. I shouldn't have. I felt the blade make contact with flesh, and then there was a wet searing sensation between my shoulder blades.

"Move."

"Freya," a voice said from behind us.

We turned to see a woman standing in the open doorway that led to the dining room. She was elderly, with short gray curly hair and a pudgy wrinkled face. Behind her round wire-rimmed glasses were kind, tear-filled eyes. She held something white in her hand that had a green light at its base. "I heard everything on the monitor, Freya. You can't do what you're thinking."

I saw Freya look to the top of the refrigerator, where a baby monitor stood, its green light matching the one in the elderly woman's hand.

"Rosie, I have to. I can't go to jail. What about Emma?" Freya sobbed.

"I won't leave Emma. Now, give me the knife, dear."

Freya dropped the knife. It clattered to the floor, just as the door opened and Officer Morgana Moss, dressed in a hospital gown, robe and slippers, stepped in, gun drawn and pointed at Freya. She was followed inside by three uniformed East Hampton Town Police officers.

"You lucked out this time, Ms. Barrett," Morgana said. "Now we're even."

I ran to her and gave her a big hug, feeling a trio of IV tubes under the robe's fabric on her right arm.

It was good to have friends in high places.

Chapter 35

I handed Elle the top from the blanket chest, which had been split in half by Frank Holden when he'd been looking for his treasure. She moaned, "Such an atrocity, I'm surprised at how great Jenna is handling everything. Heck, I'm surprised at how great you are handling everything."

"Almost losing your life makes you realize how important the people in your life are. Not things."

"Does that mean you don't care about decorating your Cottages by the Sea cottages or going vintage pickin' with moi?" she asked. "Just teasing. I know exactly what you mean. I've learned to cut Arthur a break. I know he's working hard. I just hope he shows up for the engagement party."

"He will," I said.

It was a week after Freya Rittenhouse's arrest. Roland's wake had been a small one, and so had Vicki's. Jenna hadn't combined them, but she did pay for them. She retained Emma's caretaker, Rosie, to take care of Emma, and set up a trust fund for Emma that would finance her care until her death. Jenna also planned to settle all the lawsuits against Roland with her own money. I'd seen a change in her. And it was a good one. She wasn't a wishy-washy hypochondriac who always played the victim anymore. Life events like she'd just gone through had a way of making you stronger. I could vouch for that.

"Think that's the last of it," Elle said, surveying Shepherds Cottage. "You basically have to start all over, but you have plenty of time for that. One suggestion, though," she said, looking toward the ornate bed. "I'd get rid of the bed, maybe even have Jenna find a place for it in Enderly Hall. It just doesn't fit this primitive cottage."

"I agree. But it's the only original piece that came from Gardiners Island. What if we moved it to the west wall? Then the sun would at least shine on it in the morning, lighting up all that dark mahogany."

"Can't hurt to try," Elle said as she walked to the footboard, grabbed one of the posts and pulled. "It's a heavy sucker."

"Elle Mabel Warner, do I have to remind you of all the heavy things the two of us have moved. Remember the —"

"Yes, I remember them all. So does my aching back. I just don't want to scratch the floor." She glanced down at the chipped and gouged plank floor, and we broke into laughter. "Okay, you get the headboard, I'll get the footboard. We'll shimmy it left and right to get it away from the wall. Then we can each grab one of the posts on the headboard and drag it."

The first part of Elle's plan worked perfectly. The second part, not so much. When I grabbed hold of the tall post, topped with a carved wood pineapple finial, it broke off in my hands.

Elle laughed. "It's a sign the bed doesn't belong in here."

I tried to bang the pineapple finial back in place. A big mistake. The entire post broke off the bed frame and rolled to the floor. From the post's hollow interior, a rolled document slid out, along with a small yellow stone. The stone hit the toe of my boot, then bounced under the bed.

I went scrambling for the stone. Elle untied the string around the sheaf of papers.

Surprise. Surprise.

Captain Kidd's missing yellow diamond.

And Enderly Hall's architectural renderings, signed and dated, by none other than Stanford White, the American Renaissance man himself.

Chapter 36

It was the Saturday of Memorial Day Weekend. The weather couldn't have been better. Maurice and I stood outside my walled garden, waiting for Elle to arrive. She didn't know it, but her fiancé was already inside, and he'd brought with him a surprise guest.

"Hope we can pull this off, Miss Doolittle," Elle's shopworker said in his British-accented Henry Higgins voice.

"I'm sure you made the perfect choice, you always do," I said, glancing at the puffy garment bag he held in his arms.

Music from a small quartet filtered over the garden walls. Peonies and jasmine scented the salt air. There was only one thing that could go wrong.

"Here she comes," Maurice said.

Elle pulled up in her pickup, parked, turned off the engine and opened the door. She ran, more like galloped, toward us. "Is he here? Is Arthur here? I can't believe all the cars."

"Yes, he's here," I said, laughing.

"Meg," she said, pointing to my ice blue chiffon gown, "isn't that from my closet? One of the copies of the dress Grace Kelly wore in *To Catch a Thief*? The one Edith Head had given Aunt Mabel?"

"One and the same," Maurice answered. "You see, my dear, Miss Doolittle here"—he looked down his aristocratic nose at me—"didn't know that when I sent out the invitations for your engagement party that I'd said it was black-tie. She called in a panic when she saw our first guest arrive and I flew right over with the Kelly dress. I didn't think you'd mind."

"Of course not," Elle said. "Well, that would explain why you're wearing a tuxedo, Maurice. But it doesn't explain why no one told me it was black-tie."

I laughed. "Elle, you always dress black-tie for every party you go to."

"True," she said, "but I didn't this time. You said it was a garden party, so I dressed for that." She twirled in a circle, showing off her mid-century cotton dress sprouting three-dimensional fabric daisies and an assortment of brightly colored flower brooches.

"Well, my little crumpet, Uncle Maurice to the rescue." He held up the garment bag. "Go into Meg's cottage and change. Your guests are waiting for you."

"But I have to see Arthur," she protested.

"You'll be with him soon enough," Maurice answered. "You don't want him to see you in that, do you?"

I grabbed her arm and Maurice handed me the garment bag, saying he would tell Arthur that Elle had arrived. Then I dragged her toward the cottage with little protest. Elle liked a good party dress more than anyone I knew.

When we walked inside my cottage, Sally from Montauk's Cut 'n Curl had turned my kitchen into a pop-up beauty salon.

"What's this?" Elle screeched in excitement. "Boy, Meg, you sure know how to throw an engagement party."

"Have a seat," Sally said, holding a curling iron.

Elle sat on a bar stool that faced the great room. "I wish great-aunt Mabel was here to see all this. And my parents."

"I know, sweetie. But you've got me," I said, giving her a quick kiss on the cheek. "And you've got Arthur." I hung the garment bag from a kitchen cupboard and watched the pros go to work. When they were finished, I said, "You look beautiful, Elle."

"How come there's no mirror? Let me run into the bathroom and take a look. Not that I don't trust you, Sally."

"No time for that," I said in my sternest schoolteacher voice. "You have to get your dress on. Can't keep everyone waiting."

Sally handed me a silk hood to put over Elle's head. Elle didn't protest—she knew not to get makeup on one of her vintage gowns. I unzipped the bag, took out the dress, the shoes, and even the small box of jewelry Maurice had packed. Then we went to work like we were the mice in the Disney animated cartoon *Cinderella*.

"Okay," Elle said, "you can take the hood off. I'm having a hard time breathing."

"Hold on. You need your shoes." I slipped them on. "Okay, stand up."

Sally and her assistant, Gwen, were standing in front of Elle, holding a full-length mirror.

"Here we go," I said, taking off the silk hood. "How do you think Maurice did, dear friend?"

"What. What is going on! Oh, my God! Is this what I think it is?

I'm gonna cry!"

"You can't cry, you'll ruin your mother's wedding dress." I handed her a baby blue garter. "This was *my* mother's."

"Oh, Meg! I think I'm having a heart attack."

Sally handed her a glass of champagne. "You look gorgeous, Elle. Now, buck up. Go marry that man of yours."

"Are you sure you want to go through with this?" I asked. "I'll be losing my best single friend."

Elle looked at me. Then she looked to the door. "You bet your sweet bippy I want to marry Arthur Theodore Shoner. And you will never lose me. Let's get this show on the road."

"Oh, I almost forgot. As your maid of honor, I will be holding Arthur's wedding band. I am your maid of honor, I hope?"

"Duh."

Chapter 37

"You clean up nicely, Mr. Seaton," I said into his ear as we slow-danced to one of Elle's favorite songs, Eric Clapton's "Wonderful Tonight."

I'd invited him to the wedding when my father's not-so-easy five-ingredient salmon caught fire and my kitchen almost burned down the night I was hosting the Dead Poets Society Book Club. Patrick had somehow saved the meal by adding some kind of fancy sauce to the poor salmon's charred remains. He even stayed afterward to help me clean up. Then we'd gone out to my deck and sat on my double swing, spending hours discussing poets, books and how lucky we were to live on the ocean.

A star-filled full-moon night. A night I'd never forget. Because of the kiss.

Oh, what a kiss.

I glanced toward Elle, Arthur and my father. They were standing under a pergola twinkling with fairy lights. Elle looked happier than I'd ever seen her, and I couldn't wait until her husband told her the news that he would be returning to the East Hampton Town Police with a pay raise and promotion. It seemed Arthur had been working undercover with the Suffolk County Police Department to expose a corrupt Chief Pell. Reinstated Detective Shoner wouldn't give me any details of Pell's misdeeds, but I would get it out of him somehow. Arthur had said he owed me for pulling off Elle's surprise wedding.

But when I glanced over at Elle's smiling face, I figured we were even.

Then I looked up at Patrick, who held me, even though the music had stopped.

Would it be too naïve to believe in happy endings?

For tonight, at least, I was a believer . . .

Recipes for Meg's First Dead Poets SocietyBook Club Meeting

Jeff Barrett's Roasted Shrimp Cocktail with Thai Chili Sauce
(Serves 4–6)

12–15 Jumbo shrimp, peeled, deveined, tails on
1 teaspoon olive oil
Old Bay seasoning
Bottle of Thai chili sauce

Preheat oven to 400. Toss the raw shrimp in a bowl with the olive oil and place on a baking sheet in a single layer. Lightly season the raw shrimp with Old Bay seasoning. Roast for 10–12 minutes, making sure they are just cooked through (not overcooked). Remove from cookie sheet to a serving platter and allow to cool. Serve at room temperature or even slightly chilled with the Thai chili sauce.

Jeff Barrett's Slow-Roasted Salmon with Tomato and Basil
(Serves 4)

4 tablespoons extra virgin olive oil
12 ounces cherry tomatoes, each cut in half lengthwise
2 cloves garlic, minced
3 sprigs fresh basil, leaves reserved from 2
coarse salt
pepper
4 salmon filets, skin-on, about 6 ounces each

Preheat oven to 375. In a baking dish or roasting pan, combine the olive oil, tomatoes, garlic and basil leaves, and toss well. Season with salt and pepper. Roast until tomatoes begin to wilt and concentrate, about 20 minutes. Remove from oven and reduce oven temp to 275.

Season salmon filets with salt and pepper and place, skin-side down, amid tomato mixture. Spoon some of the tomatoes over the salmon. Roast salmon in mixture for about 15 minutes, slightly less if you like rare salmon.

When salmon is done, place filets on serving platter and spoon all the tomatoes and sauce over them. Garnish with remaining basil sprig. Can be served hot or room temperature.

Jeff Barrett's Basil-Spiced Jasmine Rice
(Serves 4–6)

1 cup jasmine rice
1/2 teaspoon salt
1-1/3 cup water
3–4 fresh basil leaves, chopped

Add the rice, salt, and 1-1/3 cups water to a saucepan with a lid. I prefer using a stainless steel saucepan for this. Cover the saucepan and bring the water to boil. This should take only a few minutes.

Reduce the heat to low and let the rice simmer for another 9–10 minutes, until all the water has been absorbed. I usually use a smaller burner for simmering.

Turn off the heat and leave the saucepan covered for about 10–15 minutes. Uncover the saucepan, add the chopped basil leaves, and fluff the rice with a fork. The rice is now ready to serve.

Meg Barrett's No-Bake! Peanut Butter Pretzel Bars
(Makes 24 bars)

Peanut butter pretzel layer

3/4 cup unsalted butter (melted)
1-1/2 cups powdered sugar
1 cup creamy peanut butter
2 cups crushed pretzels (measure after crushing)

Line a 9x13-inch baking pan with parchment paper, making sure the paper goes up the pan's sides.

In a large bowl, add the melted butter, powdered sugar, peanut butter, and crushed pretzels. Mix well.

Scoop the mixture into the bottom of the lined pan and press down into one layer.

Topping

1 12-ounce package semi-sweet chocolate chips
1/4 cup creamy peanut butter

Microwave chocolate chips and peanut butter in a microwave-safe bowl until melted, stirring every thirty seconds on high until smooth.

When melted, pour the chocolate mixture evenly on top of the pretzel layer.

Cover the pan tightly. Refrigerate for at least an hour, then cut into 24 bars.

* Note from Meg—Bars can be frozen for a couple of months, but I doubt there will be any leftovers.

Meg & Elle's Think Outside the Box Guide to Vintage Decorating

Elle: For a furniture revamp, changing drawer pulls or knobs on a piece of furniture can transform and update its look. Adding a fresh coat of bold paint to a single piece of furniture is also a great way to add personality to a stale room.

Meg: Make your décor come alive by painting a vintage table with a light shade of paint and adding a rub-on transfer to the top of the table. Don't forget to add at least three coats of non-yellowing sealer to the transfer if you will be using it on your porch or balcony. Transfers come in many motifs — floral, seaside, herb, butterfly, the choices are endless — and they can also be added to the front of dressers, on mirrors, pottery, glass — the sky's the limit.

Elle: Polyester-fill pillows won't mildew when left outdoors. And if you don't own a sewing machine, pick out some great vintage-inspired outdoor fabric from your local fabric store that matches your aesthetic, then take your fabric to a dry cleaner who does tailoring and ask them to make you a pillow cover. It will cost you less than it would to buy a pillow in a pattern you don't adore.

Meg: For a fabulous outdoor decoration, find or rescue an old chair with a broken seat; remove the seat and add a potted plant to the space where the seat was. Or, if you're having a garden party, put a tin bucket in the hole of the seat and fill it with ice and beverages. You can paint the chair with a mildew-retardant paint and leave it out year-round. Also, a vintage chair with a lot of character can be placed in an unused corner of your home; it makes a great place to display a stack of coffee table books topped with a plant in a ceramic pot.

Elle: When out on the vintage trail, don't pass up amateur oil or acrylic paintings just because they are housed in an ugly frame. Take the painting out of the frame and display it on a tabletop easel. Or vice versa, don't pass up a gorgeous vintage frame because the painting in the frame is not your style. Toss the art and reuse the frame as is or paint it.

Meg: If you don't have a porch, you can create an outdoor room in your yard. Frame the space with an arched trellis and place a bistro table and chairs in front of the trellis. For romantic ambiance, hang a candelabra chandelier from an overhead tree branch and weave fairy lights through the trellis and nearby trees.

Elle: Try not to hang an oil painting over a fireplace mantel. The heat and smoke will damage it. Remember, only use a feather duster to clean oil paintings. When cleaning framed art or photos under glass, make sure not to spray glass cleaner directly on the glass. Instead, spray on paper toweling or a slightly damp cloth, then clean the glass. And if you don't have a fireplace, find a vintage mantel and create the look of a fireplace.

Meg: Take a road trip to an outdoor vintage flea market with a friend or significant other who has never been to one. You could even make it a competition—who can find the most interesting items for twenty dollars—*Now go!* There're only a few simple rules to follow: wear good walking shoes; bring cash; always bargain; never pass by something you like and plan to come back for it later—it won't be there; don't buy wobbly furniture, chances are you won't be able to repair it, and *do* remember to visit the gourmet food trucks. Bon appétit!

Elle: Mix pieces of vintage pottery by makers like McCoy, Roseville, and Rookwood with modern-day local artisan pottery. Use the pieces to add personality to your indoor or outdoor spaces. And, whether you live in a rural area or big city, remember to shop at your local vintage and home goods retailers and independent and used bookstores. They are what give your hometown its personality and impart a sense of community.

Meg: Another decorator secret is to have at least one oversized mirror in every room. Mirrors reflect the light and make things appear airy—especially if you live in a small cozy cottage like I do.

And remember, a modern home can meld perfectly with that little touch of vintage or antique.

Wishing you great finds!

About the Author

Kathleen Bridge is the national bestselling author of the Hamptons Home & Garden Mystery series and the By the Sea Mystery series. She started her writing career working at *The Michigan State University News* in East Lansing, Michigan. A member of Sisters in Crime and Mystery Writers of America, she is also the author and photographer of an antiques reference guide, *Lithographed Paper Toys, Books, and Games*. She teaches creative writing in addition to working as an antiques and vintage dealer. Kathleen blissfully lives on a barrier island in Florida. Readers can visit her on the web at www.kathleenbridge.com.

CPSIA information can be obtained
at www.ICGtesting.com
Printed in the USA
LVHW042352181120
672044LV00008B/1334

9 781950 461578